Colour Sergeant Chesney V.C.

Steven Baker

The Book Guild Ltd

First published in Great Britain in 2017 by
The Book Guild Ltd
9 Priory Business Park
Wistow Road, Kibworth
Leicestershire, LE8 0RX
Freephone: 0800 999 2982
www.bookguild.co.uk
Email: info@bookguild.co.uk
Twitter: @bookguild

Copyright © 2017 Steven Baker

The right of Steven Baker to be identified as the author of this
work has been asserted by him in accordance with the
Copyright, Design and Patents Act 1988.

All rights reserved. No part of this publication may be
reproduced, transmitted, or stored in a retrieval system, in any form or by any means,
without permission in writing from the publisher, nor be otherwise circulated in
any form of binding or cover other than that in which it is published and without
a similar condition being imposed on the subsequent purchaser.

This work is entirely fictitious and bears no resemblance to any persons living or dead.

Typeset in Aldine401 BT

Printed and bound in Great Britain by CPI Group (UK) Ltd, Croydon, CR0 4YY

ISBN 978 1910878 897

British Library Cataloguing in Publication Data.
A catalogue record for this book is available from the British Library.

*In memory of the servicemen and women of two world wars
who gave us the freedom we have today*

One

The dark streets of the dockside area of London looked strangely sombre and empty as the hansom cab slowly plodded towards its destination. There was one single lamplighter out igniting the street lights but otherwise the whole area seemed to be singularly devoid of life. Rain had been falling all day and now the road was damp and wet, and filled with puddles. The night air was decidedly chilly and there was an eerie, almost stunning silence broken only by the gentle thud of the horses' hooves against the hard surface of the road and the squeak of the wheels of the cab. From the nearby banks of the Thames River a sudden gust of wind blew a stale pungent smell into the cold night air and above the docks a spiral of thick dirty brown smoke rose into the sky from a ship's funnel.

'Not far to go now Sir,' said the cab driver pulling his jacket tight across his chest and blowing mists of breath into the air. The passenger in the cab was a gentleman somewhere in his forties, dressed in a good suit and bow tie, with a top hat. His hands were clasped round a cane. He looked outside at the cold streets and luxuriated in the warmth of the cab.

The sound of a drum roll suddenly came forth through the air, breaking the silence. Then a military band sounded off, pulsating life and warmth into what had only seconds before been a still and placid atmosphere, chillingly inhospitable. The gentleman stirred in the passenger's seat as he recognised the tune flooding the night. It was at that moment the cab turned into a side street leading to the wharves and there in full view was one of Her Majesty's flagships with hundreds of people lining the docks, waving and cheering. A military brass band was playing loudly in a rousing raucous manner that would have stimulated the coldest of hearts and the most patriotic of passions.

The cab pulled to a halt and the driver stepped down to open the door for his passenger. 'There you are Sir,' he said smiling cheerfully. He paused to gaze ahead at the spectacle on the docks. 'My word, they're getting a grand send-off aren't they?'

'You would like my fare for the evening wouldn't you?' the gentleman smiled courteously at the driver.

'Oh! Yes. Sorry Sir. I was quite taken aback by the sight of it.'

The gentleman counted the money out in the cab driver's hand and gave him a tip for good measure. 'There you are my friend and thank you for your courtesy.'

The cab driver beamed with delight. 'I can't recall having treated you any differently to any other passenger but it was very nice of you to say so Sir. Besides, what a blinking tip!'

'My pleasure,' said the man. He turned and took in the sight. 'What a grand spectacle!'

'Yes indeed,' agreed the cab driver.

The man looked around at the scene. It was one of soldiers departing for the Boer War in South Africa. The soldiers of the regiment marched aboard the ship. They were wearing the bush outfits worn by troops in the veldt. There were also soldiers on parade in ceremonial dress. The bandsmen had full colours on display in their uniforms. The brass of their side and bass drums was highly polished and glittering like mirrors. Wives, mothers and sweethearts waved to their men. The Union Jack was being waved madly from all points of the crowd, not only by the elderly but also the young and the patriotic.

The gentleman assessed the sight and turned to the cab driver who watched with interest. 'It's a familiar sight. Typical of so many regimental send-offs. The colours of the tunics and the brightly polished brass shiny buckles. The gleaming white braiding. Wives and fiancées embracing their loved ones.'

It was an emotional sight. There were mothers with tears in their eyes. Young girls waved handkerchiefs. Little children clutched flags. The band seemed to be playing louder and louder.

'Would this be your old regiment by any chance, Sir?' asked the cab driver.

The gentleman smiled at the cab driver's intuition. 'Yes. Once. A long time ago.'

'Would you have liked to have been in this show, Sir?' pursued the driver.

'No. I did my dash. Burma. India. Afghanistan. I saw it all from Ava to Bengal. I don't think they'll need me against the Boer. Tonight those young fellows will be out on the sea bound for South Africa to take part in campaigns in the Transvaal and Natal. Bound for Mafeking and Petersburg and Spelonken to take part in exploits and adventures that one day they will recount to their grandchildren.' He added sombrely, 'Those that come back of course.'

The cab driver disregarded the dire predictions of the well-dressed gentleman. 'I almost envy them you know. I envy them having the chance to go off and be part of a piece of history.'

The man smiled. 'I've seen it all before. Look around you my friend. Take up there for instance.' He pointed to the upper tiers of the ship which was thronged with soldiers who were happy and laughing, and calling out to their friends and families below on the wharves. 'I find it a terribly tragic thought that many of those eager young men, if they come back at all, will never be quite the same again in spirit or physical appearance when they return. For the moment though, I'm quite content to stand here and revel in their premature glories and recall my own memories of former battles. The looks on the people's faces are as interesting as the colours of the uniforms and the music of the band.' He pointed to the crowd, using his cane. 'Now over there in the crowds you can see plenty of young ladies wiping tears from their eyes; their thoughts no doubt amassed around future dreams of bridal trains and a white church wedding with their uniformed sweethearts. Note the older men in the crowd. Some were probably in Crimea. Nodding their heads now as another generation goes to war. Yes, it is all so familiar.'

The cabbie was a bit bemused by this man whom he was not sure how to take. 'Hard to believe you were an officer though, by the way you view things. You have all the appearance of being a well-heeled sort of man; the type that one would see in the banks or business houses of the Strand and Threadneedle Street, taking late-night suppers at Romano's, or being seen exchanging tips with the Prince of Wales at Ascot opening day.'

With a smile of amusement the gentleman realised the cab driver was no slouch in summing up people. 'You're almost right. I – NEVER – exchange tips with the Prince of Wales!' He added with a flourish as he began to walk away, 'I'm a much better judge of horseflesh than he is. Goodnight.'

The cab driver nodded his head and smiled back. 'Goodnight Sir.'

The gentleman moved amongst the people and watched the musicians playing on the wharf. The tune they were playing was different now. It was the music of *Soldiers of the Queen*. A great roar came up from the crowd as the gangplank was raised. The ship at the wharf was beginning to move away. Streamers were breaking and the band played louder and louder. At the wharf the gentleman allowed himself a smile at the poignancy of the moment. He cast his eyes around the crowd and his glance fell on someone who seemed strikingly familiar in his memory. For a moment he stared incredulously. He reassessed his study. There was no doubt in his mind. He knew this man from long ago.

He moved through the crowd, fixing his gaze on a man he had met somewhere before. Slowly it came to him where he had met the man. It had been fourteen years since they had last met. The gentleman stared at him. Beneath a cockeyed felt hat and wearing a dapper orange suit and chequered bow tie was a man with a perpetual grin, blue eyes that sparkled with good nature, and fair hair, although slightly greying at the temples. The gentleman stood close to him now. The man in the orange suit stood alone in the crowd, grinning and smoking as the refrains of *Soldiers of the Queen* rose above the noise on the dock. He was totally oblivious to the gentleman who stood by him with the top hat and cane. He was far too immersed in his own thoughts and memories.

The gentleman took one pace closer and spoke to him. 'Do you remember India, Harry?'

The soft voice seemed to cause an immediate transformation to come over the man in the orange suit. His grin collapsed. A look of shock spread over his face. Slowly he turned his head and began to lower his cigarette. A look of disbelief came across in his eyes. He struggled to find a name within the confines of his memory. Then it came.

'Mr Whittaker. By God! That's right isn't it? Mr Graham Whittaker?'

The gentleman smiled. 'Hullo.' After a pause he remembered the man's name. 'Hullo, Colour Sergeant Chesney.'

The two men shook hands with a grip of warm friendship. There on the dockside events of nearly a decade and a half ago came alive again.

In a smoky dockside public house the two men renewed their acquaintance. They were a contrasting pair. Harry Chesney and Graham Whittaker sat in silence for a moment taking sips of beer. Around them the pub was filled with a mixture of seadogs, soldiers and civilians, although the atmosphere was of a rough appearance and Whittaker in his elegant clothes was somewhat out of place there. This was not lost on a couple of ladies who gave him admiring glances. Whittaker smiled at them in a flirtatious manner. He studied the curves of their voluptuous figures for a moment, decided they were a bit too overbearing and looked across at Harry. The former colour sergeant stubbed out a cigarette and leaned across the table. Harry Chesney had a naturally happy face with what appeared to be a permanent smile. It was an appearance that never gave away his true feelings.

Harry Chesney was a genial Londoner who felt eager to speak of the past years that had elapsed since their last meeting. 'Well Mr Whittaker,' he began, 'I s'pose you came here tonight for sentimental reasons too. Nostalgia perhaps. Seeing off the old regiment and all that. Remember Rudyard Kipling's lines from *Tommy* –' he began to recite '– the troopship's on the tide, my boys, the troopship's on the tide.'

Whittaker supplied him with the next line. 'Oh it's special train for Atkins when the trooper's on the tide.' They smiled at each other. 'Yes I remember, Harry. Always an emotional sight to see a regiment off at the dockside. I've seen a few of them in my time. Sailed with a few of them too in my line of work. You'll recall that I was a military correspondent.'

'And still are,' affirmed Chesney. 'I've read your articles occasionally over the years in some of the national newspapers. 'From the Front Line' I believe they're called.'

'That is correct,' Whittaker said in a tone that indicated surprise.

'You've seen more action as a newspaperman than you did as an officer with the 25th Queen's Light Northern Regiment.'

Whittaker seemed keen to speak of his exploits. 'In recent years I've covered Omdurman. Khartoum. I was in South Africa at the time of the Jamieson Raid. I've interviewed politicians. Generals. Ministers. Governors. Ambassadors. Officers full of stupidity and arrogance. Men hell bent on sending their own regiments to a glorious death while self-seeking knighthoods, promotions and rows of medals to pin on their chests. Heaven knows the ordinary Tommy has more sense than the officers. And in all sincerity I can tell you I much prefer having a quiet ale here, away from the pomposity of it all.' He stopped for a moment and looked at his companion. 'Well Harry – that is my story. What about you? What have you been doing with your life since you left India?'

Chesney took a long swill of beer before answering. 'After I left the

Army I decided not to go home at first – at least not for a while. You see the Army and soldiering had been my life. The regiment had been my home. The men of the 25th had been my family. Well without it I was a lost soul. It was like being set adrift on a deep blue ocean without any idea of how to get back to shore. I decided to see the great British colonies of the world. I went down to Colombo, Ceylon. Then I went to Nuwara Eliya for a long time to work on a plantation. I learned about the tea trade. From there I took sail on one of the great tea clippers to New South Wales. I came home five years ago. I've got a little teashop in Horsham. I live the quiet life now.' He took another drink of beer and then spoke with a light tone of bitterness. 'You haven't forgotten I was once labelled as the VC winner who ran away.'

Whittaker remembered the incident. He gave Chesney a wry look. 'I haven't forgotten. I was there too at the battlefield on the ridge of Prakaresh.'

There was a short silence during which time Whittaker waited for Chesney to speak his mind. Chesney appeared troubled and it was obvious that past events from long ago still haunted him. There was a saying that the eyes reflect the soul and in Chesney a deep hurt could be seen, like that of a young child experiencing an emotional pain. He fidgeted and then reached for a cigarette. He lit it, blew a puff of smoke and looked around the pub at the people. Finally, more relaxed, he leaned forward and began to speak. A smile broke through as he remembered the drama and humour of his own spectacular life.

'I have quite a story to tell. I don't talk a lot about it. Maybe that's a good thing. Rudyard Kipling couldn't write or invent the chapters of my life.'

'Then tell me. I'm a good listener. It's my job to listen. Not that I'd write about it. Memories are good, Harry. They're the stories of our life that define who we are and where we get our motivation from.'

'Do you know, Mr Whittaker, I was brought up not more than a hundred yards from where we are now? My old man worked by day on the docks and sometimes in the evenings he would be the Master of Ceremonies at the local music hall. Jimmy Chesney was well known around these parts once. The music hall could get pretty rowdy in those days. If the audience didn't like an act they would boo them off with no pity or sympathy for the poor soul up on stage. Jimmy knew how to handle them. He could sing, dance and tell funny stories that would have them in stitches. He went to pieces after my mother died of consumption. Diphtheria got him and the workhouse got me. When I joined the Army – well, to me, after the workhouse, it was a life like I could not believe. A uniform instead of workhouse overalls. And it was a uniform I was proud to wear. It got me respect. I was out in India seeing things that I had never dreamed of. Mountains and lakes in Kashmir with waters that glittered and shimmered in the spellbinding light. Sunsets and sunrises like magic shows. Once a Maharajah flung his jewels on a table in front of me to show off the riches of India. I saw temples in Benares and markets in Lahore and I travelled to the Ganges Delta. I met peaceful folk in villages who never ventured far, holy men who were in constant prayer and contemplation; I clashed with fierce tribesmen, made friends with those of different castes and beliefs, loved beautiful gentle Indian maidens who wore colourful saris and danced with exotic and enticing seductive magnetism. I saw snake charmers, elephants and tigers. On top of it all I won the Victoria Cross. I couldn't believe it. Me! Harry Chesney from the Kennington workhouse – a holder of the VC and I was a colour sergeant in her Majesty's Army. I was so proud.' He stopped. His expression was grim and he delivered the next words in a voice to match. 'Then came the day of judgement.'

Rain was pattering against the window. Whittaker's face showed his sensitivity of the moment. The two men stared at each other across the table, remembering a time and experiences they had both lived through far away across the oceans of the world. It was raining heavily in the East End of London on that night but far away in another time and place it was hot and humid, and sultry. Both men's thoughts travelled back in time to India in 1885.

Two

The parade ground at Fort Valaka in Northern India was an imposing sight on one special day in 1885. The occasion was the twenty-fifth anniversary of the 25th Queen's Light Northern Regiment. There were many visitors and observers that day. A brass band played *D' Ye Ken John Peel?* in a loud and exciting manner. Soldiers in tunics and white helmets stood at ease with their rifles by their side until they were brought smartly to attention by Regimental Sergeant-Major Sandy Blackshawe. He was a huge bear of a man with a thunderous voice of authority.

Soldiers on horseback were lined up in parallel with those standing at attention. There were several marquees erected. One of these served food to the guests and officers. At one end of the parade ground were several elephants, each with a box on top in which sat a British officer and an Indian driver clad in a turban and a scarlet robe. There was a contingent of Indian troops close to the main ranks of foot soldiers. These Indian troops sat astride the most beautiful of horses. They wore grey jackets and turbans of the same colour with a peaked cone in the middle. At the command of an unseen man they rode between the ranks of the drill squad to rapturous applause from the observers who were seated beneath a shaded veranda. Amongst these people were wives, public servants, government officials and journalists, one of these being Rudyard Kipling. There was also another journalist. He was Graham Whittaker.

Whittaker was a former Army officer who had served in the regiment. He sat cool and comfortable wearing a white Victorian tropical safari outfit. Close to where he sat, there was a photographer who was faithfully recording scenes for history with his camera. A few seats along from Whittaker sat an artist who sketched the scene and added colours from a palette.

On the parade ground the colours of the regiment were presented to Colonel Duncan Anderson who took the salute. The man bearing the colours was Harry Chesney. Colonel Anderson was a rugged Scotsman with a brooding presence and a glint in his eyes that suggested he missed nothing. He strode down the parade ground inspecting the troops before entering a marquee, followed by several other officers.

After the parade had finished there was a garden party for officers, gentlemen and their ladies. Whittaker moved around the grounds making light conversation with people, and made a mental note of anything that might be useful information for his journalistic career. When he had finished talking to a public servant he went across to a table where tea was being served by an Indian waiter. Whittaker helped himself to a cup and took a sip. Turning around from the table he found himself facing Colonel Anderson.

'Colonel Anderson!' Whittaker said in genuine surprise. 'How nice to see you again Sir.' He beamed a pleasant smile and outstretched a warm handshake.

'I knew you were coming for this auspicious occasion of the twenty-fifth anniversary of the best regiment in India, the 25th Queen's Light Northern, of which I am sorry to say I shall be retiring from soon.' Colonel Anderson had spoken with real regret.

'I'm sorry to hear that, Colonel. Will you stay on in India?'

'I would have to say I've given it great depth of thought, Graham. I am widowed now. The regiment has been my life and I've given the best part of my years to service spent in India. I may go home and write my memoirs. Speaking of writing, I have to say I am most impressed with the way you have handled your newspaper career. When you left the Army and – indeed this regiment – having served with distinction I may add, I was curious of the line you would take as a journalist.' He smiled mischievously. 'I can't stand the bastards normally and their wildly inaccurate stories.'

'Just as well I'm a former officer isn't it?' Whittaker reminded him. 'I'm able to throw light on shadow and with a knowledge of strategy that is no match for any other correspondent.'

Colonel Anderson nodded in agreement and smiled. 'Your editor said in his communication that you were recently in the Sudan.'

Whittaker took on a grave expression. 'I covered various battles in the desert.'

'Really?' The colonel suddenly became very interested. 'Pretty bad was it?'

'Fearful,' came the reply. 'I was on my way to cover General Gordon's defence of the city. Only by the time I had joined Major Kitchener's men en-route there, the Mahdi's men had taken Khartoum and Gordon had become history.'

'He was one of the great characters of military history,' the colonel said in firm judgement. 'Chinese Gordon. You've heard of the story about General Gordon riding into battle wielding an umbrella?' Whittaker smiled and nodded that he had. 'Anyway Graham, what is the objective of your assignment here? Your editor stated that he wanted reports from the front. From the front? Why exactly?'

'Action, Colonel,' Whittaker replied directly to the point. 'My editor – Mr Vickers – says that we in the British Isles are not getting the full story of the ordinary Tommy. There has been far too much to do with the hierarchy around the country of India. Not enough of despatches of patrols, about the ordinary foot slogger from Stockport or Wigan.'

'And Edinburgh and Glasgow of course. Even the Hebridean island of Barra we have a lad from.' The colonel looked at him and smiled. 'Very well Graham. If there is anything happening I'll let you know. I'll make it quite clear now that if you accompany a patrol as an observer, I cannot be responsible for anything that happens in the course of events. Am I making myself abundantly clear on that point?'

'Absolutely clear. I know of the enormous risks,' Whittaker responded to the colonel's comments that at times sounded more like orders. 'But my job, like yours, is fraught with dangers, it goes with the territory.'

'My men are the best in India. Good men. You will know of course from your time here that they are the best. But I'll see that you're issued with a rifle.' He looked away at a game of polo that had just started. 'You'd better not have too many of these scones and tea. I'll be expecting you at the regimental dinner tonight and you had better have a hearty appetite old son. Some of your former compatriots from as far back as the old Burma days will be there. Now if you'll excuse me, Graham, I've a few government officials to see. Seven o'clock in the mess.'

'I'll be there Sir,' Whittaker replied in a manner befitting a salute. He refilled his cup as Colonel Anderson walked away into the crowd. For a few minutes Whittaker watched the polo game. He felt glad to be back in India. This country was exciting and fascinating.

In the midst of high breathtaking mountains that blended into a bright blue sky, there were a number of small villages where peaceful tribesmen lived with their women, children and goats. They were happy just to live off the land, to grow their own maize and to follow the traditions of their own caste.

While the British at Fort Valaka were sipping tea, eating scones and playing polo, a mere hundred miles away a lone tribesman on horseback approached a village of mud huts and straw in the Prakaresh Valley. One old man was milking a goat. He looked up and his eyes, set deep in a white-bearded face, froze at the sight of the horseman. Up on the hill less than half a mile away the rider sat still on the horse, completely motionless like a statue. The old man muttered something to himself in his native dialect and raised his eyes with dismay to the heavens. The shadowy figure in the distance just stayed there. The sunlight streamed down on the village where, apart from the old man, its inhabitants were asleep on a sweltering afternoon. Almost as if they sensed trouble the animals became aroused. A nanny goat bleated. A dog pursed its nose, lay bare its teeth, growled and then began to bark viciously. Still the man on horseback did not move.

The old man realised something was desperately wrong. He turned very slowly and stiffly walked towards his hut. Then suddenly the sound of horses' hooves hit the air like the roar of native drums. Dust was swirled into the air like turbulence from a twister. The old man stopped and turned around. Across the higher reaches of the valley there were literally dozens and dozens of swarthy, thickly-bearded warriors. The old man's eyes froze with horror. He was mesmerised by the sight before him. In one frightening moment the horsemen raced toward the villages brandishing scimitars and shrieking at the top of their voices.

That same night Graham Whittaker attended the regimental dinner at Fort Valaka. In the officers' mess there was a highly polished table placed in the centre of the room. On the table were flickering candles set in antique candelabra. Seated at the table were officers of the regiment, public servants and specially invited guests. Whittaker looked around at the guests and the elegant surroundings.

Colonel Anderson was seated at the head of the table. He was in his element on this occasion. He laughed and joked with a monocled government official, enjoyed a cigar and indulged in a scotch. Almost directly in line with the centre of the table hung a portrait of Queen Victoria, virtually above the colonel. On the left- and right-hand side of the picture were the heads of tigers. Two Indian waiters, who wore turbans that appeared to be made of a shiny silk material, stood close by to replenish empty glasses and supply the various courses of the meal. Even in the officers' mess the warmth of the summer evening still managed to filter through.

Whittaker's white suit with a gold watch chain seemed out of place amongst the medal-decorated uniforms and stiff frocked suits of the civil servants. On most occasions Whittaker made detailed observations of his surroundings and the people close by for inclusion in his journalistic notes. Around him there were officers with bristled moustaches and arrogant looks. There was also an Indian official happily chatting to an Irish major.

While Whittaker was making his close at hand study, Colonel Anderson rose to his full height and addressed the table. 'Gentlemen!' All conversation ceased immediately as they realised the colonel was about to make a toast. 'Gentlemen, I give you a toast. Would you please charge your glasses.' Almost as if rehearsed beforehand the dinner guests raised their glasses. The waiters rushed forward to ensure everyone's glass was full. The colonel waited until this had been done. 'Would you please be upstanding.' Everyone stood. 'On this most exceptional of occasions I wish to propose a toast. First of all to our monarch. The Queen.'

Everyone responded immediately. 'The Queen.'

'To the British Empire.'

The next part of the toast was repeated in unison by them all. 'To the British Empire.'

'And finally,' Colonel Anderson continued, 'but certainly not the least in order of merit. The men of the 25th Queen's Light Northern Regiment.'

Everyone spoke with pride. 'The men of the 25th Queen's Light Northern Regiment.'

The diners clinked their glasses systematically. Two bagpipers played *God Save the Queen*. The men in the officers' mess stood to attention while the national anthem was being played.

In the Prakaresh Valley where villages of peaceful tribesmen had lived untroubled only hours before, there were smouldering embers sparkling and fizzing in the black of a star-filled night. The horrifying aura of death hung over the smashed huts. Carnage was everywhere. The tribesmen who had committed the atrocity rode through the wreckage surveying the fragments of the villages that had existed.

While the slaughter was taking place in the Prakaresh Valley, the regimental dinner continued. Whittaker looked down the table and raised his glass to an old friend at the other end.

'A former colleague of yours, dear boy?' Cedric Fisher of the East India Company asked the man he was seated next to.

'Yes, Mr Fisher,' replied Whittaker. Fisher was in his fifties and a distinguished man.

'Where did you serve with him, Mr Whittaker?'

Whittaker explained. 'I served with him in Burma amongst other places. Now there's a character and a stout-hearted jovial fellow for you. The legendary Major Jack Clancy. Were it not for the fact that he rose from the slums of Dublin through the ranks to become a major, his sense of humour, passionate love of life, his deeply felt religious beliefs, outstanding courage and integrity would have placed him in the moulds of some of the great English heroes of the day.'

'A good fellow to have around you in a scrap no doubt,' Cedric Fisher remarked.

'Indeed. He's a flamboyant man loved by the ladies and admired and respected by men.' Whittaker's admiration knew no bounds. 'The most ideal combination for any man.'

'There are some good men in the ranks,' Cedric told him. 'I met RSM Sandy Blackshawe today. Good man. A real gentleman. But by jove he's fiery on the parade ground! You'd never believe, with his roaring lungs and his awesome presence, he was the son of a lay preacher.'

'You've not met Chesney?' asked Whittaker referring to the Regiment's Colour Sergeant.

'Chesney?' queried Cedric, unaware of who the man was.

'Colour Sergeant Chesney,' Whittaker stated.

Cedric Fisher's eyes sparkled. 'Oh – my goodness me – yes! Colour Sergeant Chesney, of course. Fine fellow. The Victoria Cross winner! RSM Blackshawe was telling me about it. It was on the North West Frontier. I believe a platoon was surrounded on all sides by renegade tribesmen, and as our men advanced many wounded men lay exposed in the field of fire. Chesney ran out many, many times and carried the injured men back to safety. Then he ran into attack taking on five or six men at a time. What a story that is! I would like to meet someone else who was there to confirm the truth.'

'Look no further. I was there,' said Whittaker in amusement.

'Really!' exclaimed Cedric. He was just about to probe Whittaker for more details when Colonel Anderson tapped a metal dish with a spoon to indicate he required silence. There was an immediate hush.

'Gentlemen,' Colonel Anderson said, leaning forward, 'if I may interrupt at this stage of the evening. I would like to take the opportunity to introduce you to three distinguished guests we have with us.' With a sweep of his hand he indicated Cedric. 'This gentleman I am acknowledging is Mr Cedric Fisher of the East India Company. Sir, you are most welcome here at the twenty-fifth anniversary of the regiment.'

Cedric Fisher was equally diplomatic. 'I am delighted to be here, Colonel Anderson. I've enjoyed very much meeting the fine men of your splendid regiment.'

Colonel Anderson was well briefed as to the career details of each of the invited guests. 'Mr Fisher, from Yorkshire originally, has been responsible for many of the flourishing trade practices from India. I daresay that the benefits of the company's work will continue to flow for a long time to come.' He looked down the table towards an Indian official. 'We have a gentleman with us who is most distinguished, having held high positions in public service, in diplomatic circles, and as an envoy for India. His knowledge of this country, its diversity and influences, is second to none.' Colonel Anderson continued his diplomatic words to each guest. 'Mr Matur Rajeed, your presence here and your courteous service in the cause of Her Majesty's government is greeted with thanks and respect.'

The diners acknowledged Matur Rajeed. He was an elderly Indian and a most eloquently spoken man. His primary concern was to help the British Army in an advisory capacity while best serving his own country's interest. He was a quietly spoken figure of authority who returned the colonel's compliments in his own special way.

'In my position as public servant, diplomat and envoy may I, on behalf of the Indian people for many regions in our nation, extend my good wishes to the 25th Queen's Light Northern. On a personal basis, Colonel Anderson, I would like to say how much of a pleasure it has been to meet you Sir, and the many good men and officers serving here. It would be naïve of me to suggest that the whole population welcomes the British. You and I know that is not the case. But we are – all of us – thick skinned and resilient under criticism. And speaking for myself, I have benefited from our friendship. I hope that all of the men serving here will in future years look back on their time in India with great fondness and a deep warmth.'

'I feel sure they will, Mr Rajeed,' Colonel Anderson assured him. 'Thank you for your honesty and kind words.' He looked across to Graham Whittaker. 'Finally, the last guest I wish to introduce is a gentleman well known to some of you who may have served with him in Burma and Bengal. Formerly a lieutenant in the 25th, and now a military correspondent, Graham Whittaker is making a welcome return to India. Graham was born here in India but after his father's death at the time of the Mutiny was taken back to England and raised in Cornwall and Hampshire. A Sandhurst man with a distinguished career in the organisation and intelligence aspects of our tasks, albeit too briefly I may add, he now writes articles, somewhat controversial in tone which are not necessarily the view of serving officers, but for the sake of impartiality and reasoned debate, seek to put forward different views. He recently returned from the Sudan. During his time here Mr Whittaker will be accompanying various patrols to let our friends at home know of the duties of the ordinary soldier in the field.'

Whittaker found himself in the position of having to fend off questions about his controversial articles from a couple of young officers who oozed with pomposity and arrogance, eager to make a name for themselves at someone else's expense.

One officer was unsparing in his criticism. 'Mr Whittaker I've heard that your articles have advocated changes calling for the minimum of army supervision. Isn't that rather premature?' His voice was tinged with superciliousness. 'It's almost a suggestion that the British Army should prepare to relinquish its role. If I dare challenge you, that shows gross disloyalty to the regiment you once served and the uniform you once wore.'

Whittaker rose to the occasion admirably. He realised that a couple of officers were lining up to attack him on his work as a journalist. He reacted firmly and strongly without shouting but he did not mince his words.

'I don't think a young puppy like you should dare challenge me or have the iron nerve to accuse me of disloyalty to this regiment. It was my life for many a year. With it I have served all over India. I have seen action in Afghanistan and Burma.' He paused to see what sort of reaction his words had generated. Several people, including Major Clancy and Colonel Anderson, smiled to themselves. 'I take it you have not seen action yet?'

Whittaker's words had quite thrown the young officer off balance. 'Well – no,' he replied, showing obvious signs of embarrassment. 'But that's not really the point is it?'

Again Whittaker came back quickly and firmly without rudeness or raising his voice. 'With respect to you, neither is my past service or my loyalties to this regiment, which should never come under question. It is a – GREAT – regiment and all members past and present know that. Regarding my articles calling for a minimum of army supervision in India. I will re-affirm it for you. That is something I believe should be considered now. Not for the present time. But in the next century.'

Matur Rajeed nodded his head in agreement. 'I would wholeheartedly concur with Mr Whittaker on this point. It is a good thing to plan for the future of India.'

'I do not doubt that there may be people who could misconstrue those articles that I wrote. The point was missed, as usual, and naturally some people chose to take it out of context.'

'The point being?' another young officer asked with arrogance engrained in every syllable.

'The point being that we, in this era, are at the time in our country's history when the British Empire has never been greater. We should be only too aware that eventually many of the countries under our government's authority will become independent, self-sufficient and with responsibility only to themselves at some stage in the future. Something I was trying to emphasise is that our role may become diminished, although not of lesser importance. We must prepare ourselves for the time when many of the countries of the empire will wish to become independent.' Whittaker looked at the two officers who had precipitated the conversation. 'Do any of you gentlemen wish to take me to task over this?'

There was a short silence and then Major Jack Clancy added his own point of view. Major Clancy was six feet five inches tall, dark haired, dark eyed and muscular in appearance. His voice was warm and reassuring, and projected confidence.

'I think you've made your points eloquently and concisely,' Major Clancy intervened in the conversation. 'If you want to pinpoint examples of where the authority of the empire has diminished you only have to look back as far as the American War of Independence, the War in Quebec against the Frenchies, and with respect to my friends here, the troubled history in my own homeland, Ireland. It is my fervent belief that in the next century the empire will cease to exist as we know it, although many of the countries will be the better for having been a former colony. I would say again – with great respect – to my noted and distinguished journalist friend at the end of the table, I agree with many of his comments but I disagree intensely that our presence should be smaller. On the contrary I believe our presence should be stronger and more formidable – in order to help those countries to a peaceful independence many years from now, when the will of the people will decide by ballot to give them their own constitution and self-rule.'

'It would be an excellent idea if the British government were to set a timetable to independence.' The suggestion came from Matur Rajeed.

'That will come in time Mr Rajeed,' Colonel Anderson told him. 'I have had discussions with politicians on that score. We speak in terms of decades though, not years.'

Cedric Fisher put forward his own view. 'While I appreciate the emphasis of the arguments here, have any of you considered that if there was some sort of national referendum where every person of voting age could put across their view on the matter the overwhelming majority may wish to continue as we are at the present time?' He then sought to put this in perspective. 'In any nation where there are territories and boundaries, different castes, sects, religions, dialects, tribes, there will be conflicts. Surely the objective of any resident army should not be merely to act as a defensive force but as a means of uniting people of all sections. It should be seen as a unit that can ground other members of the community in training. That is what building a nation is all about. I believe the industries of England can contribute much to India and the resources of this country can be of great advantage to many nations.'

'That is a very valid point.' Matur Rajeed seemed impressed by Cedric

Fisher's grasp of politics. 'When one looks at British industries, the tradesmen of your country can do much for our nation. I only have to list a few of the trades: glassblowing, pottery, coalmining, civil engineering; cotton and textiles in Lancashire, tin mines in Cornwall, fishing, whaling, maritime navigation. Even, dare I add, the military aspects of your army? And I genuinely believe if the British could widen their avenues of thought, there is much you could learn from our way of life.'

'Agreed,' said Cedric. 'We have certainly learned much already.'

Whittaker allowed himself a smile at the way the debate had proceeded. 'Well I think my presence here has contributed to a lively debate but I am aware that these logical discussions can degenerate into low class verbal brawls. If I could bring the topic back onto a smoother plain, I would stand by the points I made in my articles but I would concede that these gentlemen have made excellent comments about the future role of the British Army in India. Major Clancy has demonstrated his sharp mind by his awareness that the actual constitutional change of any nation comes back not to the military forces or the government but the very will of the people. Mr Fisher on the other hand is right – I feel – in emphasising that the role of the service should be to unite all the peoples rather than act as a sort of territorial policeman to different groups. There is no finer regiment in the British Army, perhaps even in the world, than the 25th and I believe that whatever the changing role in the empire the 25th will always present the way it should be done in times of peace and conflict.'

The words seemed to have touched the heart of Colonel Anderson who appeared to be glowing with pride. 'That is one comment I have absolutely no argument with. And while I have influence it will always be.'

Three

Early the next morning at Fort Valaka, a bugler played reveille. In his guest room at the barracks Whittaker woke upon hearing the sound. Already the heat was overwhelming. He took a cool jug of water and emptied the contents over his head. Slowly he rose naked from the hard bed he had attempted to sleep on and moved to the window, opening the blinds. The glaring sun flashed in his eyes which he covered quickly with his hands. He gazed out at the parade ground where soldiers lined up in formation.

'My God it's hot today,' he murmured to himself. He stared at RSM Blackshawe marching quickly across the parade ground. How on earth did the men march on parade in full regimental kit on such a scorcher of a day?

Away from the Fort, Whittaker reacquainted himself with the markets and bazaars so prevalent in India. He wandered around absorbing the sights. There were snake charmers, dancers; people seated in meditation, attractive Indian ladies in colourful saris, and a bustling street theatre. In the middle of one market a bullock stretched out while people just walked around or stepped over it. Whittaker soaked up the sights, smells and sounds of this exotic land.

Coming towards him unexpectedly he saw three English people that he knew very well. Whittaker smiled with delight at the sight of his old friends. They saw him and came across to pay their respects. The first was RSM Blackshawe. The second was Colour Sergeant Harry Chesney. The third was Lady Bernadette Shervington, the widow of a captain who had recently been killed in action.

RSM Blackshawe saluted. 'Wonderful to see you again – sah!!'

'Alright lads no need to overdo it,' said Whittaker with a touch of laughter in his voice. 'It's bloody marvellous to see you both again.'

'You remember Lady Bernadette Shervington of course,' RSM

Blackshawe said. Whittaker gazed at the beautiful blonde woman they were accompanying.

'Yes Sandy. Indeed I do,' he replied.

'We've just been escorting her to the Governor's office,' Colour Sergeant Chesney explained.

It was the perfect opportunity for Whittaker to gatecrash in on the lady's company. 'Would you mind if I look after her now lads? Lady Bernadette and I are very, very old friends.'

'Not at all Sir,' replied RSM Blackshawe. Then he turned to Lady Bernadette. 'Is that fine with you ma'am?'

Lady Bernadette looked at Whittaker with twinkling eyes and a dazzling smile that made one feel secure in its approach. 'Yes it would be Mr Blackshawe. You have been most kind and courteous. Thank you both for providing my escort.'

'An absolute pleasure lady Bernadette,' Colour Sergeant Chesney said courteously. He was equally respectful to Whittaker. 'Very nice to see you again Sir. Hope we have the opportunity to talk again.'

'We will get together I'm sure,' Whittaker said reassuringly.

The two soldiers saluted and walked off together. When they were a good way from Whittaker and Lady Bernadette they began to converse. Colour Sergeant Chesney looked at his friend and smiled.

"Ere Sandy, do you reckon those two were lovers once?' he asked in a very candid manner.

RSM Blackshawe pretended to be annoyed at the question. 'I'm surprised at you asking such a question. Really! That's neither here nor there. None of our business whatsoever.' He had spoken in a firm authoritative voice. Harry Chesney knew him much better than that. Sandy Blackshawe turned his head to Chesney who was smiling and winked. Beneath Blackshawe's moustache there beamed a mischievous smile. 'I'll lay you two bob they were! Cor, wouldn't you be, given the opportunity with a lady like that Harry my son?'

'Oh to be given the opportunity with a lady like that Sandy!'

In the shade of a tearoom Whittaker and Lady Bernadette sat in deep reminiscence of times gone by. Outside the view was of camels being led along the streets, goats, sacred cows, the bustle and flurry of a hot steamy market place. Inside, despite the sultry uncomfortable heat, Lady Bernadette appeared cool in her colonial white clothes. She wore a huge hat and carried an umbrella for a sunshade. At close to thirty years of age she was golden haired, fair skinned and a real beauty who kept her appearance in good condition.

'So. You've had tea with the Governor I take it?' asked Whittaker.

Lady Bernadette replied with a hint of sadness evident in her voice. 'I've been to pay my respects. I'm leaving India very shortly for home.' She looked at him, anticipating whether he knew of her recent bereavement. 'You know I lost my husband?'

'I heard.' Whittaker was sympathetic. 'Major Clancy told me. He and Captain Rex were great comrades.'

'Rex endured a terrible death. It's not something I want to talk about too much. I've spent longer here than I should have done. Originally I thought there was nothing back in England for me. Then I asked myself what is there here for me now. Polo and tea parties. Summer in Simla. While Rex was alive the whole world was in India for me. Not any more though. Life has to go on. I need to have meaning in my life. Some sense of purpose.'

'A long time ago in an English summer we were good friends. I thought perhaps something more.' Whittaker seemed hopeful that those old feelings might be resurrected. 'I was very fond of you once. More than fond. You do remember?'

Lady Bernadette touched his hand quickly in affection. 'I know you were. But I married Rex didn't I?'

'It was almost me Bernadette. Remember those lovely walks on the Sussex Downs?'

'I loved you once. I don't deny that. But with Rex it was very different. Women rarely go for the calm and serene man who offers stability and solidity. Rex was exciting.'

Whittaker agreed. 'Rex was a very colourful personality. The 25th Regiment is littered with them in its ranks and officers. Take Colonel Duncan Anderson for example. The archetypal Scot. A man of drama and decision. Major Jack Clancy – the Irish pugilist, poet, lover, fighter all rolled up into one. The two men you were with today. Regimental Sergeant-Major Blackshawe, a huge man with the build of a wrestler and a heart of gold belonging more to a missionary spreading the gospel than a trumpet-voiced parade ground disciplinarian. And Colour Sergeant Chesney, a rough diamond galahad who won the Victoria Cross and who loves children and animals. Stout hearted fellows.'

'And yourself of course,' smiled Lady Bernadette. 'You have quite a reputation as a newspaper journalist now. An entirely new life for yourself.'

'I could look after you back in England if you wanted,' Whittaker said with a suddenness that quite bewildered her. 'Perhaps in time maybe?'

Lady Bernadette looked at him with a deep sensitivity. Somehow she could not bring herself to say too much. Finally after a pause she spoke to him. 'I think we ought to go now Graham.'

A platoon of soldiers rode across the North-West Frontier somewhere in the vicinity of the Prakaresh Valley. They stopped as the sight of smoke rising in the distance aroused their worst fears. A sergeant took his field glasses and studied the view ahead of him. He lowered the angle of the glasses until he found himself looking at the valley floor of Prakaresh. The sight of burned out villages greeted him. He turned away and rode back through the ranks to his senior officer.

'What is it sergeant?' the officer asked, noting the serious look on the young man's face.

'It's smoke rising from the Prakaresh Valley Sir.' He hesitated. 'I think you had better take a look Sir.'

The officer took the field glasses and examined the scene himself. He lowered the glasses very slowly revealing a pained and serious expression. The sergeant made a study of the officer's face.

'Come with me sergeant,' the officer said gravely. 'We'll ride up and take a look.'

The two men rode ahead of the platoon and towards the valley. At the very edge they looked on in horror. The look on their faces was indicative of the devastation that lay before them.

'Ride back to Fort Valaka,' the officer said in an icy cold voice.

'Now Sir?' the sergeant asked. 'Yes Sir. Do you have a message?'

'I'll give you a message to hand to Colonel Anderson,' the officer said without taking his eyes away from the sight.

'Very good Sir.'

The officer turned to the sergeant. 'Take a look at this young man.' He returned the field glasses. 'Take a long hard look. That's why we're here.' He grimaced. 'This is why India needs us.'

Graham Whittaker continued his pursuit of Lady Bernadette in a more different environment. They took a pair of horses and rode over some interestingly harsh country where they arrived at a few ruined temples. Dismounting from their horses Bernadette walked away on her own. Whittaker sat on a stone contemplating the silence. There was something distinctly eerie about the place. What had taken place here in these decaying ruins? There was an aura about the fallen stones and the crumbling pillars that was different to any other architectural structure that might have existed. Perhaps lives had been lost here. It was curious and bewitching.

After a few minutes Whittaker rose and walked through the ruins. He could not see Bernadette anywhere. He looked around every pillar and post. Whittaker was very worried now and started looking frantically for her.

'Bernadette! Bernadette! Where are you?'

He was desperately worried. Where on earth could Lady Bernadette have gone? He began to run looking everywhere.

'Bernadette! Where the hell are you?'

In a moment of sheer panic he stopped for a moment to reassess the situation. Suddenly something shrieked with an animal-like cry and leapt out at him in a frightening manner. Whittaker ducked quickly. Then he turned around to see a monkey scampering away. The sound of feminine laughter came ringing out from behind a post. Lady Bernadette came into view. Her face was filled with mirth and childlike amusement. Whittaker rapidly recovered from the shock and began to laugh.

'I don't know who the cheekier monkey was,' he called out to her. 'You or that big ape that just ran away.'

Lady Bernadette teased him like a precocious school child. 'Catch me if you can!' She peeked out from a pillar. 'Catch me! You couldn't before!'

The two of them played hide and seek like children. Lady Bernadette for all of her regal bearing and aristocratic voice still possessed the nature of a child woman. Mischief sparkled in her eyes as she tried to hide from Whittaker. She peeped from behind a rock only to find him directly facing her. Whittaker took the initiative and pulled her towards him. She struggled initially. It was the pretence of a struggle though. It was obvious that she did not want to reject his advances. Her eyes were filled with a lustrous shine, the look of a woman eager for love. Splendid love. Bernadette wanted him at that moment. Gently she submitted to Whittaker's embrace. His arms clasped tightly around her. She felt his lips press gently onto hers. They indulged in a long and passionate kiss. Whittaker lowered her to the floor and glided over her. He kissed her lips slowly and passionately. He kissed her cheeks, then her neck and gently on her earlobes, setting loose a fire of passion within her that burned unchecked. They were both lost in a sea of desire amidst the ruins of these sacred temples.

Four

'A bit different to the Thames, eh Harry?' said RSM Blackshawe to Colour Sergeant Chesney who raised his eyebrows and smiled. The two men were on a barge with an Indian rowing gently along the muddy coloured waters.

The river they were travelling down ran through the centre of a town. On both sides of the river there were old shanty houses edging down towards the embankment. Some of the Indian town's people were swimming and bathing in the water. People were sitting on openings by the water. Some were in prayer. Others appeared to be meditating. There were Indians on boats with fruit and vegetables. Little children dived into the water and swam across.

Chesney and Blackshawe looked up at the homes on both sides of the river. Just on this short voyage it seemed there was the whole world to look at. Finally the boat came to rest at a house. Chesney and RSM Blackshawe stepped from the boat and entered the shanty house.

Inside, the two men were overawed. There were about half a dozen alluring Indian girls in long flowing garments, in every colour of the rainbow it seemed and a few more besides. A couple of elderly ladies sat close by waving fans up and down to keep the stifling heat in the room a few degrees cooler. Several of the Indian girls looked up at the two men and giggled.

Blackshawe turned to Chesney and gave him a quizzical look. 'Now you haven't brought me to a house of ill repute have you Harry?'

'Not exactly,' he said in a hesitant voice. 'It's more a home – well perhaps a hostel – for young ladies together with their…'

A couple of young children ran through the room without warning much to the annoyance of the elderly ladies.

'With their children you were going to say,' said Blackshawe completing Chesney's unfinished sentence.

'Orphans more like it,' Chesney mentioned. He spoke in sadness.

From a doorway with tassels hanging over it emerged an Indian lady in her late fifties.

'Welcome Harry,' she said in a voice of someone who knew him well. 'How lovely to see you again.'

'Hello Mrs Patell,' Chesney replied. 'Nice to be here too.'

Blackshawe looked at him awkwardly. 'Regular customer are you?'

'I told you. It's not that sort of a place,' Chesney protested.

'And who is this very handsome gentleman?' asked Mrs Patell, eyeing up Sandy Blackshawe from top to bottom. 'My, they make some fine looking men in the British Isles.'

Chesney introduced his comrade as if he was making an announcement at a village hall boxing match. 'Mrs Patell let me proudly introduce you to this fine piece of military colour and robust human specimen who, beneath that flickering moustache, is my good friend, drinking partner and heroic character, Regimental Sergeant-Major Sandy Blackshawe.'

Mrs Patell smiled at him admiringly. 'You should bring him again. Perhaps one of the ladies here…'

Chesney interrupted quickly. 'I think Sandy would like us to attend to the matter we've come here for.'

'Of course. Come this way then.' Mrs Patell led Blackshawe and Chesney through several rooms of the waterside shanty to an opening. There were a few children playing by the water. There was one however who looked slightly different from the rest. His skin was of a fairer complexion than the others. Mrs Patell gave the two men a knowing look. 'That is the boy.'

Blackshawe studied the boy from a distance. 'Can you call him over? He doesn't know why we're here I suppose?'

'No he doesn't,' Mrs Patell said. 'I'll call him. Ravi! Ravi! Come here Ravi! I would like you to meet two gentlemen.'

Ravi was a bouncy looking Anglo-Indian boy with sensitive eyes that could change from sadness to humour in an instant. He raced up from the embankment to the house and climbed up with all the agility and energy of a potential young athlete. When he saw Blackshawe and Chesney he seemed to be apprehensive. Ravi stood shyly by Mrs Patell who put her arm around him protectively. The two men, who stood like towering oak trees above the boy, looked at him sympathetically. Chesney and Blackshawe recognised the obvious signs that the child was the result of an Indian and English liaison. Chesney crouched down by Ravi.

'How old are you, boy?' he asked in a soft voice.

'Nine – I think Sir,' Ravi answered.

'Do you remember your father?' Chesney asked, trying to be as sensitive as he could be in such a situation.

'Yes. He's not come to see me for a while.'

Blackshawe kneeled down beside him. 'Can you tell me and my mate Harry here anything about your father? Anything in particular about him you recall more than others perhaps? The way he talked? The way he laughed? His size? His hair? The colour of his eyes?'

Ravi replied very slowly. 'He was an English officer.' The two soldiers glanced at each other quickly. 'My father was always happy. Big and smiling. Big like you.' Blackshawe laughed at the comparison. 'He had blue eyes.'

Blackshawe felt he had the young lad's confidence. He pursued the matter just a little bit further. 'We won't keep you from playing with your friends too long. Just one more question.' He glanced quickly at Chesney who was hanging on to every word. 'What was – begging your pardon – what is your father's name?'

There followed a breathtaking silence before the boy replied. Chesney swallowed. The lump in his throat was only too apparent.

'I don't know his first name,' said Ravi.

Chesney then tried to help the young boy remember. 'But – but what did you call him? Dad? Father? Pater? How was he introduced to you when he came to visit?'

Mrs Patell looked down at the boy and smiled warmly at him.

'Mrs Patell used to say,' Ravi stammered slightly, 'she used to say Ravi your father, Captain Shervington has come to see you.'

At the mention of the name Captain Shervington, Chesney appeared to sigh. Blackshawe nodded to Mrs Patell that he had heard all he needed to.

'You can go and play now Ravi,' said Mrs Patell.

'Bye-bye son. Take care.' Chesney said, ruffling the boy's hair.

They watched as Ravi ran down to the river bank to rejoin his playmates. He was a happy laughing boy who, although an orphan, was living in a warm climate and a home full of love. Surely, thought Chesney, every child should be that lucky. Warmth, love and the freedom to swim in the river and be cheeky and make mischief without hurting anyone. Chesney smiled as he watched the boy splashing up and down in the water.

'Come. Let us take tea gentlemen,' said Mrs Patell beckoning to the two men to join her in a separate room where there was tea on the table. They sat down on small wooden chairs with pink cushions while Mrs Patell poured them each a cup.

Blackshawe sipped his tea and gazed at Chesney who appeared to be thinking deeply about the young lad. 'Mrs Patell, tell me about the boy. I don't know how Harry thinks but that young boy is the spitting image of Captain Rex Shervington. I ought to know. I knew Rex well. By the heavens – that young chap is Anglo-Indian. I'll lay London to a brick on it. What's the story?'

'Captain Shervington is something of a hero in your regiment – is he not?' Mrs Patell said in a voice that sounded as if she was stating a fact more than asking a question.

'Yes he was,' replied Chesney. 'Something of a legend more like it. His exploits on and off the battlefield take some beating.'

Mrs Patell continued. 'Many years ago when Rex Shervington first came to India from England, he showed great courage and strength in the battlefield. He was, I recall, a fearless man who rode into battle at the very front of his troops. Like so many men of ego and heroic character he had his weaknesses. The drink. And women. The occasional taste for opium I am led to believe. But definitely women.'

'We know that,' smiled Blackshawe recalling his friend's wild life.

'There was a young woman,' Mrs Patell recalled. 'An Indian woman of great beauty and much desired by men. Her name was Sarah Armatradj who Captain Shervington became not only friends with but something a great deal more. They used to meet here from time to time. Anyway Captain Shervington went back to England for a while. During his stay there he wrote to Sarah to say he had married a titled Lady and would be returning to India with her.'

'Lady Bernadette,' remarked Chesney.

'Yes that is right.' Mrs Patell's voice took on a hint of anxiety. 'Sarah gave birth to a child.' She paused to look at Ravi playing. 'Ravi. Sarah continued to live here but sadly she died not long after Ravi was born. I wrote to Captain

Shervington and told him what had happened. He was astonished to learn that he had a son and saddened to learn of Sarah's death. Of course he was now married to Lady Bernadette and another woman had given birth to his child so for obvious reasons he chose to keep it quiet. Regimental honour perhaps. Or maybe he felt ashamed. It is hard to say.'

'As far as you know, did Lady Bernadette ever learn of the existence of Captain Shervington's son?' asked Chesney.

'He wanted it kept quiet,' answered Mrs Patell. 'He was an officer wasn't he? Married to a wealthy woman. If news of his relationship with Sarah had become known it could have brought disgrace to his position. Captain Shervington visited often and gave me money for the boy's upkeep. Then Harry,' she directed her words to Blackshawe, 'Harry, who is a friend of Ramajra, one of the young ladies here, told me of Captain Shervington's death on patrol. I wanted to see what we could do for the boy. He is the orphan son of a British soldier and Indian mother, although never married. What can we do Mr Blackshawe?'

For inspiration, the RSM looked to Chesney who offered none. Blackshawe appeared to be pensive. 'I almost feel duty bound to do something for the lad. Compassion for others was something my lay preacher father instilled in me. Certainly as Christians and Englishmen we'll do what we can. I'll have a discreet chat to one of the officers. It's a very tricky situation, what with Lady Bernadette and all. We wouldn't want it to reach her ears. If there's nothing official that can be done then maybe some of the lads could reach deep into their pockets to help along with the boy's future.'

A smile crept over Chesney's face. 'Blimey, if the army paid out on every indiscretion a British soldier had committed the empire would go bust.'

'The streets of Calcutta and Bombay have many children of Anglo-Indian stock,' pointed out Mrs Patell. 'Many of them without homes or parents.'

It was Chesney who had the final word showing that beneath his 'take me as you find me' attitude there lurked a man of compassion as well as steel. 'I give you my word Mrs Patell,' he said seriously and sincerely, and one knew that he meant it. 'That boy will be looked after.'

Blackshawe looked at him. He did not say a word. His expression spelled out what was on his mind. Who by? You?

Five

Things had been fairly quiet at the fort since Graham Whittaker had arrived on his assignment. He had written a few articles about India and the 25th Queen's Light Northern Regiment but as yet for the editor in London he had not been able to forward pieces on action from the front. All this was shortly to change. The news of the slaughter at Prakaresh had reached the fort.

Whittaker had been writing a brief history of the regiment when his hunt for a good strong drink had directed him to the officer's mess. He strolled along the hallway of the fort. It was a hot peppercorn summer's day. Out on the parade ground a few soldiers were practising manoeuvres. Whittaker entered the officer's mess, ordered a drink and then walked through a virtually deserted room. In the corner he espied Cedric Fisher who was sitting smoking a cigar and sipping a scotch.

'Hullo Cedric. May I join you?' he asked pleasantly, knowing that he was far too polite a man to refuse.

'Certainly dear fellow. Glad of the company,' came the almost word for word anticipated reply from Cedric.

'Hot afternoon eh Cedric?' said Whittaker seating himself.

'Very hot,' he agreed and then added a few words in a sombre voice. 'An appalling business eh?'

'What is an appalling business Cedric?' Whittaker asked, astonished that he had obviously missed something extremely important.

'You've not heard the news then Graham?'

'No! What news?'

'My goodness! I thought nothing evaded the ears of you journalists. Well old boy, on the very night of the regimental dinner, while you and I, Major Clancy and Mr Rajeed were discussing the role of the British Army in India, wholesale slaughter was taking place along the Prakaresh Valley.'

He paused, noting the look of shock on Whittaker's face. 'The colonel got the word this afternoon from a platoon sergeant who rode back with the message.'

'What happened exactly?'

'From what the colonel was saying it amounts to a sort of uprising. It seems a pagan mob without scruples or the slightest sensitivity rode into a number of villages at Prakaresh. Men. Women. Children. Their animals all cut down. Not a thing left standing.'

Whittaker was thirsting for information now. He could smell a good story. 'Any idea who – why?'

Cedric took a long drag on his cigar and blew several puffs in the air. The aroma seemed to linger in the air. He was frustratingly slow in replying. 'Colonel Anderson is meeting with Major Clancy and Matur Rajeed at the moment. I believe they have a pretty good idea who the perpetrators were. Makes our discussion the other night somewhat ironic doesn't it? I understand a great deal of the men will be moving out tomorrow. Will you be going along? No doubt that this is the perfect opportunity for you to write your articles from the front.'

'I'll be going for sure,' Whittaker said with a firm degree of certainty.

'The officers are probably planning their lines of attack at this very moment,' Cedric suggested. 'This is a sad day in the history of India but an important one for you journalists. I would go and see Colonel Anderson now if I were you.'

Whittaker finished his drink and stood up. 'Will you be around for a little while Cedric? I'd like to write an article on the East India Company.'

'Can't oblige you there old fellow. I have to leave for Calcutta.'

'When?'

'Tomorrow. If you're over there though in the not-too-distant future, come across and see me. I'll be happy to spend some time with you to help with any article you want to write.'

'Thank you Cedric. I might go and see one of the officers about tomorrow's events. Would you excuse me?' He shook Cedric's hand. 'I'll be in touch.'

In Colonel Anderson's office discussions were taking place. It was an office well suited to military conversation. On the wall there were a number of portraits featuring Queen Victoria, Prince Albert, the Duke of Wellington, William Pitt and Horatio Nelson amongst others. There was a globe on the table with the Empire clearly marked in bright red. Maps of India and geographical charts were spread out across wood panelling. On the colonel's desk there was a quill pen and books mounted to one side. The colonel stood at the wall by a map of India and discussed the situation with Major Clancy and Matur Rajeed.

Colonel Anderson admired Matur Rajeed's expert knowledge of India. He always knew that he could obtain first-hand information from him.

'Major Clancy and I have discussed the strategy that we will follow to approach the situation. The Major will take his own column out tomorrow morning and I will bring some more men the day after to provide relief or as the situation develops to further augment the numbers. One thing Mr Rajeed that you could enlighten me on. The Prakaresh Valley. The adjoining plains, the plateau and the areas along the river comprise of very peaceful villagers, people to the best of my knowledge that have no interest in warfare whatsoever. They live in small communities looking after their own families, growing their own crops. Why – tell me why – would anyone attack such people?'

Matur Rajeed rose and walked to the wall map of India. 'This area here beyond the Prakaresh Valley,' he said pointing to a region, 'until the boundaries were re-drawn by the British government, was all part of the state that Nadur Sohari ruled. When I say ruled, I mean in the sense of dominating. For a long time this fierce warrior has been attempting to take control of a number of different castes beyond this valley. Unfortunately for the British Army in India, some of those tribes have agreed on the understanding or the ridiculous assumption that Sohari would eventually overcome all opposition and become a natural leader not only of his own state but possibly even the whole of India.'

'The villagers at Prakaresh did not respond I take it?' said Major Clancy.

Matur Rajeed looked grim faced. 'I know, from my visits to that valley, Nadur Sohari has tried to entice those villagers to join him in his quest but they refused. They did not want to be part of the ferocity of war. That is totally against their nature.'

'We cannot allow this situation to continue!' Colonel Anderson snapped. His temper was fraying at the edges. 'It is intolerable that people wishing to live in peace are intimidated in this manner. I shall see the Governor and the Brigadier immediately. Jack, you might tell Graham Whittaker. This may be the story he wants. I think there's no need for further discussion gentlemen. Jack, organise the men to leave at dawn tomorrow.'

'I hope it can be brought to a swift conclusion,' said Matur.

'As swift as it can possibly be made,' the colonel assured him. 'Thank you for your help and advice Mr Rajeed.'

'I will organise the men Duncan,' Major Clancy said, rising from his chair and saluting. Colonel Anderson returned the salute. He looked deeply concerned and he considered the situation. His face reflected the tough decisions he had been called upon to make.

Outside the colonel's office, Major Clancy found himself facing Graham Whittaker who had been patiently waiting.

'Ah Jack. Can you tell me about this incident at Prakaresh?'

'We're moving out tomorrow. The colonel says that this may be the story you'll want to report. An uprising is being led by a sect leader called Nadur Sohari. We believe he may have been responsible for the skirmish in which Captain Shervington died.'

'I'll come along for sure,' said Whittaker enthused by the opportunity to report on what would surely be a rip roaring newspaper story in London.

'This is going to be a very tough exercise. There will be casualties.'

I'll still come – and I want to be with the men in the ranks.' Whittaker thought to add to that with some emphasis. 'The fighting men.'

'Very well then. Let's go to the barrack room.' Major Clancy led him through the hallways.

In the barrack room a few soldiers jostled around while Colour Sergeant Chesney and a Liverpudlian, Corporal Bill Dunham, were sparring in a friendly manner.

'Come on Dunham, I thought you Liverpool lads were fast on your feet,' he joked.

'The only thing you London boys are fast on is your jokes,' came the retort from Bill.

'How about you Bill?' Chesney jested. He danced nimbly like a bare-knuckle champ, although his poise and his movements were proof enough that he could be serious about this sport if the opportunity arose. 'You're so slow on your feet an elephant could dance faster than you.' He jabbed friendly punches at him. 'Take that – and that.'

'Call yourself nimble!' joked Bill, jumping in the air and throwing pretend punches.

'Nimble! Me! Watch this my old mate.' Chesney shuffled his feet as if to do a little dance and jumped up onto a table. 'When I was a kid my old man used to be Master of Ceremonies at a Music Hall – he used to stand up here like this on the stage with his hands spread out and he would shout out to the audience – My Lords, Ladies and Gentlemen –!!!'

That was as far as Colour Sergeant Chesney managed to get. From the back of the barrack room a soldier suddenly called out to the group. 'Attention!!'

Major Clancy and Graham Whittaker entered the barracks. Everyone stood to attention including Chesney who was on the table above everyone else. Whittaker was amused while the Major looked at Chesney with surprise.

'Colour Sergeant Chesney!' he exclaimed. 'What the hell are you doing up there?'

Chesney quickly thought out a reply. 'I was about to give a demonstration of rifle drill,' and after an immaculate pause, 'sah!!'

Major Clancy turned around and looked for a rifle. He took one from a rack against the wall, examined it from top to bottom, studied down the barrel and checked the sights. He pulled back the barrel, cocked the trigger and then slotted it back into place.

'Well, don't let me stop you Colour Sergeant Chesney,' Clancy said with a smile. 'Go ahead. Here.' He tossed the rifle to Chesney, folded his arms and watched with interest. Chesney went through the stages of presenting and shouldering arms, and bringing the rifle to the rest position.

'Very good indeed Colour Sergeant. Now get your arse down to our level.' He turned to the other men. 'Alright lads. Stand at – ease! Carry on as you were.' Then he turned back to Chesney who was now on the ground. 'Now then Chesney, you already know Mr Whittaker.'

'I do indeed Sir,' said Chesney smiling at the other.

Whittaker grinned and his glance fell upon Chesney's Victoria Cross winner's ribbon. 'I will be accompanying the troops tomorrow.'

'Tomorrow Sir?' Chesney said with surprise in his voice.

'Yes I'm sorry,' Whittaker apologised, realising Chesney was unaware of the incident at Prakaresh. 'We've only just got the details ourselves.'

Major Clancy explained to Chesney. 'You will all hear shortly but I will tell you now on the quiet, Colour Sergeant. There's been some trouble up in Prakaresh. Not far from where Captain Shervington's patrol were wiped out. Tomorrow in the very early hours several platoons will be moving out.'

'I see Sir.' Chesney appeared serious in voice and thought.

Major Clancy elaborated on the matter. 'I'll be calling you and Mr Blackshawe together but in the meantime I'm here to advise you that Mr Whittaker is going to write despatches about the ordinary fighting man in the field. I can think of no better volunteers than you and Corporal Dunham over there to accompany Mr Whittaker and give him any assistance he needs, and answer any questions he might have. Remember we want our regiment to get a good showing in the newspapers at home in the British Isles and I'd like to think you'll be able to keep an eye out for any problems that might interfere with our aims here. Alright Chesney?'

'Understood perfectly Sir.' He glanced across at Corporal Dunham with a look that suggested dismay.

'Good fellow.' Major Clancy and Whittaker turned and walked out of the barrack room.

Corporal Dunham moved forward to Chesney. 'What was that all about?'

'We're moving out first thing tomorrow to Prakaresh. I'll find out the full story shortly and then call the lads together. I think some of the tribesmen up there have been cutting up rough a bit lately. Whittaker's riding with us. He's going to write despatches back to London.'

The Corporal raised his fists mockingly. 'Where were we then Harry?'

Six

First light began to filter across the parade ground at Fort Valaka. It was the early morning hours, really the dead of night, and the temperature had hardly cooled at all from the previous day. On the horizon line a red sky was visible, blending in with the mauve and auburn colours of the surrounding scenery. Troops lined up in formation. The silence was broken in the half-light by commanding voices organising their individual squads. RSM Blackshawe strode across and consulted with Major Clancy. Then he marched across to Colonel Anderson who was standing at the edge of the parade ground.

'All present and correct Sir!' RSM Blackshawe informed the Colonel, smartly saluting him.

'Very good, Sergeant Major,' responded Colonel Anderson looking across at the sight of the regiment lined up. He looked back directly at RSM Blackshawe. There was a twinkle in his eye. 'A bloody warm morning Mr Blackshawe? Extremely bloody warm!'

'Most eloquently put, Sir!' the RSM replied, supressing a smile.

Colonel Anderson looked again at the sight of the men of his Regiment. 'Tell Mr Clancy to carry on. God speed our men, Sergeant Major.'

'I'll relay your message Sir.' He saluted Colonel Anderson and did a smart about-turn, and marched across to Major Clancy.

Colonel Anderson watched with a deep pride. On the parade ground RSM Blackshawe and Major Clancy were seen to consult at great length. The RSM then moved to one side of the contingent of troops. It was a tremendous sight and hard not to be moved by the colour and spectacle of it all. Major Clancy was on horseback at the very front of the regiment. Behind him there were numerous horse soldiers, kilted marching men, bagpipers, drummers, Indian troops; some of whom were on beautiful horses, the others would march in the rank and file. There were field guns and artillery units.

A silence fell across the parade ground. The colours of the regiment were raised high. Whittaker was on a horse and looked across at Chesney and Dunham. They could not resist smiling at the thought of being part of the occasion. The remaining darkness seemed to clear in an instant and as the early morning sun started to beam its full power, the light began to flow over the faces of every man on the parade ground, illuminating their various expressions.

RSM Blackshawe's eyes flickered from left to right. He was clear in his own mind that everyone was ready to go. Just once more he looked across at Colonel Anderson who appeared to tilt his head forward to indicate for the troops to move out.

In the stillness of the sultry early morning, RSM Blackshawe's voice fired across the parade ground. 'Parade! – Atten – shun!!'

The men responded smartly. The RSM took one pace forward. 'Colonel Anderson wishes me to relay to you – God speed the troops!! Men of the 25th Queen's Light Northern Regiment! By the right! Quick! March!!!'

Straight away the bagpipers and drummers commenced playing a rousing marching tune. RSM Blackshawe rejoined the troops.

Colonel Anderson stood in the shadows of the terrace beneath the fort, watching the troops until the last man had gone.

The men of the regiment had a difficult journey to make over very harsh country. For most of the time the sun was at its highest and most lethal, making the soldiers swelter before they had even got halfway to their destination.

Across the horizon line were some stunning mountains beyond which lay the Prakaresh Valley. Graham Whittaker rode slowly and raised his binoculars. He studied the view in the distance, knowing that somewhere out there were the errant tribesmen responsible for the carnage in the villages of Prakaresh.

At precisely the same moment, tribesmen on the opposite side had become aware that soldiers from the 25th Queen's Light Northern Regiment were approaching. A lookout safely ensconced in the rocks watched eagle-eyed as the figures in the distance became more visible. He reported his findings to a huge and muscular tribesman with a fierce and deadly look about him. The man was Nadur Sohari.

Unaware their presence had been identified the regiment proceeded on their journey to the edge of the valley. There they set up camp for the night. They knew that in all probability the next day would see them in combat. The tents were set up and the horses were roped into a corral. Sentries positioned themselves at different points around the camp. Major Clancy walked through the camp checking that all was well with the men.

RSM Blackshawe was a big burly man who in private was a quiet spiritual man. He needed moments of solitude when he could pray and seek direction from the Lord above. At Prakaresh with stunning mountains and a wide and deep valley before him, he stood by a wagon and gazed up at the stars in the night sky.

'Everything alright Sergeant-Major?' asked Clancy approaching him from behind.

The RSM turned to face him and smiled. 'Fine thank you Sir.'

'Relax for the moment,' said Major Clancy who noted the RSM standing to attention. 'No need to stand on ceremony out here Sandy. I feel like a chat. You seemed a long way from here. Deep in thought were you?'

'I was absorbing the beauty of this sky and the unending patterns of stars stretching to God knows where. Somewhere between this world and the next one I suppose.'

'You're feeling your mortality?'

Blackshawe replied from the heart. 'I always do the night before a skirmish. That's why I snatch a few quiet moments to pray and draw heavily on my faith. It will be my own instincts that carry me through the battle. It's a very strange thing you know, but when I was a lad in Brighton I would often sit by the water and look across the English Channel to France. I thought France was a million miles away. A mere drop in the ocean to where we are now though. Then I became a soldier and sailed out via the Cape of Good Hope to India, a land to me that contains beauty, passion, tragedy, exotic colours, mystery and the sights and sounds that are forever emblazoned in my memory. It's been a good life, Major. I'm a peace loving man but it was no trouble to pick up a rifle in defence of my country. I have no regrets. Soldiering is a noble profession. I know our time on earth is so short. I would like to think that in my lifetime, apart from the experience and wisdom I've gained, I somehow achieved something and contributed to the lives of others. But as I say I have no regrets.'

'Nor I for that matter,' agreed Major Clancy recognising a similar soulful trait in Blackshawe to his own. 'I can say with reflection on the past that I am glad to be a soldier, but if the Lord above was to give me my days all over again, I am sure I might have doubts about choosing this profession for my livelihood. I detest the thoughts of battles and the horrors I have seen in warfare, but my uniform gave me a duty to perform. Peace is the ultimate objective of a battle, although the cost of good mens' lives is the cross I have to bear. Now when I was a boy in Ireland, back home in Dublin, I was one of a family of eleven living in a slum tenement in a place they call Irishtown. It was a time of famine throughout Ireland. People were starving. There was civil unrest and bad blood amongst so many people. I felt there had to be a better way. From a land where the matchmaker still accompanies a courting couple to a regiment with the toughest men from the British Isles was an enormous jump. Burma, India, Afghanistan. To this place underneath the devil's own anvil. When my time is done here it'll be a cottage in Galway, a few quiet whiskys and a long sleep with only the sounds of the waves rolling in the distance.'

RSM Blackshawe allowed himself a smile at the Major's idea of heaven. Then he drew a breath to bring himself to addressing the matter of Captain Rex Shervington's orphan son. 'I wonder if I could approach you on a matter that was recently brought to my attention. Would you mind? You may think it impudent of me.'

Major Clancy looked at Blackshawe quizzically. 'Not at all Sandy. You're a direct fellow. You have my full attention.'

'In our time here in the tropics we know that as men we naturally seek the company of women.' He looked slightly embarrassed. 'Indeed men wouldn't be men would they? And naturally there have been children by these relationships. Often orphaned.'

'And naturally there are offspring. Is that what you're getting at? Offspring from our soldiers? It's no secret Sandy. I know that.'

'You've helped me there,' said a relieved RSM and then he had to proceed to the difficult part. 'I'm afraid when I tell you who the father is it won't be any laughing matter.'

The major at once assumed incorrectly that the very noble and deeply religious RSM Sandy Blackshawe was about to own up to an act of indiscretion. Clancy's eyes lit up like beacons and a broad grin spread from ear to ear. 'Not you surely!' He laughed as he spoke. 'Surely not! Shame on you! A good Christian Englishman like yourself! Did your emotions get the better of your own iron will?'

Blackshawe enjoyed the joke. He let Clancy smile and smirk. Then he told him who it really was. 'No! Not me!' He paused to let the conversation return to a more serious nature. 'I'm afraid it was a good friend of yours.' Another short pause followed. 'It's true.' In a flash the smile was wiped completely from the major's face, as he realised his friend was deadly serious. 'Captain Rex Shervington.'

Major Clancy stared back at him in shock. 'Captain Rex Shervington?'

'Yes, Major. The boy's name is Ravi. He believes he is aged about nine years old. His mother was an Indian girl who died soon after giving birth to the boy. Ravi is looked after in a place for homeless young ladies, some of whom have children. Rex married Lady Bernadette while on leave in England about nine and a half years ago. Anyway the upshot of it is that Rex did not learn about the existence of the boy until a while afterwards. Right up until his death Rex was visiting the boy regularly and paying for his upkeep.'

'How do you know this, Sandy?' There seemed to be an element of doubt in Major Clancy's voice.

'Colour Sergeant Chesney has a lady friend who lives in the same home. I went with Harry the other day to see the boy.' Clancy looked very concerned. 'The boy is the spitting image of Rex. A shade darker skinned obviously. But it's all there. The ready smile. The humorous eyes.'

At that very moment the bugler played Last Post signifying it was time for lights out.

'Hark!' said Major Clancy almost jokingly. 'I hear the bugler calling. Sandy, we'll speak about this when we've finished what we came to Prakaresh for. I will have to visit the boy myself to make my own judgement on the matter.'

'When you see fit Sir,' said RSM Blackshawe reverting back to addressing his friend with authoritive respect.

Graham Whittaker was sharing a tent with Colour Sergeant Chesney and Corporal Dunham. In one corner Whittaker filled out a journal containing detailed descriptions of the events of the past few days. He wrote in beautiful italicised writing. A candle flickered close by. Dunham and Chesney were playing cards. When they had dealt their final hand they played one last game. Whittaker waited until they had finished and stopped writing.

'Just as a matter of interest Harry. How long have you been in India?'

Colour Sergeant Chesney looked up and smiled. 'About twelve years now, Sir.'

'What do you really think of it? Anything of note I could write down about your observations in my journal that might interest the readers at home?'

'So it's India through the eyes of the footslogger you want to write about?' He took his time pondering over the question. After lighting a cigarette and blowing a ring of smoke into the air he found the words of reply. 'India to me is a lot like one's first taste of liquor I think Sir. Bitter at first. Very bitter and hard to swallow. But the more one becomes used to it, the more sweet it is to taste. It becomes addictive. Like a glass of rum or a fine leg of lamb. The flavour stays long in your mind.'

'You've no yearnings for the past?' Whittaker asked.

Colour Sergeant Chesney mused over this reply and then from this roughneck soldier came a flow of words that impressed Whittaker enormously. 'The past?' Chesney said sharply and quietly as if it was something that should be disregarded immediately. 'The past. No, I live for the thrill of the day. Not any romantic, nostalgic longings for a past that was hard, chilly and colourless. I haven't missed home so much because I've no people there. I was what you might call a child of the workhouse. An orphan in a cold inhospitable world, longing for a full stomach. I used to gaze at those rich people going past in their carriages with fine horses and drapes. The clothes of the ladies made of fine materials, shiny with colours and patterns, their faces glowing with pride and good health. The men haughty and arrogant, and oozing a swaggering confidence while inside the workhouse young children slaved away long hours, some with consumption and others with whooping cough that would echo in the middle of the night making one tremble in fear. When I was taught about the empire of Queen Victoria and the wealth of the Crown Jewels, I thought the suffering of the workhouse belonged to another planet. I couldn't believe it was all part of the same empire. The empire to me was the gold of South Africa, the riches of India. That's why I became a soldier. To be a part of that empire. The Army has been good to me. I owe it a great deal. It took me from the fog and smoke-filled streets of poverty, far away from the grime and soot and the blast furnaces of noisy industry, away from a life of tawdry overalls and resentment to a life of self-respect, excitement, pageantry and discipline.'

'You don't feel like you missed out on anything? Simple things – like marriage for example. There was never a girl that you could have exchanged this lifestyle for?'

The candle flickered. Whittaker and Corporal Dunham sat quietly listening. Chesney's eyes sparkled with the memory of a long lost love.

'I suppose you being a prim and proper gent and all that, you must find it difficult to imagine that rough and aggressive footsloggers like me and Bill over there can have sentimental and romantic thoughts.'

Whittaker put Chesney's mind at ease straight away. 'I don't find it difficult to imagine that at all Harry. Everyone has their story to tell. I also don't find you or Bill rough and aggressive. You're strong loyal soldiers with thoughts and feelings the same as any Lord or Duke's son, or peasant crofter or village blacksmith. These are the things that I am going to attempt to get across in my articles. The men of the regiment are as entitled to be sensitive and have feelings of affection and love for fine women as any other working man.'

The words seemed to strike up a flow within Chesney. It was as if he had been suppressing certain thoughts for years and had suddenly found an audience he could unleash his most private feelings to. Chesney spoke not as a man drunken with alcohol, but a man drunk with passion and emotion that had never before been evoked.

'Well I'll tell you this Sir,' Chesney said with a surge of enthusiasm, 'and Billy there will back me up when it comes to women and the sins of the flesh, if I was placed in the dock I would have to plead guilty every time. I've not been the noblest man on that score. But I've always been respectful of women and their feelings. There was one girl who stands out in my memory far beyond the dozen or so who have passed through my life. She was a nice North of England lass I met in an old cobble-stoned village in Lancashire when I was but a young soldier flushed with life and enthusiasm and bursting with good heart and cheer. This girl swept into my life as colourful as a rainbow or a fairground carousel. I was absorbed by her vulnerability and tantalising gentleness. She had the fairest long hair, friendly, smiling eyes. Her voice was sweet and gentle.' The passion that this memory carried had given way to gentility and calm reflected in Chesney's manner of speaking. 'She had the loveliest of smiles that would take away the chill on an icy cold winter's night.' The tiny audience in the tent was leaning forward, interested in his revelations. Chesney took a long drag on his cigarette and continued to speak, conjuring up a vision of the only real true love in memory. 'Alice was her name. We used to go courting down those windy old country lanes and on hot summer's days we'd walk down by the river and across the fields. Sometimes in the evenings we'd sit and talk over an ale in the village hostelry.' Then he paused and averted his eyes downwards. A look of sadness appeared in his eyes and a tremor of regret seemed to swamp the usual warmth in his voice. 'I'll never forget the day I went to see her as she was leaving the cotton mill where she worked and I told her I was going to India, and that I might never see her again. I didn't know the meaning of the word love until then. It hurt me more than being cut by the blade of a Maharajah's scimitar leaving her. Since then it's been a succession of Galahad and vagabond approaches to the fair sex from Cawnpore to Lucknow, Benares to Madras.'

Corporal Dunham quickly stepped into the silence that followed. 'Think of it like this mate. The memories we have. The places we've been. The sights we've seen. The battles we've been in from the barrack room to the mountains of Nepal. Would all that, real life in its most raw, have been worth the love of a woman?'

Chesney appeared to ponder over the words. Then he grinned. 'I will never know. Well I suppose I would never have bloody well met you, Billy you old beggar, or won the Victoria Cross.'

'Listen here Harry me old son. Who was right behind you when you won the VC? By God it was a performance to be proud of. The lads in the regiment still talk about it to this day. I shall not forget it.'

Whittaker had been there on that occasion. 'It was a situation not unlike the one we are going to be in. We were surrounded on all sides by thousands of renegade tribesmen. They came at us from all sides and we fought and fought back. I remember the ferocity and fear of it all. Do you Bill?'

'Aye that I do Sir,' Corporal Dunham recounted his own memories. 'Fourteen times they came at us with all the fury and anger of the lava of a volcano. Some men ran forward with rifles and swords to take on our attackers but they were met with overwhelming odds. By God Sir there was some real rough stuff going on that put fear and fright in the heart of any man. When the wounded fell and lay there with bullets whizzing around their heads, one man ran across the battlefield, picked the wounded up over his back and carried them to safety. It took a lot of guts Harry. I take my hat off to you. I tell you Mr Whittaker if you were going to write about one man's bravado, one man's courage, then Harry Chesney is the man you should write about.'

Chesney's eyes seemed to moisten with unwept tears at the memory. The candle flickered and the light went out. The conversation came to a sudden end.

Seven

During the night the sentries alternated their watch every hour. They were lonely figures dotted around the camp, standing poised and prepared until it was time for them to change over. In the pitch black of night only the vague silhouettes of the sentries were visible. The mountains in the distance were mere shadows but the tents were identifiable by the white canvas that gave away their position.

One sentry moved forward to take over from another. 'I'm here now mate,' a genial Lancastrian said.

'I'm glad you came. It was getting boring!' said the other. He returned to his tent while the new sentry eased himself into a rock and held his rifle at the ready. He gazed out at the nearby valley and moved his eyes from left to right. It seemed quiet enough. He relaxed. But he was unaware that in the rocks and cliff tops there were a few figures moving stealthily.

The sentry lit a cigarette; its tiny red flame sparking for an instant revealing his position. From within a crevice in the rocks a turban clad tribesman rose slowly. His sharp eyes detected the presence of lookouts and made an assiduous study of the tents and the horses. Along the rocks different figures in the night shadows rose slowly at different vantage points. Gradually more and more tribesmen materialised at different places until they were virtually surrounding the camp in large uncountable numbers.

Slowly, one agile tribesman worked his way towards the horses, carrying a knife in his hand. Just a few minutes later he was gently cutting the ropes that cordoned the horses with the intention of forcing them to run free through the camp so that they would take attention off the rest of the soldiers. The tribesmen would then move in on the unsuspecting victims of the night attack.

The sentry stared upwards at the cliffs on the other side of the valley.

He contemplated the colours of the night sky and took deep puffs on his cigarette. Then in one sudden moment of fright he began to tremble inside. He took his cigarette out of his mouth very slowly. He threw it down on the floor and stamped out the flame with his boot.

'My God!' The sentry whispered to himself. 'There's movement out there.'

Shadows moved in formation along the rocks in front of him. The sentry clasped his rifle. From the corner of his eye he saw a figure creeping towards him. In a flash he turned sharply and swung his bayonet at the attacker, jabbing at him, gritting his teeth, before felling him with a rapid thrust. Then another one came up from behind a rock and one from his opposite side. The sentry gasped with horror as the two tribesmen charged in on him. He fought with all the fury he could muster. He fired a bullet directly into the face of one. The sound of the rifle shot echoed throughout the entire valley. This spurred a soldier into action who grabbed his bugle and alerted the camp. Soldiers everywhere grabbed their guns and leapt into action.

The sentry fought like a madman as tribesman after tribesman came at him. But it was no good. He was soon struck down overwhelmed by the sheer multitude of them.

The attacking figures appeared all over the camp and every soldier found himself embroiled in the ferocity of battle. Chesney raced from his tent with Bill Dunham in hot pursuit followed by Graham Whittaker who grabbed a rifle and a hand gun. Chesney ran towards a huge wall of sandbags and fired his rifle repeatedly at the fearsome men opposing them. All around soldiers were using every weapon at their disposal; bayonets, rifles, knives, swords. A hub of violence had erupted. Explosive action raged on while soldiers and tribesmen fought. The horses ran through and several wagons were overturned in the process.

Major Clancy stormed against a group of tribesmen only to get pulled back as the horses stampeded. Some of the tribesmen were crushed under the hooves of the horses.

'They're retreating!!' screeched a soldier's voice.

The night invaders scurried away as the British lines pursued them relentlessly with rifle fire. Major Clancy looked around. There were already a few casualties. The medical orderlies started to move the wounded and the dead onto stretchers. Other soldiers attempted to round up the horses while most re-armed in the pause after battle.

'Stay by your arms men,' Clancy commanded and then he muttered under his breath, 'they'll be back.'

Chesney moved onto a pile of sandbags next to Bill Dunham. 'There must be better ways of spending an evening!'

'I can think of plenty,' Bill said with a smile, mopping his heavily perspiring brow.

The soldiers stayed ready all night long. Whittaker studied things through the eyes of a journalist. He wrote down notes and made observations. When he had finished he placed the notes inside his jacket. The night had cleared now and in the early morning sunlight, soldiers prepared themselves for what they could only assume would be a terrible onslaught. The guns and cannons were brought into line facing the direction they feared the attackers would come from.

Major Clancy took charge and organised soldiers into lines ready to combat their opponents. RSM Blackshawe handed out ammunition to the men. He checked that each of the cannons was in order. Then when he had completed this he reported to Major Clancy.

'Am I at liberty to discuss our position as regards possible tactics Sir?' RSM Blackshawe asked in a polite manner.

'By all means Sergeant-Major,' replied Major Clancy.

'Sir,' the RSM began, always in a manner of respect to his superior officers, 'to put it in layman's terms, we are currently on high ground directly facing the mountains from which Sohari and his men have challenged us. We're on a cliff-side position. If Sohari's men push us back there's nowhere for us to go except down there.' He pointed grimly to the valley floor. 'Do you think we should advance first?'

Major Clancy put one foot upon a rock and leaned forward, gazing at the mountains. The sunlight streamed across the mixed colours of the scenery. Clancy thought deeply about the situation that RSM Blackshawe had just outlined. He looked up at the crevices and his face suddenly froze with horror.

Pointing to the ridges of the mountains he said in a quiet voice, 'there you have your answer Sergeant-Major.'

RSM Blackshawe looked up. His face was ashen. 'Oh – may the Lord up above help us.'

All the way along the ridges of the mountains there seemed to be thousands of tribesmen. All the soldiers in the encampment registered looks of horror. Just as quickly as the tribesmen appeared they disappeared behind the rocks without noise or warning. It was almost as if they had stood there as a taunting show of strength to demonstrate to the men of the British regiment below what they would be up against.

Nadur Sohari in all of his awesome presence studied the British camp. He discussed details with his fellow warriors. They did not miss a single thing. They looked down and noted the entire layout of the camp: the coned tents, the field guns, the Sikh soldiers with their swords glittering in the sunlight. From the security of their safe distance they made estimates of the number of soldiers ever ready with their rifles. The horses were still being rounded up after the stampede. In Nadur Sohari's eyes there was more than just a glint of evil. He indicated to his men to move out along the rocks ready to attack the soldiers far below.

Major Clancy and RSM Blackshawe marched back along the ranks as they caught glimpses of movement in the rocks.

'Get ready men! Be on your guard!' yelled RSM Blackshawe.

Major Clancy's advice was more definite. 'This is it lads. Brace yourselves.' He carried on walking to where Graham Whittaker was situated. 'Graham, see those wagons over there?' He pointed to the supply wagons at the side of the camp. Whittaker nodded. 'Take cover beneath the wagon when the firing begins. This will be the closest to the front you'll ever get old fellow.' He looked at him with a grave face. 'This could be a tumultuous battle.'

Whittaker smiled meekly, took his rifle and headed for the cover the wagon would provide. He acknowledged that he was not a soldier any more but he knew he would be pitching in with his fair share.

Major Clancy took up his position at the head of the column as RSM Blackshawe organised the men. The soldiers were positioned into three areas: those at the front who would probably take the full fury of the attack, and the second and third ranks who were on the left- and right-hand sides of the main line, poised to attack any invaders on the cliffs. Cannons and artillery had been placed at the front. The Sikh soldiers were behind all rifle ranks prepared to give combat support.

Over by the wall of sandbags and overturned wagons that were acting as a sort of barricade, Colour Sergeant Chesney and his friends sat breathlessly with their rifles at the ready. There was a stealthy almost frightening stillness and deathly quiet. Not a sound could be heard on that limp humid morning. The faces of all the soldiers told the story. The men in the lines had varying expressions. Some were perspiring – not only from the immense heat but from the fear of the battle. Others were hawk-eyed, looking sharply from left to right. The Sikhs were leaning forward almost in anticipation. The soldiers behind the field guns betrayed their nervousness by tapping their fingers on the turrets.

RSM Blackshawe stroked his moustache habitually. Major Clancy was standing perfectly still; his eyes showed a combination of fear and fury. Whittaker rolled over beneath the wagon; his fingers lightly trembled over the carbine. A thought ran through his mind at the sight of everyone in a state of absolute stillness. From his jacket he took a journal and scribbled down some words – 'The soldiers waited in breathless silence. So still that it was like a waxworks show'. He put the journal back inside his jacket.

Whittaker waited. So still. So quiet. And God above how terribly warm it was. Then like a clap of thunder the tribesmen came down from the mountain ridges in their multitudes; fearful screaming warriors, far too many to count, racing down the rocks with guns and swords. Whittaker slid back under the wagon and took careful aim with his rifle. Major Clancy stood with his arm up in the air at the ready. The soldiers were now dripping with perspiration from fear and heat.

In the flash of an instant Clancy broke the tension and dropped his arm quickly. 'Fire at your own free will men!!!' he shouted at the top of his voice. Spontaneously the sound of volleys of rifle fire were heard roaring into the air. The sound of field guns reverberated across the valley. The ranks of the tribesmen had been drastically thinned by the effects of that first strike but they still kept coming.

'My God!' gasped Chesney. 'We'll get slaughtered.'

Rifle fire burst again. Volley after volley followed. More tribesmen fell. Many more were still coming. More rifle fire hit the air. Many more of the attackers fell. There were so many still coming and now they were only yards away. Even the devastating effects of the cannons could not keep them back.

Chesney, despite his massive surplus of courage, felt overwhelmed by it all. This was surely finality staring him in the face. It was certain death if he had ever known a certainty in his life. He was damned if he would die like an animal in hiding or a rabbit down a burrow. Colour Sergeant Chesney was determined to go out in glory right to the end and in a moment of spirit and passion which shocked his comrades he leapt onto the sandbags and stood there firing at the attackers again and again.

'You've gone mad!' shouted an astounded RSM Blackshawe. 'Get down!!'

Almost as soon as Blackshawe had yelled out to him a bullet struck Chesney in one of his calf muscles. Another bullet grazed his forehead and one more appeared to strike him in the temple. It sent him into a state of oblivion and he toppled back over the lines, immediately presumed dead by all those around him.

'Oh Harry. You poor beggar!' moaned Bill Dunham. He was shocked by the apparent death of his friend. However he had little time to mourn for him as frenzied warriors leapt over the barriers. A bitter struggle commenced. Immediately Dunham found himself in hand-to-hand combat. He used his boot, knife, rifle and sword to fend off his opponents.

RSM Blackshawe was a master of the bayonet and in a fearsome struggle he ducked and dived, and swerved from side to side as an unsavoury character waved a sword viciously at him. In a matter of seconds RSM Blackshawe had erased his opponent.

Clancy's firing lines kept on shooting until they too found themselves embroiled in terrifying combat. Their opponents kept on coming and coming. The numbers were too large even for the Sikh warriors who were cut down in their tracks. The attackers did not seem to be diminishing in numbers but the soldiers were now dwindling low.

Whittaker fired and fired from beneath the wagon where he was concealed from the battle. But one keen sharp-eyed observant native spotted him and rushed towards the wagon. The man jabbed at Whittaker, trying to spear him and missed by inches. He attempted to thrust a sabre through the wagon but Whittaker shot him quickly. Thinking he was safe he crawled beneath the other wagons. When emerging he found himself at the edge of a cliff with a sheer drop behind him. At the moment that he realised where he was, a tribesman came rushing at him. The two men fought perilously on the edge in hand-to-hand combat before Whittaker punched his opponent bareknuckle style over the side to his death. To his horror Whittaker lost his footing and found himself falling.

He tumbled over the side of the cliff. But he fell onto a ledge not more than fifty or sixty feet below. He landed with a thud in a hillside bush. He rolled over in the bush, grimaced and closed his eyes in excruciating pain. Whittaker's facial expressions registered the deep pain he was experiencing. Then as he tried to adjust himself in his position, he could hear the cries and shrieks of the battle raging up above. He was feeling pain of a different kind for above him the contingent of British soldiers were being wiped out. The noise of the tumult raged on for a while. Whittaker closed and opened his eyes in pain. The sounds of the screaming and shooting terrified him. He cried out to the sky in agony.

'Oh Lord. Dear God end this battle please.' He moaned and writhed in his state of pain. His back hurt and hurt and hurt.

The battle raged on and on until the last British soldier had dropped. Now the scene was one of a mass of soldiers lying dead in the terrifying fangs of the frontier heat. Dunham lay dead against the sandbags. Major Jack Clancy had fallen with a lance in his back. There was not, it seemed, a single person alive.

Nadur Sohari's warriors walked through the rubble of the battle individually looting the bodies and picking up guns and swords. One man reached down to Chesney's frame and pulled a rifle away from his blood-splattered body, quickly moving on. The aggressive moment of the tribesman had jolted Chesney from the state of unconsciousness he had been in. Aware of what was happening Chesney opened one eye slowly to see the backs of Nadur Sohari's men walking away from him.

Whittaker meanwhile struggled to pick himself up from where he had fallen. He attempted to wriggle free of the bush. He arched his back and legs, and let out a cry of pain. His back felt as if it had suffered a fracture. The joints in his legs seared with pain as he moved. Somehow though he had to move from the dangerous cliff ledge. Up above him the battle had ceased. A silence had fallen now. Whittaker looked towards the top of the cliff. It was far too steep to scale, and too risky at the present time. He knew Sohari's men would still be there plundering the ruins of the regiment.

He looked down over the ledge. It seemed he had no choice. Reluctantly he decided to descend. Grabbing the edge of the ledge, he slithered over the side and began the long slow climb down to the valley floor.

Several times, as Whittaker put his boots into cracks and crevices, he sighed with relief that he was managing to overcome the odds which had been thrust upon him. Down and down he moved, very slowly, not daring to avert his eyes towards the drop below for fear of being overcome by vertigo.

Suddenly he became aware of something happening above. A loose stone struck him on the shoulder, deflecting onto the cliff. Gravel and dirt rained down in his eyes and hair. He shook his head quickly. He opened and closed his eyes, gently releasing them allowing the moisture to run, taking away the dirt. His back and legs ached beyond the point of being simply unbearable. He was precariously positioned on the descent down. One wrong footing and he would be gone.

From up above there was a creaking sound and then, to Whittaker's horror, he realised that Nadur Sohari's men were pushing the empty wagons and field guns over the cliffs. He gritted his teeth, fiercely clung to the rocks and dug his heels into the crevices as the wagons and cannons tumbled down, miraculously missing him on either side. The artillery and wagons splintered and sparked as they struck the rocks. All Graham Whittaker could do was to hang there and press himself into the cliff. It seemed to go on forever as the property of the 25th Queen's Light Northern Regiment tumbled past him. Amazing, he thought, how such a formidable battery of British fighting men could suffer such an inglorious defeat at the hands of mountain tribesmen.

When it seemed that all was clear above he continued downwards. He took each step steadily and cautiously. Halfway down he paused for relief. Then unexpectedly a rock gave way beneath one of his boots. In desperation to maintain his grip he struggled to reinforce his hold. Alarmingly, one of the rocks in his hand began to come away. He was hanging on by one foot and one arm. For a few seconds he thrashed around desperately. The next moment he had completely lost his grip. He found himself sliding down a rock face. Whittaker grabbed and grasped at something to hold. He managed to clutch a ledge. There was nothing beneath his feet, not solid ground, no crevices to rest his boots in. He kicked like mad with his boots until a couple of holes had been formed in which he positioned himself. The circulation in his arms seemed to have stopped. His body was still aching in every place from the fall onto the ledge. His clothes were torn and his face was scratched and bleeding. Perspiration mingled with the blood on his body. He hung there breathing deeply. His stomach was going in and out at great rapidity. Agony was inscribed all over his face. Now his head was spinning and his mind racing like the wind.

Finally he started to allow the remaining wind in his sails to take him on the last descent. He found that he had a much firmer footing and hand grip for the rest of the way down.

Something like half an hour later with the blazing sun having taken its toll on him, a somewhat battered, sunburnt, cut and bruised Graham Whittaker gratefully fell onto the soft valley floor. He lay there for ages trying to regain his strength. He felt tired and exhausted. The sun's rays pounded down on him. Eventually he recovered and stood up, agonising at the thought of the long walk he had before him under the crucifying sun.

It was some miles away that Colonel Anderson was leading another column. He rode proudly at the front of his men, totally unaware of the devastation that had already been inflicted on the rest of his troops at Prakaresh.

Eight

Colour Sergeant Chesney lay perfectly still in the battlefield. He looked out of the side of his eyes at the tribesmen around him. At close range he was watching Nadur Sohari and his men walk through the rampage they had created. Chesney had witnessed the slaughter of the wounded. He had seen the field guns and wagons pushed over the cliffs. Now he watched Sohari. Although Chesney could not understand a word of the dialect Sohari was speaking, he could sense the aggression and menace in every syllable. There was nothing Chesney could do but lie there and patiently wait for them to go.

To his astonishment the tribesmen suddenly flocked together and began leaving the battlefield. Nadur Sohari's men took their leave and with their horses raced off leaving a trail of smoke behind them. A wave of relief flowed through Chesney and for the first time that day he rolled over. But as he turned, his relief turned to heart stopping terror. A hand shot out and grabbed Chesney's ankle.

'Oh my God!' he gasped. A voice filled his ears just as suddenly. It was an English voice. Directly behind him was a very badly wounded Sandy Blackshawe. He croaked in a voice that was barely alive, more a shadowy whisper racked with pain.

'Harry old fellow, have they all gone?'

'Yes Sandy, they've all gone.' Chesney was almost in tears. There was a trace of intense sadness evident in his eyes. His face crumpled with revulsion at the stench of death and human suffering that was there in abundance around him. He turned around to face Sandy Blackshawe and realised just how mortally wounded the RSM was. Blood soaked his tunic. 'Oh Sandy what's happened to you?'

'I'm only just hanging on.' He coughed violently. Chesney tore strips off his own uniform and wrapped them around Blackshawe's wounds. 'I don't think – I'm – going to see tomorrow.' Suddenly this courageous, sensitive man, whose parade-ground presence was normally so overpowering and formidable, looked forlorn, fragile and in need of something more than a miracle. 'Harry, my old mate, I've got four bullets – embedded in me. I'm not going to survive whatever you say.' In between bursts of broken wheezing speech and deep chesty coughs, Blackshawe shivered and breathed deeply. 'Harry I've been writing – writing …' He choked and spluttered. 'I've been writing a letter to my mother.' He took some papers from his tunic and shuffled them forward. 'I started writing this yesterday. I had the feeling it was going to be last post for me. If I don't finish this, write to her in Brighton. Don't tell her I died in pain. Say it was peaceful and easy and…'

'I'll help you Sandy,' said Chesney softly. A tear formed in one eye.

The shadows of the night fell, by which time Chesney found himself the only surviving member of the column. Sandy Blackshawe had died and gone to his maker. The voice of that strong and decent man would never echo across the parade ground at Fort Valaka again.

Chesney strode through the figures that lay all around. Somehow he needed – even felt duty bound to pay some sort of military tribute to his fallen comrades. From beneath a couple of dead soldiers he found some water carriers and a loaded rifle. Next he found a collapsed tent and tore off white strips which he used as bandages for his wounds. He wound a piece around his head where the bullet had grazed him and another strip he tied around his leg where the calf muscle had been struck by a bullet.

With the tiny amount of strength he could manage, he walked through the gruesome campsite carrying his rifle and water carriers. He stopped twice. Once to pick up a bugle with a cord that he hung around his neck and secondly to pick up the regimental colours that were lying in a corner of the battlefield. When he had checked to see if there was anyone else alive he walked up to the ridge and sat down and prayed for the men that had died.

Chesney stayed on the ridge until the next day when the sun rose with the dawn. He had been half asleep on his rifle. If anyone had stumbled across him that day they would have found the sight of a saddened and weary man with a bandage around his forehead. He rose and walked down into the battlefield.

Just once more he needed to pay his silent respects to each of his comrades. Some men looked as if they were in a peaceful dreamless sleep. Others lay around the camp with all the appearance of a child's doll; their arms outspread and heads rolled to one side. He took one final look at Sandy Blackshawe who had found the peace that eluded him the previous day. Poor Sandy, the fierce-seeming regimental sergeant-major who possessed such a deep Christian faith that he approached death with not so much as fear but a curiosity for the life beyond this one, which he strongly believed would justify his adherence to the Ten Commandments.

The sight of so many other dead comrades, including the Sikhs who had fought in the British ranks, appalled him and he could stand it no longer. He hurried back to the ridge. He was breathing heavily. The thought of the entire column having been wiped out was too much for him.

A glorious red sun rose up above the mountains and a gentle wind blew. Chesney took the regimental colours and thrust them hard into the ground. The wind suddenly blew full force, taking hold of the colours and stretched them out fully against the sky. The dazzling bulldog insignia of the 25th Queen's Light Northern Regiment fluttered in the early morning light. Most poignantly the sun rose to its fullest heights on the horizon and Harry Chesney took the bugle and blew the Last Post. The mountain valleys took the echo and the sound was that of a hundred buglers in chorus.

Chesney was the only survivor of the column. His heart was saddened to the point of despair. It was the only tribute to the fallen men of the 25th Regiment he could think of. Yet it was a great tribute. If an artist could have recorded the scene on canvas it would have been a sight for the annals of history. Like some distant, messianic figure Colour Sergeant Chesney stood on the ridge, his head bandaged, and he played the Last Post on his silver bugle. The sun caught the metallic sparkle of his instrument and the sky became a glorious blue with the regimental colours blowing in the breeze. Chesney , not a man given to shows of derring-do or emotion, could not restrain himself. The tears flowed from his eyes. When he had played the last note he stood to attention in absolute silence for one minute. He then picked up his rifle and fired into the air the maximum number of shots each cartridge contained at evenly spaced intervals. The effect as each shot rang out was to echo across the valley as if a rifle squad had fired together. The colour sergeant reloaded each cartridge as it became empty, fired off some more, and then did the same again until twenty-five bullets had been fired.

Chesney stepped back as he fired the last shot. He lowered his rifle by his side.

'Twenty five bullets for the 25th Queen's Light Northern Regiment,' he said softly. Then he saluted. 'May God bless these great men. My comrades and friends.' No sooner had he said the words than the sun seemed to illuminate his face as if someone in another place had heard him. For some reason, perhaps because of his solitude, his own survival and the trauma he had been through he found himself speaking the words of the 23rd psalm. It was as if he wanted to speak out to the spirits of all the men he had served with. The Army had once been a home for the cockneys, scouse, Irish, Scots and Home Counties boys who lay dead on the grim battlefield at Prakaresh. His voice was emotional and faltered as he spoke; his face was stained with tears.

> 'The Lord is my shepherd: I shall not want.
> He maketh me to lie down in green pastures: he
> Leadeth me beside the still waters.
> He restoreth my soul: he leadeth me in the paths
> of righteousness for his name's sake.
> Yea though I walk through the valley of the
> shadow of death
> I will fear no evil: for thou art with me:
> Thy rod and thy staff they comfort me.
> Thou preparest a table before me
> in the presence of mine enemies: thou
> anointest my head with oil: my cup
> runneth over.
> Surely goodness and mercy shall follow
> me all the days of my life: and I will dwell
> in the house of the Lord for ever.'

With some trepidation he gathered his things, including the water carriers he had earlier retrieved, and he began to walk, limping and carrying his rifle over his shoulder. He was a lonely and solitary figure leaving the battlefield. The colours of the regiment blew strongly, almost defiantly in the breeze, as if to express loudly that the spirit of the men of the 25th Queen's Light Regiment lives on.

For Graham Whittaker, his lonely journey had been a dispiriting time. He had struggled along on his own, his body racked with pain. He was hot to the point of boiling, hungry and close to exhaustion. At a boulder in this harsh frontier country, he leaned back and rested for a while. He shook his clothes from his limbs. They were wringing wet with perspiration. He mopped his brow. Up above some birds of prey circled ominously, swooping lower and lower as if they were ready to move in for the kill. He looked up at them and considered it was a sign indicating he should be on the move. This was no place to die.

Suddenly there were several bursts of rifle fire. A few birds fell to the ground. Whittaker was aware that there were horse riders approaching. He immediately took cover behind some nearby rocks. Several tribesmen rode into view. One was extremely sharp-eyed and spotted Whittaker's footprints in the ground. He could hear the dialogue between the tribesmen. Slowly he shifted round behind the rocks and studied the three men who had dismounted. At once he recognised them as Nadur Sohari's men. Whittaker steadied himself. To his horror he realised they were approaching the rocks. He had to defend himself but he had no weapons to do so. He began to move back slowly, pushing himself into a corner. How in God's name would he get out of this one? He had to think fast. One of the men pulled a scimitar from his belt and advanced with stealth. Whittaker scooped up a handful of sand and when he was certain they were almost on top of him he moved cautiously to one side and prepared himself.

Whittaker leapt out from behind the rocks and threw the sand into their eyes. He let fly with his boot and fists at each of them. Then he knocked them down. One of the tribesmen had dropped a rifle. Straightaway he grabbed the gun and then ran like mad towards one of the horses. He leapt up but as he tried to ride away one of the men came rushing at him with a sword. Whittaker had no choice. One shot fired from the rifle. The tribesman fell to the ground. Quickly he rode away. But the two remaining men recovered and mounted their horses.

Frantically he rode as fast as he could. Behind him the two tribesmen rode in hot pursuit. Shots rang out, whizzing past Whittaker's ears. He crouched in the saddle and then he turned the horse, much to the surprise of his pursuers. He straightened himself in the saddle, and raised the rifle. Taking quick careful aim he shot both of them. His heart sank. It had been a terrifying close shave. He rode away at a furious speed.

He could not take any more of the stench of death that hung over this place and as he rode not once did he cast a backward glance. It was some time later when he was well clear that he began to slow his horse down. For a while his horse gently clip-clopped along. In the distance there was a strange drone, only very slight, but it was definitely a sound breaking the hot placid atmosphere. He listened anxiously. He mopped his brow. It was hazy on the horizon. The view was blurry. Heat shimmered, obscuring the far-flung distances around him. Whittaker fixed his gaze intently. The sound was getting louder and louder. It was the sound of bagpipers playing *Lochaber No More* followed by *Cock of the North*. He allowed himself a broad smile. It was Colonel Anderson and the relief column riding towards him.

The colonel rode at the front of his beloved regiment with a fresh contingent of troops behind him. Bagpipers marched proudly. A young lieutenant rode up by the side of Colonel Anderson and pointed out Whittaker in the distance.

'Sir. There's a man over there.' He looked alarmed at the sight of only one man.

'Well, Lieutenant MacKenzie – do we know who he is? Friend or foe?'

'Sir,' Lieutenant MacKenzie said hesitantly, 'it's the military journalist Graham Whittaker.'

Colonel Anderson's face became ashen. He turned to look at the Lieutenant. The realisation that some unnatural disaster had befallen Major Clancy's column seared through him like a lightning bolt. 'On his own? Where are the rest of them?' His voice was icy cold but composed.

'There isn't anyone else Sir,' replied an equally icy Lieutenant MacKenzie.

'We'd best be prepared for the worst. Halt the men here.' The colonel rode out to greet Whittaker. He tried to smile but the look on Whittaker's face told the story.

'I'm afraid the news I have for you, Colonel, is going to be hard for you to bear.'

'Go on,' said the Colonel, adopting a serious tone. 'Don't spare me the details.'

Whittaker replied, speaking in quiet deliberation. 'Colonel, as far as I know I – I am the only survivor of the column that Major Clancy commanded.'

A look of distinct horror swept over Colonel Anderson. 'How?' He could not manage any other words.

'I'm sorry Colonel. I wish there was some easy way I could tell you.'

'Tell me!' The Colonel was tense and on edge.

Whittaker recounted the details for him. 'At the edge of the Prakaresh Valley where we camped we were attacked first by a small band of tribesmen. It was only a slight attack at first. That more or less put us on the alert. They came later in the day – in their multitudes. There were just too many. They came at us from all sides.'

'But – how did you get away?' the Colonel gasped in a shattered voice.

'I fell over the side of a cliff and onto a ledge. It was too hard and risky to scale up, so I went down to the floor of the Prakaresh Valley and I made my way back from there. I grabbed this horse from some tribesmen I encountered.'

Colonel Anderson was horrified. He swung around in the saddle and called out to Lieutenant MacKenzie who had halted the column. 'MacKenzie! Over here!'

The Lieutenant rode across to the two men. Colonel Anderson contemplated the awfulness of the news he had just heard.

'Sir?' Lieutenant MacKenzie said. He studied the colonel's expression in anticipation of the orders he was about to receive.

'It is the very worst news we could have expected.' He paused to allow the gravity of the news to sink in. 'Get some of your best men together and go up to the ridge at Prakaresh and report back to me what you find. I want every member of that column accounted for. We'll be making camp up near those mountains tonight.'

'Yes Sir,' Lieutenant MacKenzie saluted and rode away.

Colonel Anderson turned back to Whittaker. He was normally a strong spirited man, sincere and blunt speaking, who kowtowed to nobody. This time with the death of so many decent and loyal men at the hands of Nadur Sohari's tribesmen he had suffered a huge personal and strategic loss. 'I cannot find words Graham.'

Whittaker looked at him in immense sympathy. He knew that Colonel Anderson would take the loss of so many good men from his regiment with a very heavy heart. 'Sometimes Colonel, words are not necessary. Looks speak more than a thousand words of dialogue.'

Chesney's journey had not known any lucky encounters. There seemed to be no relief in sight for him. He found himself struggling in the wildest of scrubland. Chesney wandered on and on dragging his rifle and stopping every so often under the shade of a tree. He was completely lost with no idea of the direction he was heading in. Above Chesney the sun hung like a lantern, tormenting him. He took a long drink from his water carrier and continued to walk.

To further add to the difficulties of the moment, he noticed a sandstorm rising on the horizon. The sandstorm blew fiercely across the scrubland and Chesney looked anxiously for some shade. His head ached and ached from the graze wounds he had earlier received. His legs were losing the power to maintain the trek across the countryside. The stress on his wounded calf muscle was too much. Gradually the pain seeped through to his entire body. He began to keel over. Dust swirled around and around him. He tried to shield himself with his bare hands but he was near to exhaustion and collapsed on the ground.

The colour sergeant lay there for hours. Long after the storm had ceased he remained unconscious. Two hooded figures appeared in the distance. One of them saw the figure of the British soldier and pointed him out to the other. They approached him slowly. For a few minutes they circled around him before turning him over and examining his condition. They realised that he was only just barely clinging to life.

Colour Sergeant Chesney never knew what happened then. The events since the battlefield became a blank in his memory. He opened his eyes and looked around. What had happened? Where was he? Chesney felt the bed beneath him. It was made of straw. He gazed upwards at the ceiling. Except that it was not a ceiling; more of a roof made of mud and straw. Realising with utter dismay that he could quite possibly be a prisoner, he pulled himself up from his bed. To his astonishment he found that his wounds had been washed and new pieces of cloth had been tied around them.

There was light streaming through an entrance. Outside there were oxen and men working, carrying out chores in a native village. He could only see the figures in the distance. For several bewildering moments he watched the poverty-stricken villagers. Chesney let his eyes drop for a second and he fixed his gaze on the face of a small child who stared at him in puzzlement. The child was no more than five or six. He smiled at Harry Chesney and then ran outside. Chesney was bemused. The village seemed friendly enough.

'Let's see where we are,' he muttered to himself. He stepped outside and the sun caught him fully in the face. Putting his hands up to act as a shield from the sun he stood in the middle of the village and looked around him. The expression on his face changed instantaneously. 'Lepers!' Colour Sergeant Chesney stepped forward and gasped in horror. 'I'm in a leper camp!'

Miles away Colonel Anderson and Graham Whittaker were deep in conversation at a table inside a tent, talking of the tragic battle at Prakaresh.

'All those men gone, Graham. So many good ones. And Clancy. Jack Clancy was one of the best. He was a decent, likeable man, tough as a rhino with a sentimental Irish heart. A good, spirited leader who came up through the ranks and could inspire others. The regiment's going to miss those fellows. I feel almost a sense of shame. I should have led the first column. I should not have delegated it to Jack. I was so anxious to halt this trouble before it got any worse.'

'You're being too hard on yourself, Colonel,' said Whittaker, in noble defence of Colonel Anderson who he held in great respect. 'You must remember that I was not on the battleground for the entirety. I was scaling down a cliff after I lost my footing. It's quite possible there may have been a few survivors.'

Colonel Anderson turned to look out of the tent and he saw Lieutenant MacKenzie dismounting from his horse. 'We'll find out. MacKenzie's just returned.'

Lieutenant MacKenzie saluted and began to recount to Colonel Anderson. 'Sir, I'm afraid Major Clancy's column has been entirely…' He stopped short of saying the words 'wiped out' as Colonel Anderson stared upwards to the heavens, closed his eyes and brought his head down in one movement. 'My patrol could not find a solitary sign of life anywhere.'

'Every man gone.' The Colonel uttered in disbelief in a hushed broken voice. 'Did you account for everyone, Lieutenant?'

'No Sir!' came back a sharp reply.

Colonel Anderson gaped, surprised. 'What do you mean? No Sir! I thought you said the column was completely slaughtered!'

Lieutenant MacKenzie tried to explain. 'Well Sir, that's just it. My men have taken down the names of every man who died in battle. We've accounted for every last man but one and we can't find a hide nor trace of him. It's got us baffled Sir. If he's not dead I can't think of how he could have survived. Sohari's men wouldn't have taken any prisoners. The men think he must have run away.'

'I was there. I didn't see anyone run away,' said Whittaker in amazement. 'No one could have run away. The only way out was the way I went. Down a cliff.'

Colonel Anderson's Scottish temperament was being stretched to its fullest limits. He was huffing and puffing. 'Well – who in the hell is it? Who is this man you and the patrol have got it into your heads to presume that he deserted the regiment in the face of action? This is what you're saying isn't it?'

MacKenzie was slow to reply after a moment of breathtaking silence. 'The VC winner Sir. Colour Sergeant Chesney.'

Colonel Anderson looked up, aghast. His face displayed enormous shock. He clasped his hands together as if in prayer and lowered his head. When he spoke, every word was spaced, stinging the air with great effect. 'Colour Sergeant Chesney? The VC winner. The man that ran away?'

'Impossible. I am sure he was one of the first to be shot,' Whittaker stated in disbelief. 'Corpses don't get up and walk away.'

It was later that night that Graham Whittaker and Colonel Anderson rode in the darkness where the battle had taken place. Soldiers cleared the ground and took the dead away. Both men dismounted from their horses. Colonel Anderson was ashen faced. 'It was by divine providence you survived this,' Colonel Anderson said coldly. Whittaker said nothing. He looked around in dismay. 'Well Graham,' the Colonel continued, 'now I know how Lee felt at Gettysburg, Napoleon at Waterloo and Colonel General Gordon at Khartoum.'

'Don't be hard on yourself, Colonel.'

A fire burned in the background. The light seemed to illuminate Colonel Anderson's face. His face was full of crevices and his eyes had a weary tired look about them. 'Oh don't worry, I'm not feeling sorry for myself. Why should I? The colonies have run red with the blood of good men who gave their lives in combat. The soil has been fertilised and watered by the blood of the fallen in battle. Africa for example. India. The United States after the Civil War. It is isolated battles like this and the slaughter in the Prakaresh Valley that make my soul shiver. The wasted lives of good decent men. That is what angers me the most!'

Nine

The rain fell heavily on that night in 1899 as Harry Chesney and Graham Whittaker reiterated the story. Prakaresh, Northern India was a long way from the London dockside where the two middle-aged men of contrasting characters and lifestyles faced each other.

Whittaker paused in reflection. 'I can see Colonel Anderson now on that day. He was not a man given to an easy show of expression, but his voice betrayed his true feelings. He was devastated.'

'He was a good man,' Chesney remembered. 'I met him years later.' Chesney changed the subject quickly. 'Of course that was long after the humiliation of the trial I had to endure.'

'I'm sorry, really sorry, that you had to go through so much agony after Prakaresh.'

'That wasn't just it you see, Mr Whittaker. I was labelled the VC winner who ran away. When I eventually got out of that terrible leper village and found my way back to Fort Valaka, I became precisely that – a leper. No-one would believe my story and I was court martialled. It was only the work of my defence counsel who went back to the leper camp to get proof that I had been there. The prosecuting counsel couldn't disprove the case. But after all that, it left doubt in many people's minds.'

'I'd gone on another assignment by the time you'd been found and tried, Harry. I was sent with the Lancashires when they took on Sohari. We were away for months rounding on Sohari's men. It was even more fearful that I'd imagined. But Sohari's rebellion was put down.'

'My time in the Army only had a short time to go,' Chesney seemed to be speaking more in sadness than bitterness. 'It was made clear to me by some of the regiment that despite me being cleared, there would be attempts to prevent me re-enlisting. Colonel Anderson could not understand it when I chose not to stay on. I took an honourable discharge. It felt more like I had been railroaded out in a cloud of shame and disgrace. The way I look at it, my only crime was serving my Queen and country. All I got was a right royal kick up the backside.'

Whittaker gazed at him, thinking how this kindly but gruff younger man must have been shattered by being a victim of circumstances. Surely he would have had little faith in human nature.

'So – after the Army you went your own way?' he asked, interested in how the course of Chesney's life would have gone.

'I became something of a nomadic vagabond,' replied Chesney. 'Not for me discharge and the arrival home in the middle of a rainy night in Portsmouth to a life of commissioning and a soldier's measly pension. I wanted to continue tasting the spices of life. And I did! I took a journey to Darjeeling where I saw the work in the tea plantations. My wanderlust took me south to Ceylon, and it was there I found my peace and tranquillity at Nuwara Eliya, a place of soft green hills reminiscent of the lush green of the Sussex Downs but with the balmy heat of the far eastern sun warming the tea crops and the very souls of those who worked their toil in the fields. I stayed awhile to learn the trade of a tea merchant. It's a trade I learned well – so well that it stands me in good stead today.'

'Then where did you go?' Whittaker was intrigued by the spirit of this man.

'One day I decided that I should see more of the world, so I took passage aboard a tea clipper sailing from Colombo, and on a bright sunny morning with only a gentle breeze firming the sails, I cast my eyes upon the heads of Port Jackson in Sydney, New South Wales. Using my knowledge of the plantations of Darjeeling and Nuwara Eliya, I worked as an importer of tea.'

Whittaker gave him his considered opinion. 'You did not waste your life, Harry. You did not make that age-old mistake of dwelling on the past, remembering in anger the isolated incidents that through no fault of our own are inflicted upon us which make our hackles rise.' He stopped for a moment, hoping Chesney would continue the conversation but there followed a pause. 'There is something I'd like to ask you…'

'Feel free. I have no secrets Mr Whittaker.'

Whittaker was curious about one aspect of Harry Chesney's past.

'In our talk this evening, you mentioned Captain Rex Shervington.' He sought to add with emphasis. 'The late Captain Shervington.'

'Indeed I did.'

'And you made mention – of his son…'

'Ah!' Chesney said, without signs of reproach as the sensitive subject of Captain Shervington's illegitimate son moved into the conversation.

Whittaker leaned forward. 'Ravi. That was the boy's name was it not? The same boy you told Mrs Patell you would look after. What happened to him Harry?'

Chesney smiled knowingly. 'I kept my promise. Throughout my years in Ceylon and New South Wales I corresponded with the lad and sent money towards his upbringing. Eventually when I came home I sent the lad his fare and brought him to England.'

Whittaker stared incredulously. Was this man opposite him saying that he had unofficially adopted Captain Shervington's son?

Harry Chesney remembered the day he had met the young adult Ravi. It had been at Victoria Station in 1897. Chesney had returned home to England a few years previously himself. Now he was at the station waiting to renew an acquaintance of long ago. A steam train arrived. He stood there waiting anxiously for the arrival of Ravi. He wore dapper clothes and a hat; quite the fashionable gent, some would have thought. Train doors opened and slammed. Crowds moved along in a hurry. Porters and railway workers streamed across the platform. Smoke from the funnel flared over the crowd obscuring his view.

The smoke dissipated slowly. Chesney suddenly found himself gazing at a young man of obvious Anglo-Indian features. He watched as the young traveller walked through the barrier. Almost immediately he caught sight of Chesney. The mutual recognition was instantaneous in their eyes. Ravi put down his case, removed his hat and outstretched his hand. Chesney took his grip with a warm firmness.

'I will never be able to thank you enough Sir for all you have done for me.' Ravi spoke in a quiet gentlemanly voice. His appreciation embarrassed Chesney who was not used to words like this.

'The name's Harry. There's no need to call me Sir,' he said bluntly but warmly. 'I was only ever a colour sergeant. Not a captain like your father.'

'But you were a winner of the Victoria Cross. I remember Mrs Patell telling me on that occasion you came to see me with your friend Mr Blackshawe.'

'Mr Blackshawe,' Chesney repeated softly. The name brought a note of nostalgia to his memory. 'That was twelve years ago and now you are a man of twenty-one.' He picked up Ravi's bag. 'Right lad, we're going for a ride through London now and I've tickets for a Music Hall show tonight.'

Outside Victoria Station Chesney and Ravi boarded a hansom cab. Ravi was wide-eyed and interested as Chesney pointed out famous landmarks such as Big Ben and the Houses of Parliament.

'So that is the mother of all parliaments,' Ravi said with some delight.

'So they say,' Chesney replied in a manner that seemed unimpressed by the grandeur of these buildings.

'There are so many things I want to see in England,' Ravi said enthusiastically.

Chesney had seen it all so often that he could not show any real enthusiasm. With a heavy heart Chesney yearned for the blue skies and the warm sunshine of tropical lands far away from this grey place where class distinction still separated the rich and poor. 'You'll see it all in due course I'm sure,' he said kindly.

'You have been most kind to me – sending money for my upkeep, writing to Mrs Patell to see how I was getting on and bringing me to England. Why have you shown me such kindness?'

Chesney was hesitant in his reply. 'Captain Shervington was something of a widely-respected officer in the regiment. It was on his recommendation that I got my VC I owe that to his memory.' He stopped for a moment to study the Thames. 'I suppose another reason is that I was an orphan boy like you. I also made a promise to Mrs Patell and I wanted to see how you turned out. Should you go back to India you will have benefited in many ways.'

A thought crossed Ravi's mind. 'Why did you never marry and have a son of your own?'

Chesney laughed. 'I've met many a fine maiden in my time. But men like me, we travel, and we never settle.'

In this he spoke in jest but in reality he had turned down the opportunity of romantic happiness perhaps once too often.

The Music Hall show was a bright bustling occasion. It was Ravi's introduction to one of the more entertaining aspects of English life. He sat enthralled by the theatre and the audience. The pit orchestra struck up the music. The curtains sprang back on both sides of the stage revealing a painted backdrop. The scenery could not have been more nostalgic if it had been chosen especially for Ravi and Chesney. Beautifully painted and realistic were palm trees, pagodas, and a deep blue sky with attractive tropical multi-coloured birds. There were the most stunningly adorned women wearing sarongs who moved gracefully to the music which was a tune set to the words of Rudyard Kipling's famous poem *Mandalay*. Ravi sat fascinated by this colourful display. Chesney noticed a sprinkling of uniforms in the audience and his memories were stirred.

Onto the stage came a lively and cheerful entertainer with a sparkling grin and a rousing manner which put the audience into a happy mood.

'My Lords, Ladies and Gentlemen!' he boomed out loudly. 'May I bid you all a most magnificent, a most magnifying, magnificatious, magnicative, magniloquent, magnetically, magnanimous, magically, marvellous, melliferous, meritorious and memorably mesmeric welcome!!!' The audience responded happily. 'And if you understood a word of that you're a better man than I – Gunga Din!' The audience responded again with applause and laughter. 'And speaking of Gunga Din…' Drums started to beat in a sort of military rhythm. A spartan musical accompaniment began with an Indian mystical flavour about it. From one side of the stage a man appeared dressed as the mythical Indian water carrier Gunga Din and he took a position behind the entertainer. 'You've all heard of Gunga Din haven't you Ladies and Gentlemen?'

Almost as if they were trained to reply on cue, the audience responded as one, 'We've heard of Gunga Din!'

Smiles broke out everywhere. It was Ravi who had the biggest smile though as he listened to the story of Gunga Din. The entertainer launched into the poem with zest and he strode across the stage delivering the lines in an expressive manner. He was skilled in the art of showmanship and he had the audience absolutely spellbound. When he came to the last line, 'You're a better man than I am, Gunga Din' the entire audience gave him a standing ovation.

Chesney was on his feet cheering. 'More! More!' he roared.

'More! More! More!' yelled the audience.

'You want more?' The entertainer cried. 'You want to hear more?' The Music Hall was in a frenzy now. Everyone was shouting for more and stamping their feet in approval. The artist on stage smiled in approval. 'Do you want to hear *Mandalay*?' he shouted.

'We want to hear *Mandalay*!!' came back the reply from the audience so quickly and so much in unison that it sounded more rehearsed than spontaneous.

The response was so good it even surprised the entertainer. 'Cor they trained you well, didn't they?' The audience roared with laughter. 'Alright my hearty people, *Mandalay* it is! Strike up the music boys!'

Down in the pit the orchestra started to play the opening bars to *Mandalay* and the drums struck a marching rhythm. The entertainer turned to face some of the attractive women on stage who wore sarongs. 'Now then my lovelies – sway those arms – and move those hips. Isn't that great boys? I could watch it all night!' The girls swayed and moved alluringly while the entertainer played to the audience for all that he was worth. 'Come on girls! Remember ladies, you're Burmese temptresses; Far Eastern alluring oriental maidens – not Whitechapel char ladies!' Next he turned to the man appearing as the Indian water carrier at the back of the stage. 'He's a good lad!' He winked at the audience and jerked his thumb back. 'He walked all the way from Liverpool dressed like that! Forget about the water son. I'll have a beer with you later on!!!' The audience were really in a happy boisterous mood now. The entertainer, beaming a huge smile, started to march on the spot. The ladies moved like oriental dancers and the water carrier saluted as he marched. The whole stage was alive now. 'Here we go!' The orchestra moved into the first verse. Almost over-reaching himself, the entertainer expanded his voice across the Music Hall. 'By the old Moulmein Pagoda, Lookin' eastward to the sea...'

Mandalay, a place in another world. Ravi looked at Chesney. His eyes were shining. Chesney may have been a Londoner but his heart was pounding in time to the rhythm of the orient and the temple bells somewhere east of Suez.

When the entertainer had finished, he and his supporting cast took a bow to great applause. Chesney was one of the first to stand up. Ravi was stunned to see how his guardian could easily show emotion. He was standing, clapping loudly with a big grin spread-eagled over his face and a tear running from one eye. Mandalay! thought Chesney. Oh the glory to be in such a place, and to feel the warmth of that eastern sun and scent the aroma of the tropical plants. He went to sit down and noticed Ravi looking at him curiously. Chesney winked at him mischievously.

The entertainer was in peak form that night. He knew he had the audience in the palm of his hand. His smile was contagious.

'Do you like the teeth ladies and gentlemen?' He flashed them a huge smile. 'When people meet me and I smile at them they're not sure whether to pat me on the head or give me a lump of sugar!' The audience were happy and responsive. There were a sprinkling of army uniforms amongst the throngs, which he acknowledged. 'I see we have some gentlemen down there from our services. No doubt you're here for Queen Victoria's parade tomorrow. You are very welcome lads. Ladies and gentlemen, would you give our army lads a round of applause!' The audience at once gave them a loud response. The entertainer continued. 'What regiment are you from Sir?'

The reply came back swiftly, bringing a smile to Chesney's face.

'The 25th Queen's Light Northern Regiment! Sah!'

'And does your regiment have a tune associated with the ranks?' asked the man on stage.

'Yes! *D'ye Ken John Peel?*' the soldier replied.

'*D'ye Ken John Peel?*' the entertainer repeated. 'I know it well.' He looked towards the orchestra in the pit. 'Mr Conductor Sir, shall we make that our next song?' The conductor nodded and smiled back. The entertainer looked towards the audience. 'Do you all know *D'ye Ken John Peel?* Have you heard it?'

The smiling and enthusiastic audience knew exactly how to respond. 'We've heard of *D'ye Ken John Peel!*'

'Tell you what ladies and gentlemen, seeing you know it so well, I'll sit back and let you sing instead!' Then he said with a laugh in his voice, 'Let's sing it together folks. Come on everybody! Life's too short not to enjoy it. I want to hear you all sing and having a good time. Mr Conductor sir, strike up the music!'

Immediately the conductor indicated to the orchestra to start playing. The entertainer led the singing and in the best music hall tradition he managed to get everyone, young and old joining in. It was a sparkling and happy atmosphere that Ravi would remember for the rest of his life. He looked around at the audience. There were ladies in floppy hats and bustling dresses; men in bowler hats with chequered suits and bow ties;

soldiers and sailors. Everyone looked happy. Just about everyone in the audience who knew the words sang along. Most of all Harry Chesney, who sang loudly for he had heard the song played countless times by the military band on the parade grounds at Fort Valaka in India long ago.

The entertainer performed several more songs and a dance routine before coming to the finale. He walked up to the edge of the stage and the audience just knew with breathless expectation that something special was coming. One moment they were all singing along. Now there was a hush as the entertainer made an announcement.

'Ladies and gentlemen,' he began. 'This is a special day in London in this year of 1897. Many of you have travelled here to see the big parade for the Diamond Jubilee of our beloved Queen Victoria who has reigned over our great nation for sixty years.' At this point the whole audience stood up and clapped wildly. The applause went on for a moment before the entertainer indicated for quiet again. 'I know a lot of you fine folk will be there tomorrow to watch this great parade that you will tell about to your grandchildren in future years. Will you join me ladies and gentlemen... three cheers for our great Queen! Hip-hip!' The music hall audience joined in unanimously. 'Hooray! Hip-hip! Hooray! Hip-hip! Hooray!' The orchestra played *God Save the Queen*.

It had been a great night of entertainment on an historic occasion. Outside, as people left the theatre Ravi and Chesney mingled with the crowd. Chesney seemed to stop dead in his tracks. It was the sight of army uniforms that threw him off guard for a moment. Two young soldiers walked past him. On their arms were the insignia of the 25th Queen's Light Northern Regiment. The dazzling bulldog seemed to leap out at him from the colours that flickered in the early morning breeze on the ridge of the battlefield at Prakaresh. It stirred his memories suddenly and joltingly. Ravi noticed the faraway look in Chesney's eyes.

'Are you alright Mr Harry?'

The mention of Mr Harry brought a smile to his face. Chesney had never been called Mr Harry except in India where some of the natives at the various garrisons had used that title.

'I was far away in India or on the road to Mandalay,' said Chesney wistfully.

'The music brought back memories for you Mr Harry?' Ravi perceptively observed.

'You'll never know how much,' Chesney replied. He changed the subject swiftly for he had no intention of dwelling on the past. 'Anyway, I've booked a couple of rooms in a nice hotel for us tonight. Tomorrow we'll go and watch Queen Victoria's big parade. Then we will go down to leafy green Sussex.'

The two men crossed the road and entered a hansom cab.

It was truly a day for the history books on June 22nd 1897 when the most magnificent parade to ever grace London's streets took place. Harry and Ravi stood amongst the crowds of people and watched one of the most colourful pieces of pageantry take place that they would ever see in their lifetime.

What a spectacle it was too! The heads of eleven of Britain's great colonies across the world were in attendance. Princes, dukes, ambassadors and envoys were there. Representatives of all the nations of the empire joined the great parade. Australian cavalrymen from New South Wales rode past confidently in the manner that befitted the proud nature of a young and exciting country. The Gurkhas from Nepal had come. They were strong, tough and resilient men who would be loyal and supportive to the British in military campaigns throughout the next century and beyond. Soldiers from India, Canada and South Africa were amongst the fifty thousand or so troops who accompanied Queen Victoria as she was paraded in an open-top coach through the streets of the great city of London.

For Ravi this was the most wonderful introduction to Britain he could ever have imagined. Truly he thought this must surely be the best country in the world.

Ten

Chesney peered through the window of his hotel. Down below a coach and horses passed by. A lamplighter walked slowly along the street. Upstairs in the comfort of this regency style hotel, Chesney luxuriated in the warmth of a comfortable chair. He removed his tie and sat deep in thought and remembrance. His eyes felt heavy. He could feel himself drifting away.

Sleep came quickly. There were two rifle shots. A sudden splurge of pain. His head ached and ached. There were two more rifle shots. One grazed his leg. Another one bit into his calf muscle. It was burning steel striking cold flesh. Pain seared through him. He was keeling over. He was falling. Falling. Falling. Suddenly Chesney's eyes opened wide and staring. He had been dreaming about that terrible day at Prakaresh when he had been wounded early in the battle. It was a torturous memory. For a while he relived that day.

Perhaps the memory that haunted him the most was the court martial he had endured. How long ago was it? 1885. And it was now 1897. Strange how certain days and moments in life stay in the memory so visibly and often more painfully than happier times. Chesney remembered the day he had returned to Fort Valaka. He had been immediately arrested on a charge of desertion. An unjust charge which was followed by long arduous days in a military court.

1885. What a year of unexpected change that had proved to be. Chesney remembered the court martial long ago. He was lucky to have had an extremely sharp defence counsel in Lieutenant Henry Allason. The Lieutenant was a gentleman of the old school but he had the cunning of a street brawler when it came to legal technique.

Lieutenant Allason and Colour Sergeant Chesney sat at a table while the prosecution lawyer Major Gordon Irving cross-examined each witness. Above them in a very sticky courtroom a rotary fan swished around, which made very little difference to the temperature. Other people who waited to give evidence perspired in the heat. It was a closed hearing and there was not a sole judge but an Army committee making their conclusions.

Major Irving was also sharp and incisive. By his line of questioning he virtually took it for granted that the court martial was an open and shut case. He was no match for his counterpart however.

Colonel Anderson was called upon to give evidence. Major Irving approached him with a mixture of caution and respect. 'Colonel Anderson, your career in the Army has often been cited to the men in the regiment has it not?'

'In what sense?' The Colonel seemed apprehensive.

Major Irving's approach was one of flattery but hardly relevant to the court martial of Colour Sergeant Chesney. 'You are a man who rose through the ranks – from ordinary fighting Tommy to Colonel. An inspiration to many of the young lads in the ranks.'

Lieutenant Allason rose to his feet quickly. 'Objection! I do not think this line of questioning is relevant to the case.'

'Oh! But it is!' An aggrieved Major Irving turned sharply to the committee. 'If I could alert you gentlemen to the fact that Colonel Anderson would understand from his own experience the pressures on the men in the ranks when they are on the battlefield.'

The presiding committee whispered to themselves. Captain Bruce Harrison, the President of the court, nodded in acknowledgement. 'Very well. Objection overruled.'

Major Irving continued to question Colonel Anderson. 'Colonel, you have fought in the front line on many occasions. You know just exactly what your soldiers face against the enemy. How would you sum up your feelings when the combat lines are drawn? How did you feel as an ordinary Tommy under the baptism of fire?'

'Obviously I can't speak for every individual soldier. For myself especially when I was a younger man I felt a mixture of things.' Colonel Anderson always spoke in carefully measured phrases.

'Such as…?' Major Irving pressed him to be more specific.

'Excitement. Edginess. Fear. Maybe even panic.'

'Panic,' Major Irving repeated what he perceived to be a key word in this court martial. He glanced quickly at Colour Sergeant Chesney. 'The sort of panic that may have driven Colour Sergeant Chesney from the battlefield?'

'Objection!!' Lieutenant Allason barked angrily. 'Major Irving is speaking as if the accused has already been found guilty. It is unacceptable to me that the court acts in this tone.'

'Objection sustained,' Captain Harrison responded.

Major Irving felt that he had made a significant point. He would save the best for later. 'I have no further questions for the Colonel at this stage Sir.'

'Lieutenant Allason – do you wish to question Colonel Anderson?' asked Captain Harrison.

Without hesitation, Lieutenant Allason rose and moved to the front of the court. 'I most certainly do.' He positioned himself centre stage, looked hard at everyone in a show to assert his independence. He swivelled round quickly to face the witness. 'Colonel Anderson, what is your opinion of Colour Sergeant Chesney?'

He contemplated before answering. 'I believe he is a man of honour. A rough diamond maybe. That is not meant in a derogatory sense. There are some who have levelled that description at me.' He paused and then added a further degree of respect. 'The colour sergeant is a most exemplary soldier.'

'A man of courage? A good reliable man?' Lieutenant Allason suggested.

At once Major Irving rose to object. 'Objection! The defence counsel is influencing the witness with his choice of words.'

'Objection sustained,' said Captain Harrison.

Lieutenant Allason was not to be outdone. 'Let me put it another way. How would you describe Chesney's military career?'

'I think the fact that he is a Victoria Cross winner and a colour sergeant should speak for itself.'

'Would you refresh the court's memory as to how the colour sergeant won the VC?'

'Objection!' Major Irving was on his feet again. 'With respect to the colour sergeant we are not assessing his past career. Neither are we questioning his undoubted courage under fire that merited him the honour of winning the VC. We are, if I may remind the court, questioning whether Colour Sergeant Chesney deserted the regiment at Prakaresh under fire.'

'The court needs no reminding, Major, just why we are here,' Captain

Harrison said, appearing to be annoyed at Major Irving's utterance. 'I'll allow your objection. We – do – know Colour Sergeant Chesney's record. His courage winning the VC is well known.'

For a moment Lieutenant Allason seemed perplexed at the small amount of leeway the court was allowing him. Then he realised that the objection of Major Irving and Captain Harrison's statement had more or less locked themselves into a corner by acknowledging Colour Sergeant Chesney's bravery. He suddenly asserted himself with great confidence.

'Since Colour Sergeant Chesney's gallantry is acknowledged by us all I have no need to ask the colonel to tell us the story of how the accused won the VC. And to all of us here in this court today, don't just take my word for it. My very worthy opponent Major Irving says, in his own words, 'neither are we questioning his undoubted courage under fire'. The President of the court has just told the courtroom 'his courage winning the VC is well known'. Colonel Anderson has stated 'I think the fact that he is a Victoria Cross winner and a colour sergeant should speak for itself'. I put it to the honourable members of this court that Colour Sergeant Chesney, a man of undisputed courage, a man of honour – emphasized by Colonel Anderson – is not the sort of man to run away under fire.'

Captain Harrison shuffled in his chair, obviously impatient and embarrassed by his own error. 'Lieutenant, do you have any further questions of Colonel Anderson?'

'I do Sir,' Lieutenant Allason replied. 'Colonel may I ask you this?' He approached Colonel Anderson until he was almost on top of him. 'Why – did – you – instigate these court-martial proceedings? In my opinion most unnecessary proceedings.'

The question caught Colonel Anderson unaware. There was a hint of anger in his eyes. 'Because I had to in the circumstances.' His voice was firm and cold.

Lieutenant Allason closed in for the kill. 'What circumstances were they, Colonel? Be specific please for the attention of the court.'

The colonel erupted. 'The circumstances where over half my garrison was wiped out in a single battle! One man survived from that skirmish in almost improbable odds. It had to be questioned how he came to survive! The battle was comparable with the one at Isandlwana in South Africa.

The tribesmen there do not take prisoners! They are known to mutilate the dead. Do you understand me young man? Eh laddie?'

'In this court you will address me as Sir!' Lieutenant Allason came back quickly, showing a rare flash of anger amidst his normal display of calm. 'You simply could not take his word? The word of a man whom you regard as a man of honour. Do you not like or respect the soldiers under your command, Colonel? Are these whole proceedings being held to make a scapegoat out of Colour Sergeant Chesney, to save loss of face on your part for the most disastrous military and strategic decision you have ever made in what was up until recently an unblemished Army career?'

'Objection!' Major Irving was quick to find fault. 'I object most strongly. The defence counsel is intimidating the Colonel and ridiculing his authority. Some of the words he has been using are wildly speculative and borne out of pure guesswork and general assumption.'

Colour Sergeant Chesney ran his hand over his face in dismay at the awkwardness of the proceedings. At first he had likened the battle in court room to that between two unrelenting bareknuckle fighters battling on covered in blood and perspiration. Now he viewed the tactics of the court room duellists as being like that of two back street villains in the slums of London in an all-out public brawl continually resorting to gutter tactics. In a sense he was pleased about that for he knew he had a heavyweight on his side who would last the distance and fight to the bitter end.

Captain Harrison took control. 'I must allow that question,' he said. 'Lieutenant Allason I would remind you I will not tolerate the humiliation of those called upon to give evidence. Be careful of your choice of words. Remember to respect your senior officers. Mutual respect as far as a court room allows, please.'

'Sir, I will ensure my line of questioning does not degenerate to that level. I am respectful of my superior officers but as the defence counsel I have to pursue the complete facts. From time to time these jousts are bound to get fierce and forceful in order to establish the true story behind the reasons for this court martial.'

'Please carry on. We need no lecture from you, Lieutenant.'

Lieutenant Allason moved forwards to Colonel Anderson. 'Could I put that question to you again? Why could you not accept his word? Could you not see the terrible ordeal that he had been through? Can you not envisage the sheer horror of being the only survivor on a battlefield running red with the blood of good men from all parts of the British Isles who were proud to have served in your regiment under your command? Perhaps no man more than the former workhouse boy Colour Sergeant Chesney.'

Colonel Anderson was nobody's fool. He came back sharply and angry at what he saw as court room humiliation. 'I'm happy to answer that question. I am the Colonel of this regiment! Responsibility for the men lies with me! I cannot just take a man's word, no matter how much personal respect I have for him. That is not how military matters work. I have my duty to uphold. It is not an issue of whether he is a likeable man or not but of his conduct under the greatest pressure that the fighting Tommy will have to face in his service.'

'Quite,' Lieutenant Allason acknowledged. 'Chesney returned to Fort Valaka voluntarily did he not? He was brought in by an Indian horse trader who found him struggling on his own in the desert near the leper camp?'

'Yes he indeed returned of his own volition. Those were the circumstances of his return. They were the facts. But his survival on the battlefield where wholesale slaughter took place, that came under question. I cannot reiterate that enough.'

'And when he was examined by the medical officer, the wounds – the grazing of his forehead and his calf muscle – were verified.'

'They were.'

'There was no doubt then, Colonel Anderson, that Chesney saw action at Prakaresh?'

Again Major Irving was on his feet. 'Objection! Are we to assume the wounds were incurred by Colour Sergeant Chesney on that same day? Could they not have occurred in some other confrontation?'

'Sustained,' agreed Captain Harrison.

This was not satisfactory in Lieutenant Allason's view. He walked across to the committee. 'If I could appeal to you Sir. I am moving on very restricted ground here. Many of the questions I'm asking – very important questions, which could prove my client's case – are being cut off in their prime, by my opponent's objections.'

Captain Harrison showed absolutely no concession. 'Lieutenant, you know the rules in a court of law.' Lieutenant Allason nodded that he did. 'Therefore you must accept that I have the power to veto an objection if I see fit to do so. Please do not question my authority or doubt my credentials.'

'Yes Sir,' the Lieutenant said in a humbled tone. 'I have no further questions of Colonel Anderson.'

Lieutenant Allason returned to sit alongside Chesney. He appeared very solemn. In his mind a devastating thought came to the foreground. Was it possible that this court was slanted? Was it possible that a preconceived verdict of guilty had already been decided on? He would not be defeated. The dice were not totally stacked against him. He watched as the Indian official Matur Rajeed took the stand.

'Don't worry Harry,' Lieutenant Allason whispered to Chesney. 'I've got a surprise witness to produce.'

Surprise witness! Who could this possibly be? Chesney could only gasp in utter amazement. 'Who?'

Lieutenant Allason did not reply as Major Irving began his questioning of Matur Rajeed. Major Irving's courtesy concealed a courtroom killer instinct.

'First of all Mr Rajeed, thank you for agreeing to appear here. I trust you were not disrupted from your official duties to attend?'

'Not at all. I shall endeavour to answer your questions to the best of my ability.' Matur Rajeed was equally diplomatic but he was not a man to be underestimated. He had hidden reserves of courage and was capable of stating a formidable case for any cause he sincerely believed in.

'You are probably wondering Mr Rajeed just why I called upon you to attend this court martial. The reason is that you can enlighten the members here on some of the geographical aspects relating to this case.'

'The geographical…aspects?' Matur Rajeed was puzzled. Lieutenant Allason also appeared mystified. What was this angle?

'Yes. The incidents of the alleged – and I stress alleged desertion, so as the defence counsel has no cause for objection – took place in the region by the Prakaresh Valley. Colour Sergeant Chesney in his testimony has stated that upon recovering from a horrifying night he found himself the only survivor. He then proceeded to try and walk back to the Fort. He states that he passed out in a dust storm. When he regained consciousness, he found himself in a leper camp.' Major Irving felt inclined to repeat that for the emphasis of the court. 'A leper camp?' He allowed the words to sink in. Then he looked around the courtroom to see how attentive the members were. Major Irving allowed himself a long stare at Chesney. 'Do you know of a leper camp Mr Rajeed, in that vicinity?'

'I know several. It is no secret there are a number in different places. Normally they are well away from travellers' tracks.'

'What is the condition of these leper camps?'

'The people are self-sufficient. They have to be of course. Living in isolated conditions as they do, outcasts from their own tribes, they must look after each other.'

'Tragic circumstances,' Major Irving said grimly, and there was no doubting his sincerity. 'We all live in hope that medical science may one day find a cure for this most terrible of diseases.' He took a deep breath. 'Tell me Mr Rajeed, you know the areas where these lepers live – do they venture out of their colonies at any time?'

'Very rarely. Although obviously in their search for food they would have to leave their colonies. But it is rare that they do. Their illness isolates them. They are visited by compassionate tribesmen and occasionally medical teams.'

Major Irving tried to relate this information with Chesney. 'Do you think it likely that lepers from a colony seeking food, upon finding a British Army soldier lying unconscious in the middle of a harsh frontier plain, would go to his aid – even to the extent of taking him back to their own camp?'

'Objection!' Lieutenant Allason had to throw his opponent off balance somehow. 'The Major is asking Mr Rajeed to make a broad general comment on an act of human kindness. It's hardly relevant in the context of this court martial.'

The committee discussed this between them. Captain Harrison made his decision. 'I must overrule that objection. It seems a very relevant question. Please proceed with your answer Mr Rajeed.'

'They are people who have to be kind and compassionate with their own. I feel sure they would go to help any injured person. Not all frontier tribal dwellers are warriors. In every person there is an element of love.'

Slowly Major Irving was gently guiding Matur Rajeed to substantiate the case against Chesney. 'We now conclude the possibility that these people could have helped Colour Sergeant Chesney. Let us establish just where this took place. What is the nearest leper colony to Prakaresh?'

Matur Rajeed thought for a moment. 'At Kandarapah.'

Now Major Irving was going to destroy Chesney's story. 'At Kandarapah – which is in my estimation about seventy miles away from where the battle took place.' He glanced back at Chesney. 'That is a long way for a man with wounds to walk, a man with a wounded calf muscle and a head grazed by bullets. Yet somehow, according to the testimony of the colour sergeant he was rescued by lepers – he does not recall how or where! These lepers who on a rare occasion journeyed out from their colony. It's quite a story isn't it? Who would have believed it?' He was emphatic now and became contemptuously dismissive of Chesney's story. 'In fact I say to the court now, who can possibly believe it? Thank you Mr Rajeed. I've concluded my examination.'

Major Irving strode to his table. Lieutenant Allason immediately rose and walked to the front of the room. He did not address Matur Rajeed but pitched his oratory to everyone.

'I would like to thank my admirable opponent for his clarity in stating exactly what happened to Colour Sergeant Chesney. I agree. Who can possibly believe it?' There was a short pause as Lieutenant Allason allowed the words to take their desired effect. The members of the court were bewildered. Not least of all Harry Chesney. The officer's big moment had arrived. He was about to dominate the courtroom in an explosive manner. 'I believe Colour Sergeant Chesney's story! Do you know why? It is an extraordinary story about an extraordinary man. In years to come, when the full history of India has been written and the role of the British soldier is fully defined, there will be many stories of legend that are impossible to believe. Rather than doubt the plausibility of the colour sergeant's story, the authenticity of it should be considered.' He removed a letter from his jacket and held it up to the court. 'I have here a statement signed under oath by one person who was on the battlefield with Chesney. Someone who also survived.' From another pocket he produced a second letter. 'I also have a letter written by a dying man who survived the night and passed away in the early hours of the morning. He gave this letter to be passed on to his elderly mother in Brighton. Chesney consoled the man on that terrible battle-scarred place.' Lieutenant Allason strode around the court with the letters and placed them on the table before the committee. There was a hush as the officers read the two letters.
Chesney looked concerned for he knew that it was crucial evidence that would almost certainly tip the scales of this biased courtroom. Colonel

Anderson showed a look of interest, while Major Irving mentally calculated what his next move would be. Lieutenant Allason now turned his full attention to the committee. He looked directly at Captain Harrison. 'Sir, you now have before you the two letters. The first one was written by the distinguished newspaper journalist Mr Graham Whittaker. Mr Whittaker is currently with the Royal Lancashires who are pursuing Nadur Sohari in the North-West of this country. In his absence while he is reporting for a London newspaper he left a signed statement in which he testifies that he saw Chesney struck down at the very front of the lines. Mr Whittaker states that Colour Sergeant Chesney leapt onto the sandbags at the commencement of the confrontation, firing over and over again at his opponents before being apparently struck in the leg and head by bullets. Chesney fell back over the lines, presumed to have died.' The officers on the committee looked up sharply, as did Major Irving. The story intrigued them more for its content than in its context as evidence. With a dash of the theatrical he began to tear the legal fabric apart. 'Gentlemen, I believe from my heart, not only in my role as the defence counsel, but also as a man who believes in fair play, that the statement alone from Mr Whittaker should be sufficient proof for the court to conclude that the accused is innocent. Colour Sergeant Chesney should not be in this room in a court martial on a charge of deserting the battlefield under fire! By God gentlemen! He should be recommended for another Victoria Cross!' He was very angry but strove to keep his temper under control. He allowed the words to sting the air.

'Mr Whittaker's story, his written testimony, was conducted under oath. He was on the battlefield long enough to see the start of the battle, before falling onto a ledge. It was impossible for him to scale back to the battle scene. The full details are in the letter. Let us consider the second letter. Consider if you will the scene at Prakaresh. Nadur Sohari and his tribesmen have caused devastation. They have left the field, believing every soldier to have perished. Chesney is lying still amidst the ruins of this group of men; a terrifying scene of carnage! Then to his amazement – and perhaps horror – he finds he is not the only person alive. A very badly wounded Regimental Sergeant Major Sandy Blackshawe is barely clinging to life. This fine man, whose voice boomed over the parade ground with such resonance, could scarcely raise a whisper to his good friend Harry Chesney, except to ask him if he could thank his mother for all the kindness and love that a mother could give a son.' Lieutenant Allason picked up some notes that he had strategically placed on a table. 'RSM Blackshawe scrawled a letter to his elderly mother. I am not going to dishonour the RSM by reading out all the contents of a very private and emotional letter in the public arena of this courtroom. However, I have made some notes and I will quote one line from his personal letter; one line that makes it very clear that the accused was on the battlefield.'

He addressed the committee now more than the courtroom. 'I refer to the line in which Mr Blackshawe has written of – and let me quote to you with great emphasis – Colour Sergeant Chesney's welcoming presence and warm confident friendship giving me support and strength in my final hours between this rich, rewarding, satisfying life I have led to entering the Kingdom of the Lord; the Lord whose love for me has never wavered, like the immense love I have for you my own dear mother.' The Lieutenant lowered the notes. The court was moved. 'The rest of this letter was of a personal nature. It was important to the dignity of this court that I quoted the one line only. It is a very relevant line. Note the statement, 'Colour Sergeant Chesney's welcoming presence'. Note too if you will the words 'in my final hours'. Now tell me. Now prove to me that the colour sergeant deserted under fire. He was there in the thick of things and he stayed on supporting a comrade who had suffered a long drawn out end.' He then turned round to face Matur Rajeed. 'Sir, I'm sorry that you have been kept waiting while I detailed the contents of those two letters.'

'I understand Lieutenant,' said Matur Rajeed who had been impressed by his interrogator's performance.

Lieutenant Allason was completely in control now. He had the courtroom mesmerised. 'I want to speak to you about the leper camp at Kandarapah where Mr Chesney found himself. Apart from an excellent command of the English language you speak several dialects. Is that correct?'

'Yes. It is.'

'Mr Rajeed, do you speak the same dialect as those at Kandarapah?'

'Yes I do, Lieutenant.'

'Fine,' Lieutenant Allason said with a smile. 'If I were to produce a witness from that camp would you be able to converse in that same dialect with the man?'

Chesney was almost beside himself with horror at the thought of a witness being brought from Kandarapah's leper camp. It was unspeakable that a terribly sick person, afraid of showing his afflictions to anyone, could be wheeled out for public display and interrogated in a courtroom.

'If you wish me to act as an interpreter I will do so,' Matur Rajeed said politely, but even he looked concerned.

Before the questioning could go on any further Captain Harrison interjected sharply. 'I must interrupt there! Lieutenant Allason! Do I understand you correctly? You – are going to produce a witness – from…?'

Lieutenant Allason replied without any show of expression. 'That is correct Sir. I intend to bring a witness from Kandarpah who will confirm for you that Mr Chesney was there. Someone who was in the leper camp…'

Anger glowed in Captain Harrison's eyes. 'This court is suspended for fifteen minutes!' he snapped. 'I want to see you and Major Irving in my office immediately.'

Major Irving looked across to Lieutenant Allason and raised his eyes in dismay. What was happening now? The two officers followed Captain Harrison into the ante-room where they sat down opposite him. Surprisingly the atmosphere of formality and procedure in the courtroom was more relaxed now. Captain Harrison did not show any anger now. He was in reality suppressing it. He smiled almost slyly at them.

Lieutenant Allason kept on considering the possibility that this court had been directed by Army headquarters in India to find Chesney guilty. So many factors seemed to indicate that. An obvious bias against Lieutenant Allason's objections. An obvious favourable response to any objections that Major Irving raised. The result of this had created huge restrictions against Lieutenant Allason's case for the defence. Now he was fighting back and the evidence provided by Lieutenant Allason would undoubtedly prove Colour Sergeant Chesney's innocence.

'Relax gentlemen. We're temporarily out of court,' said the presiding officer in an amicable manner. It was too amiable for Lieutenant Allason. 'I'm sorry we didn't have any formal introductions before this fiasco got under way. I was brought in by Army HQ to act as the President of the court for these proceedings. The committee have to make a decision based on the evidence we have heard so far.' He hesitated for a moment to look them both in the eye. 'I've admired your work gentlemen. Really! It's been intriguing to watch your different styles.' His expression changed suddenly. 'This is a court martial unlike any I have had to deal with before. I mean it is extraordinary. I sympathise with Colonel Anderson. He really had no choice; much of his regiment wiped out in a single battle, a VC winner missing from the field and this incredible story of how he woke up in a leper colony seventy miles away from Prakaresh in Kandarapah.' He let out a laugh that sounded false. 'It tests the imagination doesn't it? An incredible piece of fiction don't you think?'

Lieutenant Allason was astounded. He could hardly believe his ears. The obvious bias from Captain Harrison was clear beyond belief. 'But the letters – the statements!' Lieutenant Allason protested. 'They are proof beyond absolute doubt. Chesney did not desert!'

Captain Harrison's arrogance and unattractive patrician air came to the surface. 'You've worked well, Lieutenant. You've presented your case well. Surely you don't expect the court to swallow this cock 'n' bull story piecemeal do you? How do you think Army Headquarters will react to a Not Guilty verdict with a story like this? Chesney has nothing sufficient to back him up with.'

Even Major Irving felt inclined to protest. 'I may be the prosecuting counsel – but it sounds to me if you've already made up your mind. With due respect Sir, Lieutenant Allason wishes to produce another witness. Under cross-examination we can verify or disprove the last part of Chesney's story. This trial is by no means over.'

'We cannot allow this court martial to drag on and on without making a conclusive verdict!' Captain Harrison was agitated. 'Are we really here purely and simply for the benefit of one man, to preserve his reputation as against the men of the regiment who died valiantly in the field!'

It was no use. Lieutenant Allason could not restrain himself any longer. He unleashed his anger. 'What on earth are you talking about? Do you mean to sit there and tell me that because of one disastrous battle – one gross military misjudgement – that an ordinary British Tommy, Colour Sergeant Chesney has to be found guilty of desertion!!! What sort of court is this? The evidence overwhelmingly points to the colour sergeant's innocence! And not only his innocence – it is testimony to his courage and endurance! Are you going to slant history as well as the verdict, Captain? Does that mean newspaper stories will be carrying headlines like "Brave men of the 25th Queen's Light Northern Regiment Die Valiantly While Colour Sergeant Chesney deserts"? Tell me, Captain Harrison, does that take the gloss off the true picture? How about the true story? Men of the 25th Regiment die in military miscalculation. Colour Sergeant Chesney is the only survivor!'

'Lieutenant !' Captain Harrison shouted frantically. 'Do not speak to me in this tone!'

'Hear me out!!!' the Lieutenant shouted back, the full fury of his anger making him go red in the face.

'I will not tolerate this insubordinate, impudent, aggressive…'

'For God's sake Captain Harrison, let him speak!!' Interjected Major Irving, standing up and coming between the two men. There was now a deathly silence and the men with frayed tempers attempted to calm down. Both men huffed and puffed; their faces were crimson red, with a fearful anger still bubbling on the surface.

Lieutenant Allason spoke in a calmer tone but his voice was deadly cold with intent. 'And I will not tolerate this court martial making Colour Sergeant Chesney a scapegoat for a disastrous battle. It's abundantly clear that the court is slanted.'

'Are you suggesting that this court has already agreed on a Guilty verdict?' Captain Harrison was authoritive now.

'Yes I damn well am!' retorted Lieutenant Allason.

'I shall obviously have to recommend your removal as the defence counsel in that case,' Captain Harrison responded smugly.

In this he made a serious misjudgement. It was Major Irving who stepped in now to sway the balance. 'And if you do that Captain Harrison, in the interests of a fair and reasonable hearing you will have me to contend with. I shall join my colleague here in protesting most thoroughly at the way this whole disgraceful episode has been carried out. It is not the purpose of a judge, magistrate, lawyer or member of a jury to stroll into court with a preconceived verdict of Guilty or to interfere with the due processes of law!'

'Furthermore,' added Lieutenant Allason, 'if in the course of time it becomes clear that the officers in the court were instructed to obtain a Guilty verdict by the Army, I shall make representations to the Queen, the Governor of this state, the Prime Minister, and I shall advise Mr Graham Whittaker of the London Echo to issue a series of articles reproducing the two letters in print. I will also challenge the legality of the verdict in a private lawsuit.'

After this Captain Harrison stood up and walked across to the window.

He looked out at the parade ground, apparently deep in thought. Major Irving glanced at Lieutenant Allason. Captain Harrison walked to the door and opened it.

'Well gentlemen,' he said with a flourish, 'let us return to the courtroom – and you can call your witness.'

Quietly the men returned to the court. Lieutenant Allason took up his position next to Colour Sergeant Chesney. Inside the court there was a lot of murmuring while they waited for the court martial to resume.

Colour Sergeant Chesney leaned across to Lieutenant Allason. 'Henry, who is this surprise witness?' he whispered.

'I went to Kandarapah,' came the hushed reply.

'Kandarapah? The leper colony!'

'Yes. I took an Indian soldier to the colony to substantiate your story. We have a man. Nashid Khan. He was there when you were.'

Chesney appeared to be visibly shaken. 'When are you going to bring him here?'

Lieutenant Allason looked straight ahead. 'He's outside.'

'Outside!' Chesney was stunned. Outside the courtroom. This couldn't be.

Lieutenant Allason stood up and walked to the front of the court. He turned to face the committee. 'I request of the presiding officer that I may call a witness not present in the courtroom. I also request that I call Mr Matur Rajeed to act as an interpreter when the witness delivers his testimony.'

The silence that followed was almost deadly. Captain Harrison appeared to be seeking approval from his two fellow officers. He looked up sharply when he had made his decision.

'Approval is granted. When do you intend to bring your witness?'

Lieutenant Allason replied in a quiet and effective manner. 'This morning I had two NCOs bring him in a tanned covered waggonette to Fort Valaka. Nashid Khan from Kandarapah is currently with two Army surgeons and a military doctor, being attended to. I have spoken to Colonel Anderson who agrees the surgeons should accompany the witness back to the colony with food and medical supplies, and as much compassion as we can show these unfortunate people.' He moved forward. 'With your permission Sir, I would like Mr Rajeed to take the seat.' He indicated the witness chair. 'I would like to call Mr Nashid Khan to enter the courtroom.' The Lieutenant called out to an NCO by the door at the end of the room. 'Sergeant Skinner, would you bring in Mr Khan.'

The Sergeant left the room closing the door behind him. All eyes were focussed on the door. Matur Rajeed positioned himself in the witness chair. Captain Harrison turned a pencil over several times on the table, betraying his nervousness. Chesney stared straight ahead, preparing himself for the shock that would follow. He, more than anyone, knew what was going to happen now. Colonel Anderson from a somewhat isolated position pondered the outcome of this controversial trial. Lieutenant Allason's eyes suddenly became alert as the door opened.

'This way Mr Khan,' said Sergeant Skinner at the back of the room. Almost at once the entire members of the court turned around to face the door. Major Irving's eyes froze with a look that showed a mixture of fear and amazement. Colonel Anderson lowered his mouth in shock. Colour Sergeant Chesney changed his facial expression from shock to sadness as the shadow of the man fell across him. The members of the committee looked on in amazement at the member of the Kandarapah leper colony.

'Thank you for coming, Mr Khan,' said Lieutenant Allason who smiled at him gently, but the tragedy of this sight brought moisture to his eyes. Matur Rajeed repeated the words of thanks in an Indian dialect. Tears rolled from Colour Sergeant Chesney's eyes.

Chesney sprang up from his seat in the hotel. He had been half dozing – half remembering. What a terrible memory that had been to recall. All that had been twelve years before, in 1885. But once the memories had been triggered he seemed to want to keep remembering, almost as if it was something he needed to desperately purge from his system.

Eleven

All night long Chesney sat in the chair thinking of the past. If it had not been for Lieutenant Henry Allason's fervent belief in his innocence and some skilful defensive work in the courtroom, Chesney would almost certainly have been found guilty of desertion under fire. The penalty would have been death by firing squad. It was harrowing to think about.

He remembered the spectre of Nashid Khan delivering his testimony. It was tragic and heartbreaking that the court had been brought to such a level. Then when Matur Rajeed had fully interpreted Nashid Khan's statements, the committee made their decision. The tension in the court had been electric. Captain Harrison delivered his findings while Colour Sergeant Chesney and Lieutenant Allason sat on the edge of their chairs. The Captain spoke, occasionally glancing down at notes.

'The evidence we have heard has been wide and detailed. The story related to Colour Sergeant Chesney's experiences is quite extraordinary. But the court would conclude we are living in a country, a time of history in the British Empire, and the type of circumstances that create legends. The contents of Mr Whittaker's statement are sufficient in themselves to confirm the whereabouts of the colour sergeant on the battlefield. The letter written by the late Regimental Sergeant Major Blackshawe also further substantiates Chesney's presence through long hours of what we can only determine must have been torturous and despairing for any man.' He looked up for a moment. 'The life of a British soldier in India – the ordinary 'Tommy', a description we have heard much in this courtroom, is not all parade ground drill in the spellbinding sunshine, or band practice beneath Asian awnings. Neither is it the spit and polish of dazzling regimental tunics and ceremonial dress uniforms.' He drew a breath and his voice took on a tone with a hint of anger evident. 'It is often being placed in the front line of the harsh reality of enemy fire and human suffering. I know that from personal experience! The members of the court know this! The colour sergeant more than anyone here knows this! The unusual testimony by the witness brought in from the leper colony at Kandarapah only further clarifies Colour Sergeant Chesney's own version of the events. It may have appeared to some people present that the colour sergeant was singled out in a vindictive manner. This was not the intention of the court.' Captain Harrison closed some notes he had on the table. 'The court finds that on the charge of desertion under fire the evidence is overwhelmingly indicative of the colour sergeant's innocence. We, the committee appointed by Army headquarters, find the defendant – Colour Sergeant Chesney…' There followed a breathtaking silence '…Not Guilty.'

Not guilty. The words seemed to flow over the heads of everyone in the court. Suddenly everyone was standing and the committee left the room. Chesney stood up, hardly believing he had survived all this. Major Irving crossed over and shook hands with his courtroom opponent Lieutenant Allason.

'Congratulations Henry. You won,' Major Irving conceded gracefully.

'We won, Gordon,' Lieutenant Allason corrected him. He indicated with a knowing look the departing members of the committee. 'We beat the real enemy. Thank you for your support in our meeting with Captain Harrison.' He turned to Colour Sergeant Chesney. 'You've come through, Harry.'

Chesney wore a grim expression on his face. 'I'd have preferred to have fought in another battle rather than go through all that again.'

'You won't have to,' Lieutenant Allason said with confidence in his voice. 'You've been exonerated. You're free to return to duty. I believe this verdict has come just in time.'

'Yes. My time in the Army is almost up.'

'You'll be re-enlisting then, Colour Sergeant?' The question had been asked by Colonel Anderson who approached from behind.

Chesney turned around to face the Colonel but he was unable to say anything. His expression showed that he was still considering his decision.

At a very crowded railway station two Englishmen were very distinctive by their appearance amongst such an array of Indian colour. One was Harry Chesney in civilian clothes and the other was Lieutenant Allason in uniform. Chesney carried a bag of his belongings and made his way through the swarms of people. A train slowly approached the platform. Chesney turned to Lieutenant Allason.

'I hope you didn't think I was a lost cause, Henry. I wanted to leave the regiment with some dignity. I was innocent of the charges and you proved it. I'll always be grateful for that.'

'I'd do the same again. I believed strongly in your case. Not only was justice done but, more importantly, right.'

'Well, perhaps I'll see you in a London magistrate's court one day.' He held his hand out and shook Henry Allason's hand with a warm grip. 'Goodbye Henry. Thank you for everything.'

'Are you going home Harry? Back to blighty's green fields and oak-beamed ale hostelries and fresh-faced maidens wearing bonnets and carrying baskets?'

Chesney walked to a train carriage and called out as he opened the door, 'I'm going to see the world!'

He stepped into the carriage. People flooded inside the train. Doors closed and banged. Some Indians climbed up and sat on the roof of the train carriage. The train started to move out slowly. Lieutenant Allason stepped forward and shouted to Chesney as his carriage passed by. 'Don't forget to see Mandalay!'

From within the carriage Chesney beamed a happy smile. One chapter of his life had closed and a new one had begun.

On that journey Chesney took in the view of the varying countryside. Since his arrival in India many years before, he had developed a real passion for this land. From his window he could see the diversity of this country in all of its many multi-coloured images. He felt different, travelling as a civilian now. Perhaps his point of view had changed with the shedding of a military uniform.

Before him lay poverty-stricken villages, bullocks in fields, elephants at watering holes, paddy fields, mountain ranges, glistening lakes and streams. Everywhere there were the strange sights, sounds and colours of India. It was stiflingly hot in the carriage and Chesney mopped his brow.

At an out-of-the-way station the train stopped suddenly, jerking Chesney out of a heat induced sleep. He opened his eyes and stifled a yawn. Doors opened, closed and banged as passengers departed and entered. An elderly English gentleman entered the carriage. Chesney nodded and smiled politely. The man responded with a smile and then opened out an English newspaper. It was a copy of the Indian Chronicle.

The headlines of the newspaper mesmerised Chesney. He scanned the article eagerly. Bold headlines almost jumped out at him.

NADUR SOHARI CAPTURED. ROYAL LANCASHIRE REGIMENT STEM UPRISING.

Chesney drew back in shock. He noticed that the article had been written by Graham Whittaker. Almost as suddenly the train jolted into action and began to move from the confines of the railway station into the depths of the night. Occasionally the light from the moon flickered through the shutters of the railway carriage, igniting Chesney's face which was a picture of thought. That fearful time in Prakaresh had changed his life forever.

Now that he was a civilian traveller Chesney seemed to have all the time in the world to explore and re-explore India. Before long he would have to find a new direction in life. Just what he would do with the rest of his life he felt unsure about. In the meantime he would casually meander through this exotic land. He kept reminding himself that he was no longer Colour Sergeant Chesney of the 25th Queen's Light Northern Regiment, winner of the Victoria Cross and ex-orphan boy made good. He was just plain old Harry Chesney – itinerant wanderer and civilian.

His heart missed a beat when he thought of the regimental colours being paraded at Fort Valaka. Things would never be the same at that garrison any more. All the old characters had gone. Blackshawe, Dunham, Clancy; fine men, but now legends in the history of the regiment.

Chesney travelled first to see the Taj Mahal. He was enthralled by the fascinating sight of this gleaming building. He looked up and down its structures in admiration. Certainly he was more at home as a man in uniform, but he was an admirer of beauty whether it be physical or in the eye of the beholder. The Taj Mahal was a stunning sight at any time.

His journey through India took him further afield. Chesney found himself in a holy city. He wandered through, absorbing the curious sights. There were masses of winding narrow alleys, crowded mystical lanes full of colourful pilgrims, snake charmers, wandering holy men with craggy interesting faces, Hindu priests and Brahmins giving offerings to the gods.

At the Ganges, the very distinctive figure of Harry Chesney mingled with the colourful figures who moved down to the water. He was fascinated by the sight of the women bathing in their saris. There were children with impish smiles and twinkling eyes, playing together. There were men and women in prayer, meditation and worship.

During his travels Chesney visited many towns and villages. At one place he trudged wearily through some colourful lanes looking for somewhere to stay the night. He found himself outside a Christian church, which seemed to be strangely out of place in an area that was so predominantly Hindu. From within he could hear the words of a hymn, *Give me the faith which I can move*. He listened with interest. Then he carried on walking the streets with the words of the hymn still ringing in his ears.

For many weeks he travelled at leisure across India until his journey took him to a spectacular area. There was a friend Chesney wanted to see. This man had served in the regiment with Chesney but since leaving the Army had forged a new career for himself as a tea planter in Darjeeling. Chesney's old comrade Richard Wise greeted him warmly and took him round the fields.

Darjeeling was a hill station spreading along a mountain slope and surrounded by green hills and coniferous trees. Chesney looked on with interest as Richard Wise pointed out different things to him. The workers in the fields were enthusiastically filling their baskets with tea plants. It was a trade and a profitable business. Chesney could recognise that straight away.

'Look at all this!' beamed Richard Wise. 'Marvellous isn't it old fellow? All over the world they drink the stuff. Tea, beautiful tea.'

Chesney considered the possibility of working there. 'A few people in your old regiment might disagree with you. They prefer a drop of the hard stuff. Gin and beer. Of course Mr Wise, the officers like their whisky and a fair ration of grog.'

'Ah – but tea is the drink of the masses,' Richard pointed out. 'And drop the Mr Wise; Richard, old man, that's my name. They call me Richard the Lionheart.'

'It's a good trade this,' Chesney said, viewing the possibility of life in Darjeeling with a keen optimism.

Richard recognised the anticipation in Chesney's voice. 'Aye. It is that. Will you be working with me? Do you think you'll enjoy helping me to manage the place? I'll teach you all the ropes.'

Chesney took one pace forward and looked at the workers in the fields. It was a scene of much activity but there was also something serene and tranquil about its setting amidst such lush scenery.

He smiled warmly. He felt that a new life was beginning to open for him. 'I won't let you down Richard. I'm going to enjoy working here. I think this is what I've been looking for.'

Chesney was in his element. In his new-found career he approached every day with enthusiasm. The working days were long and full. Every aspect of the tea trade became something to be learned and studied by Chesney.

Harry Chesney stayed at Darjeeling for five of the happiest years of his life. After his years in uniform he enjoyed the peacefulness of life in this lovely part of the world. There was something wonderful about the twilight at the end of the day when the workers returned from their labour in the fields. Chesney would watch and feel good that he had performed a rewarding day's work.

One night in 1890 Chesney sat sipping tea on the veranda of a tea planter's house. He was handed a letter by one of the servants. Slowly he read the contents. The letter was offering him a position in Ceylon at a tea plantation called Nuwara Eliya. He mused over the offer. It seemed too good to refuse. Besides, restlessness was creeping into his wandering soul. Perhaps it was time to move on. From behind Richard Wise approached him. Chesney looked up somewhat apprehensively.

'Some good news Harry?' Richard asked, pouring himself a drink.

'Depends,' said Harry handing him the letter. 'I've been offered a tea plantation job in Ceylon.'

Richard scanned through the letter without giving away his innermost feelings. 'You must have made a good impression on those visitors we had last month. Are you going to take it? It's a good offer.'

'I've been here nearly five years now. I'm very grateful to you for all the help you gave me.' Chesney was in no doubt that he should accept the offer but he felt much indebted to Richard.

'Don't let loyalty bind you Harry. I'll be sorry to see you go, of course. But I would like to be the first to wish you long life and happiness.'

'Thank you old friend,' Chesney said, acknowledging his friend's sincere words. He stood up and looked at the tea plantation below. 'Do you know something Richard? I'm really going to miss this place.'

Ceylon was another experience for Harry Chesney. He had left India with much regret. Yet as always there was the feeling that a new challenge and a change of environment would do much to sharpen the senses, and boost enthusiasm in life again.

After his vessel had docked at Colombo, Chesney had begun a train journey across Ceylon. His first impressions of this island were that it was something radiant and exotic. Lakes and jungles were passed quickly. He knew that this was a place he was going to enjoy.

At one station a beautiful dark-haired girl of English appearance boarded the carriage. She had brown eyes and a warmth that quite entranced Chesney, even from a distance. Her clothes were fine garments of the sort worn by rich English ladies and her huge floppy hat, peaked at an angle, gave her an aura that Harry Chesney found hard to resist. Quickly he rose from his seat to help her with her bags.

'Here, let me give you a hand love,' he said amiably.

She looked up and smiled at him. This girl bedazzled him. 'Thank you very much Sir.' Her voice had a pleasant lilt to it. In an instant Chesney felt drawn to her like iron filings to a magnet. She oozed warmth with a hint of vulnerability.

Chesney placed her bags in the luggage compartment. He was not going to miss an opportunity like this. 'There's a spare seat opposite me. Would you like to join me?'

'Yes. Why not?' she said with a smile.

The two sat down opposite each other. Chesney was dazzled by this girl. In his years of philandering he had never experienced love at first sight quite like this before. The lady in front of him removed her hat. Immediately a long mane of glistening fine dark hair fell down over her face. She pushed it back, smoothing it into place. There was a gleam in her eyes which Chesney interpreted quickly. Was he wrong or did he imagine that she was thinking he was a man she would like to know better?

'I'm Harry Chesney,' he said after a while. She said nothing, but smiled at him in an admiring fashion. 'I'm on my way to work on a tea plantation at Nuwara Eliya.'

Her eyes sparkled with delight. 'I shall probably be seeing a lot of you then. That's where I'm going! I've a brother there.' Chesney felt happy at the thought of seeing this girl frequently. Then without prompting she introduced herself. 'My name is Karen Kelleher.'

'Karen Kelleher,' Chesney repeated. 'You're fresh out of England then?'

'Ireland to be exact,' Karen corrected him with a twinkle in her eye. 'I come from Belfast originally. Although I've been living in Kilmacrennan in Donegal. I lived in England for a while too at a place called Enfield.'

'I should have realised you were a young colleen. I've not been home in fifteen years or more. I was a boy soldier, a ten-year man, and this five years past I've been tea planting in Northern India. I'm taking up a new job here.'

'We'll be able to get to know the place together then,' Karen said with eagerness.

Chesney smiled at the prospect. During the train journey they talked a great deal. Karen exuded warmth and allure. She was the sort of girl men admired in every respect. Not only was she natural and attractive but she combined the ideal qualities of wife, lover, friend, possible mother and companion. Chesney recognised this immediately. He wondered initially if there was a possibility of this relationship blossoming into something strong and permanent.

It surprised Chesney to lean that Karen was in her late twenties and still unmarried. Particularly surprising when he considered just what a marriageable girl she was. But he was to learn much later that Karen Kelleher had an independent and assertive streak in her. She was something of a rebel, who would defy the restrictive Victorian conventions of the era and marry a man of her choosing if and when she chose to do so.

At Nuwara Eliya, Karen and Chesney spent a lot of time together. Chesney was fast approaching forty and almost a decade older than Karen. He kept thinking of the age gap. Could that be a problem in later years? He himself could not have given a fig for convention. But there was always the question of doubt in his mind. Harry Chesney – a married man? Never?

There was no doubt that Karen's presence made life in Ceylon very happy for him. He enjoyed working in the fields and he loved the peace of this lush green area. The tea plantation was set amidst scenery that was reminiscent of fine English countryside. This was not lost on Chesney who loved his work and his surroundings. Here in Ceylon he was a man with authority and respect. Back home it would be a life of lower class living and low grade jobs. He doubted if he would ever return to England.

One day Chesney was overseeing a Ceylonese lady worker when Karen rode towards him. Karen was a splendid sight on horseback. She wore a pith helmet, riding breeches and a safari top. Whatever she wore, she wore it well. On the plantation she worked in the office, occasionally riding out on chores for the staff. Life here agreed well with her too. Her face was ruddy with good health. Chesney looked up and winked at her.

'Hello Harry. I've been asked to tell you to come to the house tonight for dinner.'

'Why? Is there something special on?'

'Oh, I believe there's an ex-Army officer coming. A man of some standing.'

Chesney was immediately curious. 'You didn't catch the man's name did you? Or his regiment I suppose?'

'No I didn't. You'll be sitting next to me tonight. You will be my man for the night! How do you feel about that? You know you want to.'

The Ceylonese lady giggled at the way Karen openly flirted with Chesney.

'How could I refuse such a tempting offer?' Chesney grinned.

Karen smiled at him deliciously and rode away. 'See you later…darling.'

'I think she likes you very much,' the tea picker said to Chesney, fluttering her eyes sensually. 'Maybe you and she get married perhaps? Have lots of babies!'

The thought had been on Chesney's mind but he wasn't going to tell anyone. 'Not me, my dear little Ceylonese maiden!' he joked. 'One day the wanderlust will get the better of me and I'll board a clipper. Men like me – we love them, and we leave them!'

'You leave nice girl that like?' the astonished Indian lady tea picker gasped in honest amazement. 'Where will you go?'

Chesney's imagination took over. He had a knack of fulfilling his dreams, so perhaps he wasn't telling a lie when he replied, 'The South Seas, my darling girl! Australia's sunny shore perhaps. Maybe those faraway islands. Palm trees. Coconuts. Clear blue waters in lovely lagoons. Yes, that's where I'll go.'

In the evening Chesney went along to the manager's huge colonial house to attend a dinner party for the special guest that Karen had mentioned. A number of guests were standing around talking. Karen was looking glamourous in a long cool gown. She spotted Chesney as soon as he came through the door.

'Hello. I was wondering where you'd got to. You look more like an ex-officer in your nice clothes.' She looked him over with much admiration and it was obvious she had fallen in love with him. He really did look an entirely different man in evening clothes. 'You're quite a gentleman aren't you Harry Chesney?'

'Don't deceive yourself. You're a real lady. But me, I'm a workhouse boy. I'll always be one.'

'I think at times Harry, you deceive yourself. Not me. Come on then you big workhouse boy. I'll introduce you to our guest.'

Karen took his arm and led him towards a group of people. Chesney did not see the man from the front. He only saw a grey-haired man from the back. Karen tapped the man on the shoulder.

'Harry, I'd like to introduce you to our guest.' The man turned around. 'This is Duncan Anderson, formerly a Colonel in the 25th Queen's Light Northern Regiment.'

Chesney was mesmerised as he found himself facing his old commanding officer. Colonel Anderson was himself shocked. His expression changed from one of disbelief to a slow smile.

'Well, I am amazed to see you again, Colour Sergeant.' He held out his hand courteously to shake. 'I'm glad to see you well.'

Chesney shook hands with him. 'And you Sir. I'm as surprised as you are.'

Karen looked on in amazement. 'You two – know each other?'

'Oh yes,' said Chesney, not sure how he should feel about greeting his old CO He looked at Duncan Anderson and thought of past memories. 'Perhaps we could talk about old times – after dinner, if that's alright with you?'

Colonel Anderson, who was a wily old fox and nobody's fool, was quick to understand the reasoning behind Chesney's words.

'I'd like to,' he replied in a genuine, sympathetic tone. 'We have a lot to catch up on.'

The two men did get together after the dinner. They took drinks to a quiet smoking room where for a few moments they sat in silence. The room was well decorated, complete with Victorian pictures, a world globe and wicker furniture. In the room next door a string quartet played while the rest of the diners circulated.

'Well Sir,' Chesney said after a while. 'What brings you back to these parts?'

'Memories,' Colonel Anderson replied without hesitation. 'Memories.

Plenty of them. When I retired from the Army I went home to Scotland; rested up for a wee while, found myself a quiet cottage overlooking a loch and surrounded by the heather of my distant boyhood.' He stopped to light a cigar. 'Ah – it was so bonny for a while – tasting the chill of the air and being free of the responsibilities of command. But do you know something Chesney? I began to miss the life we had once.'

'How do you mean, Sir?'

'I missed being part of real life. Being in the thick of adventure. Mountains, tropical heat. The parade ground at Fort Valaka. I wanted to see it all again before I left this world. So I came travelling back to see Burma and Afghanistan, India and Ceylon. I've missed it.' He took a sip of his drink and a long puff on his cigar. 'I was at Darjeeling a while back. Met your old comrade-at-arms Richard Wise. He didn'a mention that you'd moved on to here. Quite a shock to me when I saw you.'

Chesney seized an opportunity to speak his mind. 'If you don't mind, I was haunted by the memories of what happened at Prakaresh and my court martial. It was humiliation that caused me more pain than I ever felt on the battlefield. I'm talking to you on equal terms now as one ex-soldier to another, not as an inferior. I fought long and hard to rebuild my life. Tell me, Sir – tell me, after all that I went through on the battlefield, why was I put through a court martial?'

Colonel Anderson lowered his glass and rested his cigar in an ash tray. He looked at Chesney, his expression showing a mixture of sadness and seriousness.

'If you knew just how many times I have thought of that particular time, over and over again.'

He had spoken as if he was attempting to justify his past actions. That was it! Chesney snapped at him aggressively as an old wound surfaced. 'Listen to me!' His voice was a clap of thunder. 'I want to tell you how I felt!'

Just as furiously Colonel Anderson's Scottish temperament boiled. Not for him a soulful reply from beneath still waters. He responded in equal anger. 'No! You listen to me! I know the private pain you have suffered! I am not insensitive and cold-hearted, Chesney. I know the traumatic experience you would have been through! When I rode through the ranks of what had been my soldiers and I saw many good men I had known lying in that sweltering carnage, I felt a sense of guilt and humiliation far greater than you would ever have felt. And I'll tell you why! It was on my command that the troops under Major Clancy went first. Can you imagine what that feels like? To know that your command, a gross error of misjudgement, was responsible for the loss of many good men's lives?'

Chesney could see the Colonel's point of view. 'I understand Sir,' he said unreservedly, without loss of face or concession. 'I've got a pent-up anger in my life that is taking its time to go away. But the terrible memories of that time don't go away, nor does the humiliation of a trial that sought to degrade me and exonerate the regiment!'

'Don't apologise. You've every right. But I was compelled by my responsibilities. As Colonel of the 25th I had no choice. Senior officers could not accept the circumstances as they stood. Having you on a charge was one of the worst things I have ever had to do. Shortly after you resigned I had to face a tribunal in Delhi over my handling of the situation. Between you and me, it was only my impending retirement that saved me from being removed from command. That disaster at Prakaresh affected both our lives.'

'I didn't know. I have a lot of memories of the Army but I wish I could forget that time when I stood on the ridge above the slaughter. It haunts me still.'

'For both of us it will,' Colonel Anderson said with a voice that still commanded authority. 'It's well in the past now. I've learned to live with it.'

'Believe me, I've tried,' Chesney said bluntly. 'I don't like being humbled by the arrogance of the superiors who think everyone else is their inferior. And if I ever cross the path of any of those who tried to find me guilty, I shall let them know in no uncertain terms what I think of them!! But I've done pretty well for myself. I've done much with my time.'

Colonel Anderson raised his glass as if to propose a toast. 'This is my last night here Chesney. I'll be away travelling in the morn to Kandy and Colombo.' He took a decanter and filled both their glasses. 'Will you have a toast and raise your glass with me to the better memories we had as soldiers of the 25th? I'm not asking you now, Colour Sergeant Chesney. I'm speaking to you as the former colonel of your regiment.'

'Is that an order then?' Chesney asked, with a glint of humour in his eyes.

'It is.' The colonel smiled broadly. 'I hope I command some respect.'

This time it was Chesney who gave the orders. 'You were my colonel, and you have my respect Sir. However, I'll have to disobey you on one score. I'll raise a glass with you.' He brought his glass to the colonel's. 'The toast is mine. To the men that fell at Prakaresh – fine fellows all – but more to the point, Colonel – to you and I, the men whose lives are affected still.'

A look of deep pride spread across Colonel Anderson's face. 'Fine words. Fine sentiments. Somehow we have to learn from this and enjoy every minute of our lives, because we live now for the fallen.'

The two men had a joyous reunion that night. They had both spoken their minds. The tribulations of long ago had dissipated now. They spoke as old comrades and friends recalling battles lost and won. When they shook hands and made their farewells later that night many memories had been renewed. Chesney went to his room in very good spirits that night. He made no pretence to sleep. For several hours he lay awake just revelling in the happy thoughts that had been generated by the reunion. It was a particularly hot and sticky night. Sleep would not come easily anyway. A few times in the early morning hours, he rose naked from his bed and splashed himself all over with water from a jug. Chesney had just returned to his bed when in the midst of a deathly night silence he became aware of someone attempting to enter his room. The door handle swivelled several times. Chesney took out a pistol from a drawer by his bed. He sat up and pointed the gun towards the door.

Slowly the door began to open. The shadows of the night obscured the figure as it came into the room. First of all a pair of tiny white feet could be seen. Then in the next instant a long nightdress became visible. Chesney kept his eyes firmly fixed on the figure as it came nearer and nearer. The light from the moon flooded through at that second, revealing the person's face. It was Karen. She stood there smiling at him, an absolute vision of loveliness.

Chesney lowered the pistol and put it to one side. He was struck dumb by her unexpected presence. All he could do was to look at Karen in amazement. She moved closer to him. The night was warm and his senses of desire for her were stronger now than they had ever been.

At last he found words. 'Karen. Why!' It was all he could mumble stupidly. He saw Karen lower her nightdress and stand there before him naked, a picture of beauty and warmth. Her face came down to meet his.

The passion of her lips on his was explosive. He felt the gentle warm touch of her hands as they ran up and down his neck. The love he felt for this girl was so powerful. Chesney pulled her down towards him, gripping her tightly. He stroked her long hair gently and kissed her lips; then her forehead, followed by her cheeks and her shoulders. He was lost in desire and yearning. In the dark shadows of the night they made love in slow, unhurried passion. Karen's eyes shone brightly in the dark. Her cheeks flushed crimson red. Chesney felt himself being enveloped by the warmth and emotion of it all.

This was different from other affairs he had experienced. This was real love from a woman who cared for him deeply. It was something that frightened him. Chesney found her love and need of him so powerful that he knew she wanted a commitment. The commitment of marriage was a powerful bind, a sacrament and sacred obligation as strong as molten metal that once entered into he knew must last forever.

Harry Chesney loved Karen. But marry her? Wed her with God's blessing? He could not do this. Chesney wrestled with his conscience. He tried to find excuses in his own mind. He convinced himself he was still a vagabond and soldier of fortune, even though in reality he was now a forty-year-old plantation team overseer. Furthermore, Chesney told himself over and over again that Karen was a fine, kind, loving lady who did not deserve a man with a past such as his. Every time he did this it seemed false. He did not believe himself.

Finally he found the excuse he needed. Chesney learned that a tea clipper would be sailing from Colombo Harbour in a few weeks' time, bound for Australia. He decided there and then that he would be on this voyage to the great southern continent.

Karen was not to be deterred. She accompanied him as far as the harbour in the vain hope that Chesney would change his mind. It was not to be. The two of them stood at the dock. It was a difficult farewell for both of them.

'I didn't think you'd leave,' Karen said to him sadly. 'I don't believe you want to go, Harry. Something haunts you from the past. I don't know what it is, but I could help you. I'm loyal and supportive. We could be good for each other.'

Chesney looked down into her eyes. He realised that he probably loved this girl far more than he had loved anyone in his life. The thought disturbed him. He couldn't understand himself just why he was leaving her.

'Harry – I don't want you to go,' Karen said. There was just a hint of a plea in her voice. 'I love you. I should have told you earlier. If you go now you will be throwing away your chance of love and happiness for ever.'

Chesney put his arms around her and pulled her close. 'What do you see in a big lump like me?' he asked her, in a voice that indicated he was agonising over his decision. 'I'm not good enough for you.'

Karen was almost despairing. 'Oh – Harry!' She hugged and kissed him. 'You're always moving on. Why? What are you afraid of?'

Chesney attempted to explain. But he was lying to himself more than Karen. 'It's just – just the way I am. By instinct I'm a born wanderer.'

Karen stood there with tears in her eyes. 'Take this,' she said suddenly. She gave him a small locket. 'It'll remind you of someone who loves you.'

Chesney took the locket, examined it and put it in his pocket. For a few moments he held her tightly, savouring the warmth of her love. The time had come for him to go. He released his grip, picked up his bag and walked to the gangway. Just before he boarded the boat he turned around.

'Goodbye Karen,' he said chokingly.

Karen's reply was firmer. 'You'll always be in my thoughts Harry.'

Chesney gave her one last longing look and then he walked aboard the tea clipper. The crew were busy aboard the vessel preparing to sail. Other passengers boarded the clipper. Chesney walked along and gazed down at Karen on the harbour wharf. He realised with the utmost dismay that he was making one of the worst decisions he had ever made.

It was several weeks later when the coastline of Australia came into view. Chesney looked over the side of the boat at this strange brown coastline before him. A sailor came up beside him.

'Looking forward to landfall eh Sir?' he asked pleasantly.

'Yes. I've not been there before,' Chesney replied.

'Oh I have – several times as a matter of fact,' the sailor stated proudly. 'An interesting place. Mind you, still in its infancy. But it's a big place. Not many people. Very hot. Stinking hot sometimes. Wait 'til you see those heads of Port Sydney. On one side there's Watson's Bay. On the other there's Manly. Beautiful sight for the eyes of any man.'

Chesney had been drifting away in the past. He realised that the past should be left behind. The future suddenly seemed interesting. 'Do we dock at either of those places? This Manly? Watson's Bay is it?'

'Nah. When I've been there before, the ship's pulled in to Woolloomooloo. Roughneck docks them are. This time the clipper will be putting down its tea cargo at Circular Quay. Now there's a fine dock, that Circular Quay.'

'Tea eh?' Chesney mused. 'That's been my profession a while.'

'You'll be able to get a job working for a tea company on one of the wharves I s'pect,' the sailor remarked. 'Are you starting a new life there?'

Chesney looked straight ahead. His thoughts were still of Karen whom he regretted leaving behind. A hint of agony and frustration crept into the tone of his voice. 'I'm always starting a new life.'

In his cabin that night, Chesney lay in his bunk listening to the waves and the roll of the vessel. He thought of Karen. Her voice seemed to echo in his mind.

'You'll always be in my thoughts. Harry – you'll always be in my thoughts. In my thoughts Harry. Harry – Harry – Harry'.

Chesney opened his hand. He was holding the locket that Karen had given him. Still her voice haunted his mind.

'Take this. It'll remind you of someone who loves you'.

Chesney rolled over in his bunk, still clutching the locket and he closed his eyes. He tried desperately to blot out the pain of so many memories.

It was 1897. Chesney had been half dreaming, half remembering the preceding years. He opened his eyes slowly. He was in the room of his London hotel, a world away from India, Ceylon and Australia. For a moment he stared around the room at the flickering candle-light and then lowered his glance to his hand. He had been clutching the locket that Karen had given him all those years before. Where was that fine girl he had once loved? How sad it was for him now to realise that he would never find a love like that again.

Twelve

It hardly seemed possible. Queen Victoria had reigned for sixty years. On that day in 1897 there was enormous celebration in London for the Queen's Diamond Jubilee. People had converged on the centre of the city to see Queen Victoria ride through the streets in a carriage. There were huge parades comprising of representatives from all over the Empire. In the parade were Gurkhas, Sikhs, Indians, troops from New South Wales, New Zealand, Canada and the West Indies. There was pomp and circumstance, and pageantry at every level.

In the crowd Chesney and Ravi watched. Their eyes sparkled as they soaked up this never-to-be-forgotten historical occasion. Finally Queen Victoria came into view. Ravi could hardly believe just what he was seeing. Approaching him was the Queen of all the dominions. In an open-topped carriage, flanked by two soldiers in Glengarry caps, came Queen Victoria. The crowds erupted into spontaneous cheers and applause, and bouts of flag waving patriotism, the like of which had never been seen in London before.

Ravi removed his hat and doffed it in courtesy. He almost bowed, so taken was he by the spectacle. Chesney immediately did the same. He smiled broadly at his young friend from India.

Chesney and Ravi took the train out of London later that day. They boarded a train for Chesney's home in the Sussex town of Horsham where he had established a new life for himself. There were many passengers carrying flags and memorabilia of the day. Both men were equally enthusiastic about the day which had been a colourful and momentous piece of history. It was one of the first occasions involving pageantry that had been filmed by early moving-picture cameras and for years to come would be shown for historical note.

'What a superb day, eh young Ravi! That's one for the memories,' remarked Chesney.

Ravi agreed. 'A really wonderful day Mr Harry! Now I have seen the Empress of India.'

There was a short pause as Chesney gathered his thoughts. 'I hope you don't mind staying at my lodgings for a while,' he said almost apologetically.

'No. You have been more than kind.'

'My place is a few rooms above the teashop I run in Horsham. There's a tea warehouse at the back where I employ a few lads. We import tea from Assam and Lukwah, Darjeeling and Nuwara Eliya, and flog it off to the locals at a reasonable price. Maybe you might like to lend a hand?'

'I'd be delighted,' smiled Ravi, excited at the prospect of his new life.

Chesney was a fair man. 'I'd pay you as one of the staff of course. I'll try and get you something good, Ravi. A good job in service in one of those good houses.'

Harry Chesney was as good as his word. A few days later he set out to obtain some advice from a titled lady who lived in a large country house in the village of Storrington nestled in the Sussex Downs. This lady, more than anyone, could advise Chesney just where Ravi would be able to obtain work in the employ of a large house. The particular person he was going to see was Lady Bernadette Shervington; the woman who in effect was Ravi's stepmother.

It had been something of a miraculous coincidence when Lady Bernadette had entered Chesney's teashop in Horsham the year before. On seeing Chesney behind the counter, checking account books and ledgers, Lady Bernadette had approached him until she was virtually nose to nose. The two had been lost for words as they gaped with amazement at each other. Chesney had not seen her since 1885 when Lady Bernadette had left India, following the death of her husband Captain Rex Shervington.

Chesney learned that Lady Bernadette had returned to the family home in Storrington to run the estates and several companies. She had issued him an invitation to visit which until now he had never taken up. It had been on the tip of his tongue to tell Lady Bernadette about the son her late husband had sired during an association with an Indian woman. Somehow he could not tell this fine and gracious lady of her husband's past affair. He was sensitive enough to recognise that news of Ravi's existence could come as one almighty shock to her.

Still, he had needed an excuse to visit the Shervington manor house if only to reminisce about India. Lady Bernadette, with her easily contactable friends with large houses and estate staff, would be bound to know of someone who could employ Ravi. Chesney would be cautious if the subject of Ravi's parentage came up. He would merely state that he was a friend of the young man's mother and father in India.

A horse-drawn cab took Chesney from the train station at Pulborough to Shervington Manor, which was at the very top of the Sussex Downs with a wonderful view on a clear day of this beautiful agricultural county below. This part of England was somewhere special. There were dairy farms and cornfields stretching out as far as the eye could see, from Amberley to Bognor Regis, Pulborough to Portsmouth. Chesney considered that Lady Bernadette had plenty to get up for in the morning with a spectacular view such as this to sample every day over breakfast.

Chesney stepped out of the cab, paid the driver with a substantial tip and then walked up to the front door of this rather imposing house. He rapped on the door, fully expecting a footman to reply. Instead he was pleasantly surprised when a young parlour maid of about twenty-one came to the door.

'Good morning Sir,' she said politely. 'Tradesmen's entrance is round the back.'

The remark brought a smile to Chesney's face. 'I'm not a tradesman miss,' he said good naturedly. Not in this fine cut of clothes, he thought. 'I'm here to see the lady of the house.'

The parlour maid, a young lady called Jessica looked at him with a quizzical expression. 'I knew Lady Bernadette in India many years ago. I served under the command of her late husband Rex.'

'Oh I see,' Jessica said but she still seemed unconvinced.

'Yes,' Chesney sought to explain to this mere slip of a girl. 'I'm Harry Chesney. Now of Chesney's teashop and tea import warehouse in Horsham, but once Colour Sergeant Harry Chesney of the 25th Queen's Light Northern Regiment at Fort Valaka in India and veteran of skirmishes in the North-West Frontier, Afghanistan and Burma.' Jessica began to smile. 'I met Lady Bernadette again last year when she came in by chance to my teashop. She told me that she was living here and if I was ever round this way to drop round. So here I am.'

Jessica pulled the door wide open, exposing a long hallway into the house. 'Well she's out riding at the moment. But I'm sure she would like to see you. The staff are just having a pot of tea at the moment. Would you like to join us while you're waiting?'

'That's very nice of you luv,' he said, clutching his hat and entering the house. 'A cuppa would go down just nicely.'

Jessica took Chesney through to the kitchen. At a table the 'below stairs' staff were seated drinking tea. He was about to meet some of the pleasantest people he could have wished to know. There was a jovial, smiling faced middle-aged lady called Mrs Price who was the cook of the house. Then there was the cheerful butler Jimmy Brown, a London cockney in his forties, and a man very much like Chesney in many ways. The mutual respect between them was instantaneous. Bobby Grey, in his late fifties, was the general handyman for the manor and on occasion he would double as the house footman. Jessica was much younger than the staff.

'This is Harry Chesney everyone,' she said introducing him to her fellow staff. 'Mr Chesney is a friend of Lady Bernadette's from India. I said it would be alright if he joined us for a cup of tea while he waits for Lady Bernadette to come back.'

Bobby Grey stood up. 'Take a seat then 'Arry.' He spoke in a warm Sussex burr.

Chesney sat down. Mrs Price poured him a cup of tea. 'Not often we have company. Help yourself to sugar and milk.'

'Thank you very much,' Chesney said, pouring a dash of milk he knew would have been fresh from a local dairy farm, and adding one sugar. His throat was so parched that he virtually sunk the cup's contents in two mouthfuls. 'Ah – that's beautiful. Hot but refreshing still on a hot day. Where are you all from then?'

Mrs Price spoke up for everybody. 'Me and Mr Grey there, we were brought up in and around Sussex. Young Jessica is a Surrey lass. And that fine figure of a lad is Jimmy Brown, the house's trusty butler who is a Londoner through and through.'

'From the Old Kent Road Mrs Price!' Jimmy boomed from the other side of the table.

'Now there's a lad after my own heart!' Chesney smiled. 'I was brought up in a workhouse not too far from there.'

Jimmy was a chipper fellow who sparkled in good conversation. 'It was a good place to come from. Wouldn't go back there to live for quids.

What will it all be like in a hundred years I say? Probably mansions with gardens and those new cars they're talking about. Imagine them roads up in London with cars instead of horses and carriages.'

'Never!' Bobby Grey rebuked him pleasantly. 'While man is alive the 'orse'll always have a place. Cars! Flight o' fancy. That's what they'll be. You mark my words – not because I was reared on 'orses and because I love 'em like my fellow man, but you look at what they do. They transport man to his place of work. They pull coal. Then there's the farm pony. My word, after the dog, the 'orse is a man's finest companion.'

Jimmy gently chided him. 'Don't know that I agree with you there Bobby. I reckon the car is the coming invention. Come the next century I think there will be one on every street corner.'

'I saw a car the other day,' said Jessica. 'Ooh, it made a noise like you wouldn't believe.'

'More tea Mr Chesney?' Mrs Price asked. Harry smiled and his cup was refilled. 'Now then Jessica, where did you see this car?'

'At Stopham Bridge near Pulborough.'

'Really?' Now there's a thing.' Mrs Price spoke in a motherly caring fashion. 'My we've seen some changes this century haven't we?'

'What do you do here Mrs Price?' asked Chesney, impressed by the kindliness of this lady.

'I'm the house cook.'

Chesney was genuinely interested in these people. 'Are you all happy here in your work? Is it a good life in service?'

'Wouldn't have it any other way,' Bobby answered enthusiastically. 'I work with my hands, doing all the home repairs. Little bit of carpentry. Do some leather work. I'm the footman also.'

'And,' added Jimmy, 'you look after your good mates the horses as well. You speak their language almost!'

'They speak sense, Jimmy me lad. 'Orse sense!'

'Sorry you've got to wait Mr Chesney,' Jessica said in a polite aside.

'That's alright love,' he replied. Chesney felt comfortable with these people. 'Did you all get up to London then to see old Queen Vic at her big parade?'

'Ooh we did!' Mrs Price seemed enthralled by the thought of it. 'Lady Bernadette let us have the day off and we all went up together. Wasn't it a wonderful day? All those uniforms and all that colour. Marvellous stuff.

Everybody looked happy. Flags waving. Smashing!'

'She passed by in her carriage right by us too,' Jessica recalled. This prompted Jimmy and Bobby to add their comments.

'Jessica reckons one of the soldiers with the Glengarry hat on who was sitting in the Queen's carriage winked at her! Beamed a beautiful smile at her and made her quiver all over.'

'Right made young Jessie blush too! Turning bright crimson she was!'

'Oh I was not!' Jessica was red faced and embarrassed.

Mrs Price laughed and came to the rescue. 'They're only joking. I thought it was me he smiled at! He was a handsome man too I'll be bound!'

Jessica looked up at the window quickly on hearing a horse whinny. Outside, Lady Bernadette rode by. Chesney caught a quick glance of her in riding clothes and wearing a top hat.

'Here she is now,' said Jessica. 'I'll take you through Mr Chesney.'

He got up from the table and smiled warmly at everyone. 'It's been very nice to have met you all. Perhaps I'll see you again sometime.'

'If you drop in again do come down and join us for a pot of tea and a scone.'

'That sounds most inviting,' Chesney said in response to Mrs Price's suggestion. 'I will make a point of it. Goodbye to you all.'

Jessica took Chesney through to an elegantly furnished lounge where he re-acquainted himself with Lady Bernadette. They talked for a long time in terms of pleasantries. Chesney noticed how well Lady Bernadette had kept for her age. Although there were flashes of silver in her hair, it had not reduced her natural attractiveness. Rather more, it had enhanced her and added character to a face that glowed with enthusiasm.

'I must say Harry I was most surprised when I came into your teashop a year ago and saw you behind the counter.'

'It was something of a shock to me. A very nice one of course. Rex told me that Shervington house was in Sussex but I never expected to bump into you.'

'It is nice to see you Harry. You are a reminder to me of a life I once knew. Long gone now of course. India. Dear Rex. But I prefer to live for the day and plan for the future. God knows life is short enough.'

'I quite agree.' Chesney paused to look at a painting of the late Captain Rex Shervington that hung on an opposite wall. In terms of profile and features Ravi bore strong similarities to his father. Where Captain Rex had been tall and well built, Ravi was lithe and slim. It was the boy's Indian upbringing that really separated them. 'Could I ask your advice on something, Lady Bernadette?'

'By all means.'

If she only knew, thought Chesney. 'I have this young lad staying with me. Just turned twenty-one. He's an Indian.' Lady Bernadette suddenly seemed very interested. 'I knew his mother and father in India.' This was half true at least. 'They're both dead now, sadly. Anyway for much of his life I've been what you might call his unofficial guardian. I sent money for his upkeep to the home he was adopted into. Even when I was working in Darjeeling and Ceylon and when I was out in Australia I looked after the lad.'

'That was very noble of you Harry,' Lady Bernadette was astonished.

'I never married you see. I never had the joy of any children of my own. I brought the lad to England. Thought I might try and get him some work in house service somewhere. He's got very good references. He worked as a waiter in the Officer's Club in Calcutta for a while. He's a right dapper little gent. I was wondering if you knew of somewhere he might be able to find work?'

'You say he's very good?'

'Very polite too. He's adopted my surname, by the way.'

Lady Bernadette stood up and clasped her hands together. 'Well that settles it then. When can he start?'

'You know of someone who can employ Ravi? That's wonderful!' Chesney was delighted.

'Here!' exclaimed Lady Bernadette. 'I'd like him to start work here!'

Chesney recoiled in horror, realising what he had done. 'Oh I couldn't impose on you, Lady Bernadette.'

'Nonsense! I'll be pleased to help him. I'm short of a permanent footman and an assistant butler. It would be my great pleasure to have him here. So that's final then. I'll hear no protest from you Harry!'

Chesney stood up, attempting to smile but in reality he felt sick inside. He could not explain this one away. On his way back to Horsham Chesney considered how his blunder could be turned into an advantage for both Ravi and Lady Bernadette.

Back in Horsham Chesney wandered around to the back of his tea warehouse. Ravi was putting packets of tea on the shelves. He turned around and smiled as Chesney entered.

'Hullo Mr Harry.'

'Wotcha me old mate,' Chesney said affably. 'Guess what I've gone and done?'

'You have found me work?' Ravi guessed correctly.

'I have.' Chesney looked apprehensive. 'That I have.'

'That is wonderful. Who is it with?' Chesney tried to calculate his words carefully. He was slow to reply. 'Something wrong Mr Harry?'

At last Chesney started to explain. 'I s'pose it is something of an irony. A poetic irony if it truly be realised. About a year ago into this very teashop came a Lady – by that I man a real titled Lady with a fair ancestry and heritage behind her. I knew her in India. I went to see her at her manor in Storrington, purely for some advice as to where I could get you a job in service. To my surprise she insisted that a job is on offer for you at her home.'

'Why are you so grim faced then, Mr Harry?'

'Because this Lady of grace, dignity and warmth was married to an officer in my regiment.' He took a deep breath. 'The officer, Ravi my good friend, was your father.' He looked at the young man square on, who registered a look of astonishment. 'Captain Rex Shervington.'

'This Lady was the one who married Captain Rex in England?' stammered Ravi.

'Yes. You must remember that he did not know, when he married Lady Bernadette, that your mother Sarah was expecting you.'

'I understand that,' Ravi said.

Chesney was cautious now. 'Listen Ravi. At first I thought it was a ridiculous idea. I was thinking I'd made a naïve and stupid blunder. Now I'm not so sure. The more I think about it, the more I think it would be a good thing for you to work in the house. At least for a while, to gain some experience. The other staff are smashing. I met them. Lady Bernadette is splendid. Don't reveal what we know to Lady Bernadette. It would be insensitive and could hurt her badly. Remember too, it is your late father's house. Honour his memory.'

Ravi's face was such that his expression was difficult to interpret. 'I will honour his memory Mr Harry,' he said after a while. Chesney knew that the young lad would do his best.

Thirteen

Ravi took up the position with Lady Bernadette Shervington's household and several months on he had progressed well. The staff had warmed to this polite, gentle and dark-skinned man. His lack of aggression and peaceful soul had made him an easy person to work with. Ravi was learning his new trade from Jimmy Brown who watched over him with a fatherly eye. Although they were opposites in character, for some curious unknown reason, they got on together famously.

Lady Bernadette frequently held garden parties at Shervington Manor when all manner of guests would be invited. These would be not only people who were of a wealthy class, but local people who contributed to the way of life in Storrington. At one of these parties Ravi was to experience how titled people could demean themselves as much as any street vagabond.

During the meal Lady Bernadette sat at the centre of a long table in the garden. She spoke to another woman of affluence and position who was the wealthy if somewhat delightfully eccentric widow of an estate owner. This person was Lady Geraldine Lambert. She had a great fondness for wine and a sense of humour bordering on hilarity. Unfortunately, on this occasion Lady Geraldine had refilled her glass perhaps once too much. Ravi filled it while Jimmy watched from a safe distance. He realised that the Lady was obviously 'three sheets to the wind'. Jimmy winked at him reassuringly.

Ravi returned to the kitchen where Mrs Price and Jessica were busy working. Jessica turned around and smiled very warmly at Ravi. It was a smile that indicated more than warmth. Often she would steal a quick glance at him. It was clear to anyone who saw her how much she adored him.

'How are you getting on out there Ravi?' she asked and looked at him admiringly as he filled his tray with pastries, cakes and clean glasses.

'I'm busy Miss Jessica,' Ravi replied. 'Very busy. There is a Lady at the table who is gradually drinking Lady Bernadette's wine cellar dry.'

'That sounds like Lady Geraldine Lambert.' Jessica giggled. 'Oh she's a jolly sort. Likes a fair tipple though. Gosh can she get tippled too! She fell over once and slid across the wet grass on her bottom!'

'Never mind, young man,' Mrs Price said warmly. 'It's your afternoon off tomorrow isn't it? What are you going to do?'

Ravi pondered in thought. 'I might go walking over the Downs. I've not really got to know the countryside.'

Mrs Price was quick to offer her own suggestion. 'Young Jess has got the afternoon off. Why don't you show Ravi around?'

Ravi turned to Jessica quickly. 'Would you?'

Jessica smiled at him almost shyly. 'I'd love to.'

Jimmy suddenly entered the room. 'Blimey! What a show eh! Can you fill my tray up with desserts then Jessica, there's a good girl.' He mopped his brow and relaxed for a moment. 'A right party of Lords and Ladies out there. They've had more than their fair share of the wine.'

Mrs Price nodded her head. 'Sounds like I must put some good hot coffee on the boil.'

'Very strong I think,' agreed Jimmy. 'My goodness, they say the working class love their ale but the upper class certainly know how to enjoy their liquor.'

'Everyone's the same Jimmy boy,' said Mrs Price, filling up kettles to boil water for coffee. 'It's only their wealth that separates them.'

Ravi found this comment interesting. 'It's strange when you say that. In India we have many castes. We also have wealthy people like maharajahs and princes. Yet we never think of ourselves as the same as each other.'

Jessica added a couple more dishes of food to Ravi's tray. 'I am ready now Mr Jimmy.'

Jimmy was keen to look after his young protégé. 'I'll give you a tip Ravi. When the guests are considerably the worse for wear, as indeed they are at the moment, and the conversation is verging on the frivolous if not the damn ridiculous, hold yourself in good stead. Be cautious and courteous at all times. More importantly, be respectful. Right lad, we'll give them some service. Remember Ravi, caution.'

The two men returned to the outside table and continued to serve the guests. After they had distributed the food and drink they took up their position at the back of the table where they would be at the beck and call of the guests. Lady Geraldine turned around and waved with her fingers to indicate to Ravi. Reluctantly he responded and went across to her.

'Yes m' Lady what can I get you?'

Lady Geraldine eyed him curiously. 'Tell me young man, you're from India aren't you?'

'Yes m' Lady I am.'

'You look a bit of mixture actually,' she said, slurring her words. 'Were both your parents Indian – or some other breed perhaps?'

Ravi was slightly unnerved. 'I did not know my parents m' Lady. They died when I was young.' He was anxious to end this conversation. 'Will that be all now?'

Lady Geraldine was persistent. 'I thought you must be from an Anglo-Indian union. Perhaps your father was a British soldier?' She was terribly drunk now and not aware of the stinging effect of her words. 'Do you know who your father is?'

Ravi froze in horror. She had struck a raw nerve. Even a patient and gentle man such as he had a limit as to how much he could take of this nonsense. 'You really must excuse me, I have other guests to serve, m' Lady.'

He walked away, angry and disgusted. Jimmy was quick to notice and followed him across the garden. Lady Bernadette too noticed and asked Lady Geraldine just what exactly she had said.

Jimmy ran after Ravi who was walking in the direction of the kitchen. He was an old street fighter who could tell by people's expressions just what they were feeling. Jimmy called Ravi.

'Hey! Hey Ravi! Stop for a moment will you?'

Ravi turned around and stopped. 'I'm sorry Jimmy.' His face was ashen. 'That Lady. She was…'

Jimmy looked on in sympathy. He was a kind man with much feeling for his young friend. 'I know son. She can be a handful at times. Forget it. Let's get back. We've got a job to do.'

Ravi looked at him, realising he had to return to his duties. He and Jimmy walked back to the garden party as if nothing had happened.

It was during the evening that Ravi found his employer was also a very compassionate person. He had always thought of English ladies as ice cold and aloof, not warm blooded or passionate like the women of the orient. Ravi did not realise that the English were not made of stone and that beneath their sometimes frosty surfaces lurked warmth and goodwill. In fact, English women were known for their compassion, service and dedication.

Lady Bernadette was at work in her study writing letters and entering notes in her diaries. Ravi knocked on the door and entered carrying a tray with a pot of tea and several cups on it.

'I have your evening tea, m' Lady,' he said politely.

Lady Bernadette continued to write without looking up. 'Thank you Ravi. Would you place it on the side table?'

'Certainly,' he replied. He placed it on the table and proceeded to pour a cup for her. Lady Bernadette turned to face him.

'Would you care to join me for a cup?' she asked him unexpectedly. Ravi looked surprised. He was aware that staff and employees always had a great distance between them. Servant and master had wide divisions. 'Please. Take a seat. Pour yourself a cup.'

He followed her instruction and sat down opposite her. She noticed the worried expression on Ravi's face.

'I believe one of the guests was rude to you this afternoon.' Ravi opened his mouth to speak but Lady Bernadette placated him with a wave of her hand. 'It's alright. No need for you to worry. I am apologising on behalf of her to you.'

'It's very kind of you,' Ravi said humbly.

'That particular person should have shown considerably more consideration for a person's feelings.'

Ravi suddenly felt more relaxed. 'It's alright. I think it was just one of those things. I really would like to take this opportunity to thank you for giving me the chance to work here. I am very happy to be employed here. The staff have been very nice to me.'

Lady Bernadette was obviously pleased. 'I am glad to hear that. As you know I am a widow of some years standing and this house, the staff, the horses and the dogs, well it's my family. I want everybody to be happy here. Feel free to come and see me if you ever have any problems.' Ravi started to rise. 'Don't get up. There is something I would like to ask you. Forgive me for returning to the earlier subject. I noticed when Lady Geraldine spoke to you, she asked you about your origins. I must apologise for her asking that question. I don't mean to be intrusive, but as your employer –

would you be offended if I asked you a bit more about yourself?'

Ravi was hesitant in replying. This was not lost on Lady Bernadette, who smiled reassuringly at him. Finally he volunteered.

'My mother was an Indian lady called Sarah. My father...was a British soldier. Both of them died when I was quite young. Mr Chesney very kindly became my guardian. While he was away in other countries he paid for my upbringing and wrote letters to me as would a father to his son.' Ravi had told her the truth without actually naming the man who was his real father. For a moment he anticipated that Lady Bernadette would ask him the identity of the man. Ravi would not lie. It was not in the make-up of his character to do so. He would tell the truth whatever the consequences.

Lady Bernadette merely pondered on what she had just heard. 'I see,' she murmured quietly.

'Mr Chesney was most kind,' Ravi added.

'Certainly,' agreed Lady Bernadette. 'He is a fine man. A hearty soul with much feeling for his fellow man.' She seemed keen to keep the cosy chat bubbling over. 'I knew many of the soldiers of the 25th Queen's Light Northern regiment. My late husband was a Captain you see.'

'Yes m'Lady,' Ravi answered quietly with a tremble in his voice. The thought occurred to him: did she suspect who he was? He felt alarm within.

If she did know, she wasn't saying anything. She smiled at him in such a way that he responded in kind. 'I won't keep you now Ravi. Thank you for joining me.'

Ravi rose from his chair and as always responded to politeness with equal respect. 'Thank you for allowing me to join you.' He turned and left the room.

Lady Bernadette watched him leave. From her chair in the study she rose to her feet and went across to the wall where a painting hung of her late husband Captain Rex Shervington. She was far too intuitive not to notice the likeness.

Fourteen

Ravi had been looking forward to his day away from household duties. He and Jessica were going to walk across the country footpaths of the Sussex Downs. In the short time he had been in England he had fallen in love with Sussex. It was beyond his dreams to live in such a peaceful, prosperous English county that contained so much natural beauty. He was surprised that the cold grey land he had heard about as a boy in India could evoke so much warmth and brightness. His free days were rare but he always spent his time well.

Bobby Grey took Ravi and Jessica for a ride in an open carriage drawn by a proud strutting horse. Down an old winding country lane, Bobby steered his way until he came to a tiny stile. From there a narrow path meandered across the lush green downs.

'There you'll be then, my young lad and lass.' Bobby stopped the carriage. Ravi and Jessica climbed down. 'Follow that path all the way and ye'll arrive in Bognor – if you're feeling a trifle energetic that is.'

'No fear Bobby!' Jessica smiled at this wonderful Sussex character. 'We're just going walking. I'm going to show Ravi some of the best of the English countryside.'

'Right, I'll be gone now. Take care of young Ravi then Jess. Be seeing you later then.' Bobby lifted up the reins and moved off down the path.

'Come on then,' Jessica said almost playfully.

Ravi and Jessica walked across the Downs. It was a very sunny day and the two of them skipped like children across the fields. The attraction between the two was so obvious.

It was a pleasant walk. The Downs were high up and they slowly wandered along the path, taking in the rustic view far below. Pathways meandered in and out of clumps of trees. Sleepy villages nestled at different points of the outspreading scenery. Jessica pointed out all the villages she knew by name: Nutley, Alfriston, Ardingly, Washington, Findon, Amberley, Arundel. Trees in clusters of hundreds seemed to spring up at uneven intervals. Some of the pathways they followed had once been trod centuries before by legions of Romans. A soft blue sky formed a beautiful backdrop to the golden sparkle of barley growing in the occasional field amidst the lush rich green rectangles that spread out all the way to the coast.

'You should see it at harvest time Ravi,' Jessica said, proudly showing off her adopted county which she too passionately adored.

Ravi smiled at her. He had feelings of adoration for this happy laughing young lady. Looking out at the market towns, the flour mills, dairy and sheep farms, Ravi found this way of life so peaceful after the teeming crowds of India. Truly, paradise could be found in such unexpected places, enhanced by that first glorious flush of the excitement of love.

Above them, all the signs of a summer storm about to break with a thunderous effect became apparent. Ravi and Jessica took cover from the sudden downpour of heavy rain that seemed to come tumbling down in torrents. Beneath a clump of thickly wooded trees they sat in silence. Ravi watched the cloud of rain enveloping the green contours of the Downs. He was oblivious to the fact that Jessica, sitting very close, was looking at him with a mixture of admiration and affection. He turned suddenly and caught the loving look in her eyes. Jessica started to blush, but from behind them there was a sudden rustling noise. An animal about the size of a dog scurried away quickly.

'What is that?' gasped Ravi, astonished at the creature which he had never known existed.

Jessica smiled at the sight of it. 'Oh he won't do us any harm. It's a lovely old badger. Don't see too many of them. They come out at night usually. Poor old things, badgers. Out in the cold foraging for food. Not as exciting as the animals in India I bet.'

At this Ravi smiled. 'I don't know what you English people think of India. They all seem to think tigers roam in the street.' Jessica laughed. 'England is very, very different to what I imagined. I see now how green it is. There is so much history here. It is a lovely land in so many ways.'

'Yes is it,' Jessica said wistfully. 'I've not been anywhere else though. I'd like to go somewhere exciting like India. Somewhere warm and sunny. When I saw you come to the house that first day I thought you were an

Indian prince come to visit. I couldn't believe it when Lady Bernadette said you were to be the assistant butler working with Mr Brown. I thought you were the most handsome man I had ever seen.'

It was Ravi's turn to blush. 'That is a very nice thing for you to say,' he remarked rather shyly. 'You are a very pretty girl.' Jessica seemed to be thrilled at the compliment. She kissed him quickly. Ravi savoured the moment. He was left speechless by her action but he managed a smile. 'You'd better show me some more of the English countryside. Otherwise I might run away with you.'

Jessica smiled at him again. She was obviously very much in love with him. When the rain had eased off the two of them continued their walk across the countryside. A little way in front of them were two farm workers making their way home. Both of them were unsavoury characters and local troublemakers. One of them was a mere five feet tall but he had a nasty aggressive nature. He would pick on anyone for a fight to demonstrate that what he lacked in height he could more than make up for by way of fighting. The tragedy was that he would invariably fight people taller than he was who were quiet and defenceless, and had no interest in fisticuffs. His name was Danny Blackwell and he was often accompanied by his big burly brute of a brother Dave, who was also possessed of a vicious nature. Dave Blackwell wasn't with his brother on this occasion. Danny Blackwell was with a mutual friend, Mick Bloodlace. Mick was about five feet five, as thin as a rake, with long unkempt black matted hair, dark brown eyes that gleamed with hate and a face shrouded in stubble.

'Hullo there!' Mick called out, on seeing Jessica. It wasn't a friendly cry though. Even from a distance the two could sense aggression.

'Oh no,' murmured Jessica, flinching at the sight of the two young men.

'What's wrong?' Ravi could see the change in her expression.

Jessica looked at him worriedly. 'Those two are the local mischief makers. The one on the left is Mick Bloodlace and the other little rogue is Danny Blackwell. They're always picking fights in the village.'

While she had been explaining, the two men had come right up to them. They stood virtually blocking their way.

'How would you be then? Still working in the big house with all them snobs eh?' Mick smiled at them. It was a twisted smile though.

Ravi stepped forward calmly. 'Would you two show some courtesy and allow the lady and me to pass?'

Almost at once Danny Blackwell seized the opportunity to demonstrate his thorough nastiness and ignorance. 'Who do you think you are then!? You're a bit hoity-toity ain't ya? You walk and talk funny. Don't 'e eh Mick?'

'E's an Indie boy,' sneered Mick. 'Fresh out the bleedin' jungle if you ask me.'

Ravi stood his ground. But he did not raise his voice or show any signs of temper. 'It doesn't matter where I come from or what I do. The lady and I have done you no harm.'

Danny rubbed the lapel of Ravi's suit and eyed him with contempt. 'Think you're a gent do you? You're all smooth words and good clothes eh. You don't seem to be anything much to me.'

'He's all show. Bet he's never done a real day's work in his life,' Mick jeered and he casually spat at Ravi's shoes.

Jessica showed a rare flash of anger. 'You two are a nasty pair. You're always picking on people for no reason. Usually defenceless people who've done you no harm!'

'If he were a real man 'e'd 'ave a bleedin' fight wiv me!' Danny said in protest, as if he was the person who had been wronged.

Ravi, ever calm, spoke to him quietly. 'And if you were a real man you would not pick fights with those you think are more vulnerable and weaker than you. The sign of a real man is one who has gentleness mixed in with compassion, sensitivity to others and who can show strength under pressure. All you have shown to me is that you are a man lacking in kindness; someone who would rather throw punches for no other reason than to be vicious. You are ignorant of what you do not understand.'

Danny Blackwell was seething with anger at Ravi's calm courage. 'You make me bleedin' sick with your posh talk!' Danny snarled at him. 'I'll tell you what a real man is! Someone who can hold his liquor. Someone who can hold his woman and can fight any man!'

Ravi looked at this spiteful young man for whom he could only feel pity. 'Then you are even more ignorant, I am sorry to say. I feel sorry for you. You are a bully, a jeering lout, and Jessica and I have done you no harm. We will pass if you don't mind.'

Ravi and Jessica made an attempt to pass but Danny raised his fists angrily. 'You nancy boy!' he screeched. In a moment of sheer madness, Danny was raining blows and heavy punches on Ravi.

Jessica recoiled in horror. 'Stop it!' she cried. 'Stop it!'

Mick went forward and pulled Danny away from Ravi who had been sent crashing to the floor, and was almost unconscious. He was bleeding. Jessica knelt down and mopped Ravi's head. She looked around at the two thugs who were walking away.

'You two are filth! Call yourselves men! You're disgusting! You're miserable mistakes for human beings. Ravi is far more of a man than you two wicked swine!' Jessica caressed Ravi and took care of him. Her face was tear stained. She could not understand the way of human nature that two thugs could hurt a man such as Ravi who had a peace loving and gentle nature.

It took her a while to get Ravi back to the house. Jessica had a struggle as Ravi had taken a fair beating, but eventually she got him into the kitchen of the house. Thankfully Lady Bernadette and Mrs Price were both out of the house. If they had seen Ravi in his present condition it would have upset them deeply. Jessica swabbed Ravi down with water and soap. She positioned him in a chair and stroked his bruised face with her soft gentle hands.

From behind, Bobby Grey and Jimmy Brown entered the kitchen. They were both speechless. The looks on their faces were full of shock. It was Bobby who broke the silence. He was aghast.

'Wha's 'appened 'ere then Jessie my love?'

'How did young Ravi get like this?' Jimmy asked coldly, but studying the bruises on his friend's face, he knew the question was not so much as 'how' but 'who' did this?

Jessica looked up with tears welling in her eyes. 'It was one of the Blackwell brothers from Storrington village and his friend Mick Bloodlace. We were walking across the fields and Danny Blackwell started hitting Ravi. He didn't like the way Ravi talked and walked. That Blackwell sours this nice village.'

Jimmy got down and looked at Ravi. 'Are you alright son?'

'Just about,' Ravi croaked, trying to appear in a better manner than he really was.

'Well you hang in here old mate.' Jimmy gripped Ravi's shoulder with a sense of reassurance. 'Do you want us to let Constable Treadwell know what's happened?'

'No, I will be alright Mr Jimmy,' Ravi said in a very low voice.

Bobby came across to look at him. 'Look Ravi,' he said, 'I know you've just had a bit o' bad bother an' all but I reckon we'd better get you cleaned up in my quarters. If Mrs Price and Lady Bernadette see you like this they'll be right shocked. Jess, you take young Ravi to my rooms and get him to lie down and rest awhile.'

'I will. Come on Ravi.' Jessica and Ravi left the room. When they had gone Jimmy and Bobby looked at each other in anticipation of their thoughts.

'What are you thinking then?' Bobby asked.

Jimmy glanced down at the floor and then directly at Bobby. 'I think we'll have a quiet word with these lads.'

Bobby appeared flabbergasted. 'A word is it then Jim? A word! By God, them Blackwell brothers need a damn good thrashing! Only bullies and savages would do to Ravi what they did. This is the fairest village in all these parts and scum like them Blackwells go round putting fear and fright into the hearts o' decent folk.'

'Alright Bobby you've made your point. I'll roll up my sleeves.'

'No!' snapped Bobby. 'I didn't mean that. Let's see the local bobby and get those mongrels in the dock. Transportation would be too good for them. Three terms plus ten for them'd be more like it in a lock-up with no keys.'

Jimmy had other ideas. 'I might enjoy letting off a bit of steam. I thought I'd given away the fisticuffs years ago when I got out of Newgate. I started myself a nice new life away from the thieving and the street fighting. This home, this place, everyone here – it's been happy times. I've learned decency and I'm proud of being a butler in this fine house.'

'So fighting blood still surges through the veins eh?'

'You know what they say.'

'What do they say then Jim?'

'It's not what anybody says. It's what I think. I'm knocking on to my forties. But I know how to land a few punches the Blackwells don't. I'm fond of Ravi. He's a good lad. Hasn't had an easy life by all accounts. But old Harry Chesney wanted to give him a good start over here. I think we ought to put the lad's mind at ease.'

Bobby eyed him curiously. 'How are we going to do this?'

'Listen now Bobby. There's a bare-knuckle fight on behind the pub tonight?'

'Right Jim. So?'

'Half the village will be there to place a bet.'

Bobby was slowly getting the picture. 'You and me included. A sovereign or two each way. Including – dare I say, Danny and Dave Blackwell, and Mick Bloodlace.'

'Now you've got it. When we get down there, start collecting the bets. Me at a hundred to one to take all three of them on and beat them.'

'All three of them? You're mad you silly beggar!' Suddenly Bobby's look of astonishment changed to one of amusement. 'If you beat the swine we could trump a few aces my old boy.'

Jimmy and Bobby grinned at the thought of what they could achieve in an evening; revenge and a pocket full of money.

Late in the night Jimmy and Bobby made their way to the Half Moon pub. It was a local with a very unsavoury reputation. Once it had been a smugglers' haunt and a stopping off point for coaches from Portsmouth to London. Now it was a roughneck drinking den and gambling house where bets could be placed on anything from cock fighting to bare-knuckle scrapping.

On this night two heavily-built bare-chested bare-knuckle fighters were in the centre of a group of villagers. The men slugged it out in ferocious traditional style. Several villagers held blazing beacons, the light of which illuminated the agony of the two fighters whose faces were becoming exceedingly bloody and bruised.

Jimmy watched from amongst the crowd. He gazed across and his eyes focussed on Danny and Dave Blackwell, both of whom were unshaven and filthy in appearance. Then his gaze switched to Mick Bloodlace who, even in the dark, had a satanic look about him. While the fight was going on, Bobby Grey went around with a hat amongst the villagers, taking bets for the bout to come. He was careful to avoid Jimmy's opponents, who would get the biggest shock of the evening.

Bobby looked across at Jimmy and shook his hat, indicating the stakes they could clean up on. The hat was filled to overflowing. It was going to be one hell of a fight.

Meanwhile the bare-knuckle bout was drawing to a close. The punches were flying thick and fast but one of the pugilists was stumbling on his feet and he dropped to his knees. He attempted to rise. He was just about on his feet when his opponent landed one more heavy punch, sending him flying back into a state of oblivion.

The villagers cheered and gave the victor a huge round of applause. The people who had placed bets started to gather in their winnings. Someone tossed a bucket of water over the loser who was carried away to quietly recover in one of the rooms of the inn. This signalled the opportunity for Jimmy and Bobby to proceed with their plans.

Jimmy walked into the area that had served as the ring for the contestants. He removed his jacket and shirt, revealing a very sturdy physique. Then he started sparring with an imaginary opponent for practice.

Behind the crowd, Bobby Grey made the announcement that was about to startle the Blackwell brothers and Mick Bloodlace.

'Gentlemen! Gather round!' he cried at the top of his voice, indicating with his hands for the crowd to draw in. 'In this 'ere 'at I've been taking bets for the best scrapping bout we'll be seeing for many a while in this fair village of ours. It's not just one of our local lads squaring off at the other. It's a contest between one gallant fellow versus three.'

Unaware of who was going to be an unwilling participant in the bout, Danny Blackwell reacted in his usual sneering manner. 'Who's that then Bobby? You?'

Some of the villagers laughed. Bobby smiled too, for he had the last laugh. 'Behind me, good folk, you'll see my sparring friend Jimmy Brown. Come on down Jim!' Jimmy flung his arms up and jumped into the centre of the group. 'This 'ere fine fellow Jimmy is going to take three of you lads on; three lads who've been doing a bit of bullying. And who might they be Jim?'

'I'll tell you who the blighters are. Danny and Dave Blackwell and their accomplice Mick Bloodlace. This afternoon Danny Blackwell damn near knocked the life blood out of a young fellow I work with, because he speaks more nicely than he does.'

Danny pouted his lip defiantly. 'Oh yeah! He was a blackface in a good suit.'

'The odds are against me – true,' Jimmy said, stating the obvious. 'But it's a good bet if anyone's interested. You three scum can either settle with me or, on the other hand, we can let the good constable know and you can take your chances in the dock. I fancy you'll not enjoy a prison cell too much.' Some more villagers started placing bets with Bobby. 'Come on then boys, you normally make a point of picking on the weak, the timid, the meek; those you sneeringly say aren't men because they won't fight you. Well I'll give you a bit of fair competition.'

Bobby wasn't going to give anyone options. 'Let the fight commence!'

At this Jimmy moved forward. The Blackwell brothers realised they had no choice and were being seriously challenged. Reluctantly they came out, swinging their fists. Mick Bloodlace started to come forward. Bobby indicated to the crowd to spread out. Danny took a swing at Jimmy but he was too slow. Jimmy ducked and then plunged forward, striking Danny firm on the chin, following it up with two quick punches to the stomach and a kick up the backside for good measure. Mick Bloodlace and Dave Blackwell realised with shock that they had good competition. They both moved forward viciously. Jimmy struck at each of them with rapid movement, using both his left and right fists forcefully.

The crowd by now was enthralled with this spectacle of the near-middle-aged battling butler knocking the stuffing out of these three young hooligans who, it was rumoured, even the local constable was afraid of tackling.

All hell broke loose. Punches were traded on all sides. Jimmy was knocked to the floor and as he attempted to regain his lost ground he took a great deal of punishment. But in the world of street fighting Jimmy was no slouch. He sprang back into action, and with a lot of ducking and weaving and striking he soon flattened his opponents into submission. The brutes were no match for this middle-aged connoisseur of the pugilistic arts. Jimmy knocked both men out with clean well-placed punches.

The fight was not over yet. Danny recovered, and with vengeance clearly on his mind poised to strike. Once again he missed. Jimmy came back, using all his remaining strength in final jabs that floored his vicious opponent.

It was all over. The Blackwell brothers and Mick Bloodlace lay flat on their backs, beaten by a surprisingly formidable opponent. Jimmy very wearily walked across to the three men lying on the ground. He knelt down by Danny Blackwell.

'Listen to me Blackwell, you're a nasty piece of work and if you even attempt to bully anyone in this village – especially my mate you so viciously beat up this afternoon – then by heavens I'll make sure criminal charges are brought against you. Do I make myself clear?' There was no answer. Jimmy leaned down and shook Danny a few times. 'Do I make myself clear?'

'There'll be no trouble,' Danny croaked meekly.

Jimmy got up and put his shirt and jacket back on. A few villagers patted him on the back. Jimmy half smiled and turned to look back at the three men. Bobby raised the hat full of money in front of him and the two men left the area behind the Half Moon pub. Jimmy saw two men with fighting cocks preparing for the next bout of the evening.

The two men headed back towards Shervington Manor. Bobby held the reins of the horse and open carriage. He noticed that Jimmy had been a remarkably quiet passenger on this journey.

'What's wrong there, Jimmy boy?' Bobby asked. 'You've been as quiet as the gravestones in the cemetery in St. Mary's church. You're not fretting are you?'

'I am.'

'Why? For your trouble, you and I have made a couple of months' wages, Jim.'

Jimmy seemed to be more sad than angry. 'I'm fretting because I'm disgusted with myself! When I came out of prison – and the memory of it still haunts me – I decided to walk the straight and narrow. I was ashamed of my past. Petty theft. Brawling. Fighting. Villainy. That was my lot. I was born into poverty. That's my excuse which is no excuse at all.'

'We've all got things in our life that maybe we do not wish to remember.'

'Not like I have. I served my time in Newgate Prison. Told myself no more fighting. No more of the rough stuff. Sixteen years of clean living and living decently. And what do I do? Tonight I get down to my old trade. Fisticuffs.'

Bobby tried to sooth Jimmy's mood. 'You brought it out for one night. One night only. Forget it. Don't dwell on it. Tomorrow you go back to being the best butler in these parts.'

'I will,' said Jimmy firmly. He wanted to close the incident out of his mind forever. 'I shall never raise my fists again. It's back to the good life we know at the old manor house; good manners and decency.'

Fifteen

The kitchen in Shervington Manor was a flurry of activity the next morning. Mrs Price was preparing pastry and cakes. Ravi was quietly cleaning glasses; he was desperately trying to maintain a cool composure after the beating he had taken the previous day. Jessica was dusting shelves and every so often she would glance over and smile at Ravi to let him know she was there for him. Outside, Bobby Grey waved through the window as he walked past leading some horses. Jimmy walked into the kitchen. Out of earshot of the others, he had a quiet word to Ravi.

'How are you feeling this morning?' he whispered.

'I am fine Mr Jimmy.' He didn't sound very convincing. Jimmy looked at him in quiet disbelief. Ravi noticed this and tried to reassure him. 'Really, I am fine.'

'If you tell me you are I believe you. But I've got a good idea of how you must be feeling. Ravi, I want you to put what happened yesterday out of your mind.' He looked at this young man with sympathy. 'I had a chat to the lads concerned.' Some chat, thought he! 'They'll not trouble you again.'

'You went to see them?' Ravi gasped in amazement.

'In a manner of speaking,' Jimmy replied. Ravi looked at him, instinctively knowing Jimmy was not telling him everything. He smiled in return and tried to put Ravi in a good mood. 'So come on then son, put your best foot forward, smile, be happy and get your tasks done. In a minute when Bobby's groomed the horses we'll go down the markets and get some more food in.' Jimmy turned around and called out to the cook. 'Mrs Price!'

'What are you two whispering about over there? You're like Guy Fawkes plotting.' Mrs Price was permanently good natured.

'You know Ravi and I are off to the markets this morning?'

'I had to remind you didn't I Jim? You nearly forgot. Don't you be forgetting the prime beef or the sack of flour. And we need plenty of fresh fruit, vegetables, fine potatoes, peaches…'

'Whoa! Whoa!' Jimmy was flabbergasted by the list of food. He knew it was a special occasion when so much was required. 'I've got all that on my list. Lady Bernadette said we have some special guests on Saturday. Any idea who they are?'

Mrs Price smiled one of her cheekiest smiles. 'I've no idea. But I've been trying to work it out. Do you know what I think?'

'I bet many a man's wanted to know in your time Mrs Price,' Jimmy said mischievously.

'You cheeky beggar! I'll tell you what I think. I reckon it's royalty m'self. What do you think?'

There were special guests coming for dinner at Shervington Manor. Lady Bernadette was inviting a cross-section of people to that particular function; one of them would be Harry Chesney.

Lady Bernadette paid a surprise visit to Harry Chesney's warehouse. She looked very vivacious and well-dressed that day. It was to be a surprise, and Lady Bernadette went to the door of the warehouse and peered inside. There were a number of men working very hard, packing tea. From outside she called to one of the men.

'Excuse me.' There was no reply. She called out again, this time a bit louder. 'Excuse me! You there! I say young man!'

A tea packer turned around and on seeing Lady Bernadette pointed to himself as if to say 'who, me?' Lady Bernadette smiled and nodded. The tea packer came across to the door and removed his flat cap as a sign of courtesy.

'Blimey!' The tea packer was breathtaken by Lady Bernadette's appearance. 'Begging your pardon madam we don't often see such a splendidly dressed lady as yourself in a place like this.'

'I'm sorry to disturb you in your labour young man,' she said pleasantly. 'I'm looking for the proprietor.'

'The – proprietor?' That was a new word for the tea packer. 'Oh! – you mean the guv'nor!'

'That's him. The proprietor. Manager. Owner. Leader. Guv. Whatever you call him. Last known as Mr H. Chesney.'

'E's in the teashop miss. I'll take you through. All the lads call 'im young 'Arry. 'E might be the guv'nor but 'e's like one of the blokes really.'

The tea packer took Lady Bernadette into Harry Chesney's teashop. It was doing good business that morning. Amidst the oak beams people sat at tables eating pastries and cakes, and drinking teas from the variety of imports that Harry stored in his warehouse.

'There he is,' said the tea packer. 'His royal eminence Mr Harold Chesney esquire.'

'Thank you,' said Lady Bernadette. Harry Chesney was standing behind the counter filling in a ledger book. He was concentrating hard and was unaware of her presence. Lady Bernadette surprised him by emulating a cockney accent. 'Allo young 'Arry. I 'ear yer the guv'nor. Got a kiss fer yer old muvver then?'

Chesney looked up from behind the counter. He was stunned at first, then burst out laughing. 'Lady Bernadette! How nice to see you. To what do I owe the pleasure of this visit?'

'Can we sit down Harry?'

'By all means.' He showed her to a table and they sat down. A waitress walked past and Chesney called out to her. 'Linda, can we have some tea over here.' The waitress acknowledged him. 'Well now, Lady Bernadette. A most unexpected visit. How is young Ravi?'

'An excellent butler-in-training,' she replied. 'Extremely diplomatic. He's rather shy, which I suppose with his background is to be expected. I'm very glad he came to us.'

'I am pleased,' said Chesney, and one could tell that he really meant what he said. 'When I met your staff I thought they were a lovely group.'

Lady Bernadette came straight to the point. 'I'd like you to come to the house and visit him. It's been a while now.'

'I wouldn't want to put you to any trouble.' The waitress placed a tray on the table and began pouring them a cup.

'I would be very pleased to have you visit. In fact, I'm here to give you a special invitation.' She handed him a card. Chesney opened it and appeared flattered. 'There is a point-to-point race meeting on Saturday in the village. Afterwards there will be a dinner party at Shervington Manor. I'd rather like you to be there. I have two very special guests coming. Please stay overnight.'

'I'll be pleased to come – that's if you think a rough-hewn fellow like me will fit into your gilded cage.'

'Of course you will,' Lady Bernadette said, tapping Chesney's hand lightly.

'Who are these – these special guests?'

Lady Bernadette's face beamed with delight. 'The Prince of Wales and Mr Rudyard Kipling.'

Chesney's eyes showed disbelief. 'Good God almighty! You jest surely?'

'No not at all,' Lady Bernadette said, smiling deliciously at him. 'There will be a few local guests from the village. I'd be delighted if you would come.'

'The Prince of Wales and Rudyard Kipling eh?' Chesney could not comprehend this. 'Me in the company of those two gentlemen! Who would have ever believed it?'

Sixteen

It was the Saturday of the race meeting at Storrington village. The dinner party at Shervington Manor was also in preparation. All the staff were busy in the kitchen, cutting vegetables and sorting out the best silver service for the long highly polished dining-room table.

Everyone was at their most industrious. Bobby Grey anxiously repaired shelves in the kitchen. Jimmy and Ravi put together fine silver cutlery, crystal clear glasses and oriental decorated crockery. Jessica was running around with a brush, cleaning every nook and cranny. Mrs Price was surrounded by vegetables which she cut and sliced carefully.

Always with a motherly eye, she watched Jessica getting flustered in the kitchen. 'Don't get working y'self in a tizz now Jess.'

Jessica turned around and smiled at Mrs Price. The truth was that young Jessica felt thrilled beyond belief at the thought of the two distinguished guests who would be arriving. 'The Prince of Wales and Rudyard Kipling eh! Me in the company of those two gentlemen. Who would have ever believed it?' She was absolutely ecstatic.

From the main door of the kitchen came the sound of laughter. Everyone looked up as Harry Chesney entered the room.

'That's exactly what I said!' he chuckled. 'Hello everyone.'

'Lovely to see you again Mr Chesney,' Mrs Price said, looking at him admiringly. Now if she'd been ten years younger…

'And you darling,' Chesney responded.

Jessica, ever respectful of guests to the house, curtsied. 'Good morning Sir.'

'Good morning to you sweetheart,' Chesney said. Ravi turned to greet him. 'Hello young man.' The two shook hands and embraced.

'Welcome to the house Mr Harry,' Ravi said proudly.

'It's good to be here.' Chesney felt glad that Ravi was in the best of company. He turned to the other men. 'Nice to see you Mr Grey.'

'A pleasure to see you too Sir,' Bobby replied.

Chesney walked across to Jimmy and shook his hand. 'Jimmy, I had a chat to a lad in the village on my way up here. He was telling me about a good deed you did for someone's peace of mind.' The two men looked at each other. Jimmy instinctively knew that Chesney was referring to the recent fight behind the pub, where the three thugs who had attacked Ravi had been despatched. 'I'd just like to say I'm proud to know you and delighted that Ravi is working with such good people. You're a fine man, Jimmy Brown.'

Jimmy showed no shred of embarrassment or response to Chesney's compliment, but as with most generous men merely shrugged his shoulders and smiled. 'It's a privilege to have him on board Sir.'

Mrs Price, who was always eager to please, was overwhelmed with food to cook that day. She liked Harry Chesney and felt inclined to offer her apologies for not being able to offer him refreshment. 'We would offer you a cup of tea Mr Chesney, but we're flat out this morn. Got a right special dinner on tonight as you know. The Prince of Wales is coming up here tonight after opening the point-to-point, and Rudyard Kipling will be here too.'

'Well I won't keep you all from your work,' Chesney said politely. 'To tell you the truth I think I would probably be more at home having tea and scones with you all, rather than going to the dinner tonight.'

'You can be a sort of ambassador Sir,' suggested Bobby. 'If you want to look at it in that sort of way. An ambassador of our class at theirs.'

'I like the idea Bobby,' Chesney said. 'I'm off to the point-to-point. I'll see you good people later.'

The point-to-point races were a colourful meeting in Storrington. All the local villagers attended, some in their Sunday best and others in costumes of a time gone by. A brass band was playing. There were side stalls and tents beneath which people sold food and drink. Beautiful horses were led back and forwards between each of the races.

Chesney stood in the crowd, with a good view of the proceedings. From a distance he could see a man in a top hat being greeted by several dignitaries. He immediately recognised the man who was the heir to the throne: the Prince of Wales. The crowd in attendance at the race meeting automatically cheered and clapped wildly. The prince removed his hat as a sign of courtesy and walked to the podium. Everyone stood still as the band struck up *God Save the Queen*.

The race meeting continued, with Chesney exchanging bets at every opportunity. He was a good judge on many things in life but he could never have been a gambler. Not one of the horses he put money on even came in for a place. It had been fun though. Chesney enjoyed the afternoon.

There was one final race. Perhaps he might get lucky. Chesney watched from the sidelines. The horses were in the starting blocks. The jockeys were poised. The starter raised his gun in the air. There was an air of expectancy; a breathtaking silence followed by the shot from the starter's gun and the sound of horses' hooves thudding the turf. Several laps were covered but Chesney smiled when he realised his horse had lost too.

He watched the winning rider ascend the podium to shake hands and receive a cup from the Prince of Wales. With the race meeting now officially over the prince took the opportunity to mingle with the local people. Ladies bowed and curtsied. Chesney stood back as the prince passed by. Chesney removed his cap and grinned. The prince did the same, acknowledging him.

Back at Shervington Manor, preparations for the evening were well under way. Everything was laid out on a long highly-polished table. There were candelabra set at equidistant intervals, table napkins set at each place setting and beautiful shiny silver serving platters. Even the tablecloth was elegant in design, appearing more like mosaic tapestry than linen material.

Jimmy and Ravi laid the table with silver cutlery. On completion they stood back and looked at the magnificently set table which in a short while would be filled with luxurious food. Jimmy winked at Ravi who smiled in return. They both picked up silver trays and left the room. No sooner had they departed than Lady Bernadette and Mrs Price entered. For a moment Lady Bernadette stood and looked at the layout, beaming with pride. She turned to Mrs Price, who acknowledged the fine presentation.

'Beautifully laid out,' said Lady Bernadette, giving it her seal of approval.

'It is indeed m'Lady,' replied Mrs Price.

Lady Bernadette conferred with Mrs Price as to the food selection available for the evening's guests. 'Now just tell me again the courses for tonight's menu.'

'To begin with m'Lady we have a choice of soups. They include oxtail, harvest vegetable, mushroom, brown Windsor or a fine rich vegetable freshly picked only this morn. This is followed by the first course of salmon and sliced lemon, or whiting if preferred. If those are not partial to a guest's palate, I have a standby fish course of shrimps; trout in a raisin, sultana and almond sauce. I can always serve up a mixed plate of the fish if anybody requires it. When we come to the main course I've cooked and prepared some fine meats: a pheasant so succulent I drool to think of it ma'am; some prime beef and guinea fowl still being cooked lightly but long and slowly, juicy red in colour and tender to taste. There is also smoked ham. I leave that to the discretion of the guests whether they have one or the other or a fair mixture of all. It looks mighty tasty too. The ham has been cooked and coated in honey and demerara sugar. I realise that not everyone at the table will be a lover of good meats, so as a precaution I took the liberty of taking receipt of and cooking crab, lobster and oysters, which came up from Worthing this afternoon. Vegetables served alongside the main course, Jim brought from our markets and the nurseries in Findon Valley. There are runner beans, garden peas, cauliflower in a creamy milk or cream cheese sauce, pumpkin, carrots, turnips, swedes and parsnips. I have a rich tangy gravy to add. I have a choice of potatoes which have been either roasted, boiled or cooked in their jackets. Several freshly-baked crispy crusty loaves were taken from the oven not less than fifteen minutes ago. There is some fresh cheese to follow. For dessert I've made plum tarts, mince and apple pies, and a three-tiered cake. I've also fresh fruit. I have a separate dish of peaches and apple in cream cheese. Coffee and tea to follow. Mr Grey has organised the wine and spirits. That's the full menu m'Lady. I hope it's a menu fit for a King.'

'For a future King I'm sure it will be,' Lady Bernadette said, impressed by Mrs Price's obviously marathon efforts. 'I know the prince has an extremely hearty appetite. Not only for food but for life it seems. When I met him at the garden party at Buckingham Palace last year, I suggested if he was ever in the area that we would show him hospitality. Never in my wildest dreams did I imagine he would seriously accept the invitation. Mr Kipling too! I met him on the same occasion. I was delighted he accepted.

I'm sure the meeting of the two men will be interesting.' She reflected on her words. Then she looked at Mrs Price with affection. 'You've done wonders at such short notice Mrs Price. Obviously, I'm sure not all the food will be eaten. Tomorrow when all the staff have finished their duties I would like you all to eat whatever is remaining. And if it's too much for all of you I'm sure you know a few needy people in the village who might appreciate a meal on our behalf. You'll see to it then Mrs Price?'

'I will m'Lady.'

'Well ...' Lady Bernadette gazed at the clock striking six-thirty. 'We have half an hour until the prince arrives. Would you get yourself ready? I'm going to present all the staff as well as the other guests.'

'Very good m'Lady,' said Mrs Price, and left the room. Ravi entered the room.

'Yes Ravi,' Lady Bernadette said, fully expecting him to advise her that a distinguished guest was about to arrive.

'The guests have begun to arrive m'Lady. Mr Grey tells me Mr Rudyard Kipling and his wife are coming up the road in a carriage.'

'Thank you Ravi. I shall be there straightaway.'

Harry Chesney had arrived back at Shervington Manor now. Before the main meal all the guests were introduced in a separate room. Jimmy handed out drinks to everyone. They began to mingle and strike up casual conversation. There were eight people, landowners and their ladies together with Chesney, who stood apart from the rest. He gazed through the window, taking the occasional sip of his drink. He looked quite dynamic in his evening dress and bow tie. His physical features had filled out. Together with the flashes of silver in his hair he had an aura about him, a presence that he was naively unaware he possessed. Yet he stood alone in the room, feeling a world apart from the other people. He looked at the attractive women in the room. It struck a chord in his memory.

Chesney remembered with some pain his childhood in the workhouse of long ago. He could not fail to be reminded that the ladies close by him now, in fine clothes and good complexion, were of a different class to the one he had been brought up in. He remembered the times when he, as a scruffy young boy in workhouse overalls, would climb onto a chair and stare out at that distant, complicated, sometimes exotic land that adults live in. Here in Shervington Manor, with the pending visit of the heir to the throne and a distinguished scribe whose name would become immortal,

Chesney was the young boy gazing at a carriage passing by. The words he had once spoken to a journalist in India regarding his background flooded his mind.

'I was what you might call a child of the workhouse. An orphan in a cold inhospitable world, longing for a full stomach. I used to gaze at those rich people going past in their carriages with fine horses and drapes. The clothes of the ladies, made of fine materials, shiny with colours and patterns, their faces glowing with pride and good health. The men haughty and arrogant, and oozing with a swaggering confidence, while inside the workhouse young children slaved away long hours, some with consumption and others with whooping cough that would echo in the middle of the night, making one tremble with fear'.

Chesney remembered. He felt that he didn't fit in here at this venue. Before he could drift away on more negative thoughts, Jimmy came up to him with a tray full of glasses.

'Would you like another one Sir?' he asked.

'Thank you Jimmy,' Chesney said, appreciating the butler's presence; for here was a man of a similar background to his own. He took a glass from the tray. 'That's the shot.'

'I just thought you would be interested to know that Mr Rudyard Kipling and his good lady wife have arrived.'

'Better prepare myself, Jim. I'm not sure I fit in here.'

'You'll be alright Sir,' Jimmy assured him. 'I think you've probably got the capacity to fit in anywhere.'

From the doorway Bobby, in his other role as a footman, addressed the room. 'Ladies and gentlemen, it is our privilege to welcome to Shervington Manor and present to you all – Mr and Mrs Rudyard Kipling.'

Chesney turned around to see Rudyard Kipling and his wife enter the room, closely followed by Lady Bernadette.

The distinguished couple were introduced to everybody. Was it really so long, thought Chesney, that he had last seen Kipling as one of the invited journalists at the twenty-fifth anniversary of the 25th Queen's Light Northern Regiment. Chesney was in awe of the distinguished couple and stood apart from the rest of the people in the room. However, Lady Bernadette was quick to spot Chesney's isolation. She led the Kiplings across the room to meet him. Chesney straightened himself up, ramrod style, and attempted to smile at the Kiplings.

'How do you do Sir? How do you do Mrs Kipling?' The two of them shook hands with Chesney.

Rudyard Kipling seemed warmer than he had imagined. 'I'm very pleased to meet you Mr – ?'

Lady Bernadette did the informal introduction. 'This is Harry Chesney, formerly a colour sergeant in India, and now owner of Chesney's tea warehouse and teashop in Horsham.'

'Now that's a name I recall from somewhere.' Kipling appeared to study Chesney's face for signs of recognition. 'Is it possible we met in India, Mr Chesney?'

'We've never actually met on a personal basis Sir, but I do recall you were present at Fort Valaka for the twenty-fifth anniversary of the 25th Queen's Light Northern in 1885.'

'By jove!' exclaimed Kipling. 'Of course! Chesney! Chesney...' His voice tapered off, almost in distaste. Chesney's eyes froze in horror as he anticipated that Kipling may have known of his court martial. A stern look crossed the famous writer's face. Then almost as suddenly Kipling's eyes sparkled and he smiled in such a dazzling manner Chesney felt secure once again. 'Harry Chesney! Now I know. You were the Victoria Cross winner. You were under the command of Colonel Duncan Anderson.'

'That's right!' Chesney was surprised at how retentive Rudyard Kipling's memory must have been.

'I remember reading about your exploits in the regimental despatches. My word, you've had a colourful career! Nasty show that at Prakaresh?'

'It was Sir.' Chesney looked glum. So he did know after all.

'Still it's a sad episode that need not be resurrected.' Almost as if to put aside any fears Chesney may have had, Kipling added, 'Your courage was never under question.' Chesney nodded. 'I'll look forward to you telling me at dinner how you've spent the intervening years.'

'It will be my pleasure Sir.'

Chesney felt relaxed now. He spoke at length with Rudyard Kipling and his American wife. After a while Chesney felt that maybe there was not a great deal of difference between him and the other guests.

Outside, a carriage approached Shervington Manor. The Prince of Wales sat in it with several equerries. From inside the house Lady Bernadette emerged with Bobby Grey. The carriage drew up in front of the house. Bobby moved forward, opened the carriage door and bowed towards the prince. Lady Bernadette walked forward. The prince stepped down from the carriage followed by three of the equerries. Lady Bernadette curtsied in a manner befitting the presence of royalty. The prince doffed his hat politely and bowed slightly.

'Welcome to Shervington Manor, your Royal Highness,' Lady Bernadette said.

The prince's voice resounded at her in a distinctive rolling tone. 'How very nice to see you again my dear. May I say Lady Bernadette, it is most kind of you to have invited me here. I am sincerely looking forward to this evening.'

'Come Sir. I will introduce you to everyone.'

Inside the house the entire household, guests and staff were standing in a line waiting to be introduced. Lady Bernadette brought the prince into the hallway. With a sweep of her hand she introduced each person.

'Sir, you already know Mr and Mrs Rudyard Kipling.'

'What a pleasure it is to see you Mr Kipling – and in the company of your wife.' The prince beamed with admiration. Rudyard Kipling bowed and Mrs Kipling curtsied. 'May I say how much I've admired your work.'

'Thank you your Royal Highness.'

The Prince of Wales turned to Mrs Kipling. 'Are you the inspiration behind your husband my dear?'

Mrs Kipling replied in a soft American accent. 'No Sir. I think my husband has a drive and inspiration of his own.'

A smile of wry amusement crossed the prince's face. 'There are some who say I have a mind of my own. I think there are some who say I should listen to my wife Alex more often!'

This remark sparked some amusement amongst the others who knew of the prince's penchant for lively living.

Lady Bernadette then moved along the line. 'May I introduce Squire Peter Raven and Mrs Raven.'

The Prince of Wales acknowledged their bow and curtsy. 'Good evening to you both.' He was then ushered along to the next couple.

Lady Bernadette, who was well briefed on the background of all of her guests, gave details to the prince. 'This couple are two of the hardest working farmer and wife teams in the district. Mr and Mrs Lindley.' They in turn bowed and curtsied as did the previous couple. 'They often supply all the vegetable produce to our local markets.'

'Really!' The prince seemed genuinely interested. 'A good trade to be in. Very nice to meet you.'

In cautious style Lady Bernadette quickly moved along the line. 'One final couple for you to meet, but not the least in stature. Sir, this is George Rattray our town councillor, and George's daughter –.' Lady Bernadette was momentarily flummoxed as she stumbled to remember the name of the councillor's daughter. 'You must forgive me. I've forgotten your name?'

'My name is Georgia, Lady Bernadette.' Georgia was a stunning-looking woman with dark hair, in her late thirties. The prince, who was obviously enamoured, took her hand and kissed it.

'George and Georgia,' the prince said with a smile. 'That's a combination of names I won't forget. I am delighted to meet you. And what a pretty girl you are, Georgia.'

Lady Bernadette moved in front of Chesney, who was very conspicuous at the end of the line between the guests and the staff.

'This gentleman – ' Lady Bernadette began.

'– was at the races this afternoon,' the prince cut in quickly, recognising Chesney. 'Did you win much this afternoon? I saw you placing bets enthusiastically.'

'Not a brass coin to even scratch my backside with, your Royal Highness,' Chesney replied unpretentiously. He spoke in such an easy manner it could not possibly cause offence.

The prince appeared to warm to him instantly. 'You appear to be unaccompanied. No lady accompanying you?'

Once again Chesney could not resist showing good humour. 'No your Royal Highness, I always travel light!'

A pause of deafening silence followed. The Prince of Wales looked startled for a moment, giving Chesney cause for serious thought. He thought that for one terrifying moment he had overplayed his hand. But just in time a smile crossed the prince's face and he broke out into a peal of laughter which triggered off smiles elsewhere.

'Splendid! A good humoured fellow indeed! Who might you be?'

Lady Bernadette proceeded to introduce him. 'Sir, allow me to introduce you to Harry Chesney; a former soldier in India, Victoria Cross winner and now a tea merchant.'

The two men shook hands. Although there was a towering difference between them both socially and intellectually, the prince was quick to recognise in Chesney a fun-loving man with similar characteristics to his own.

'A Victoria Cross winner! Did you hold a commission Mr Chesney?'

'No Sir. I came from the workhouse and rose to the rank of colour sergeant.'

'And now you're a tea merchant. You're an enterprising fellow Mr Chesney. I shall enjoy talking to you later on.'

Lady Bernadette moved the prince along to meet her staff. She cast a glance back at Chesney and smiled. Chesney ,who had thought that he would be out of place at the dinner, felt much more at home now.

Seventeen

The evening meal was served very shortly after the prince arrived. It had been a very carefully arranged dinner with all the guests informed prior to their arrival just where they would be sitting. Lady Bernadette was seated opposite the prince, Mr and Mrs Kipling were seated next to the prince, Chesney was seated next to Lady Bernadette and the other couples, together with the three equerries, were interspersed around the table.

The soup dishes were gathered up by Ravi and Jimmy at one end. In a carefully co-ordinated manner the two men moved down the table on opposite sides, picking up the empty dishes, placing them on their individual trays, and moving out uniformly towards the kitchen.

When Ravi and Jimmy left the room this was the signal for Bobby Grey to enter, carrying a huge tray of breathtaking, mouth-watering prime beef. The sight of it was enough for some of the guests to turn and look at what would only be part of the main course. Shortly Bobby would return with another tray on which would be a pheasant and then a further platter which would contain roast guinea fowl. Bobby placed the first tray at one end of the table while Mrs Price emerged from a door on the opposite side carrying a tray of the fish course she had so carefully put together: salmon and sliced lemon, and whiting. Jimmy and Jessica also entered the room. Their trays were variously filled with shrimps and trout in a most exotic sauce.

Chesney had never eaten like this in all of his life. He was totally mesmerised by the food. Not only for the quality of it all but the sheer volume that gradually filled the long dining-room table in Shervington Manor. It was staggering that the wealthy people of this land could eat like this while the poorer classes would never have even seen food of this calibre, let alone feast on it.

It was a splendid night, however, for all concerned. While the guests enjoyed the meal the staff were extremely busy in the kitchen. Jessica and Mrs Price were busy for apart from serving the food they were busy washing the dishes and plates. Every so often Jessica would take a quick peep from the kitchen at the dining-room guests. She smiled, almost bubbling with excitement at the thought of serving the prince and Mr Kipling. Jessica turned around and looked at Mrs Price who in reality was over-awed by their distinguished guests.

'Do you know Mrs Price?' she said in sheer delight. 'I will remember this night all my born days.'

'You'll be able to tell your grandchildren you served the Prince of Wales and Rudyard Kipling at the same dinner table.' Mrs Price too could hardly contain her excitement at the occasion.

Jessica's eyes sparkled at the thought. Although marriage was a fair way ahead of her, she already had dreams as to who the man for her might be. She let her dreams rule her head for one glorious moment. Perhaps in years to come Jessica and her own prince, Ravi, would remember this occasion together.

During the course of the evening the conversation at the dining-room table had become quite convivial. The prince had been very diplomatic and made a point of conversing with everyone. It soon became apparent that the Prince of Wales enjoyed these more informal occasions away from the rigours of official palace duties. He had a love of sailing and outdoor sports as well as a taste for high living and showed no airs or graces, conversing freely and easily.

Harry Chesney was at heart a rebel who could not have cared a fig for royalty. He could never understand why the wealthy people and the aristocracy of the land were put on a pedestal and revered. Chesney was of the belief that it was the ordinary working men and women who had made this country great but tonight he felt that he could put his bias aside. The Prince of Wales was only flesh and blood; a sporting man at that, and although Chesney wore the workhouse-boy chip on his shoulder he would never deny respect to those of a different class. He found the prince to be a warm, affable man, not perhaps the remote distant figure he had originally envisaged.

Chesney listened politely to the banter between the guests. Squire Peter Raven and Mrs Raven were talking quite happily in an engaging manner with the Kiplings. Ravi and Jimmy attended to the needs of the guests, replenishing their drinks, and Bobby stood close to the table, bringing more food servings as required. Jimmy looked across at Ravi and in his usual reassuring manner winked at him good-naturedly. Jimmy was also keeping an eye on Ravi and helping him whenever possible. Chesney was only half listening to the guests' chatter when he suddenly became aware that all eyes from the prince's end of the table were directed at him.

'What do you think, Mr Chesney?' the Prince of Wales asked him.

Chesney's face showed he had not heard the subject matter of the conversation. Kipling was quick to recognise this.

'Squire Peter Raven was just remarking that England means different things to different people. To the good squire and his kind lady it means the acres of unspoiled land they love and cherish. For me it's the peace and tranquillity of my home in Rottingdean. For Lady Bernadette no doubt it's the beauty of the Sussex Downs and this very pleasant home of hers.' Lady Bernadette smiled and nodded her approval. 'It's an interesting question.'

Chesney considered his answer. He felt inclined to reply in his usual straightforward fashion, even though he knew it may offend someone. 'I agree with you Sir. It is an interesting question. I could give you a few interesting answers.' The prince looked curious. 'Some of you might take offence if I was to answer that question straight out. I don't mean to sound disloyal or unpatriotic. That's not the case. I love England. I was proud to serve in Her Majesty's forces, and I would do so again if age was on my side. I think for me the England of my workhouse childhood and the England I know today as an affluent self-made man are two very different places.'

There was a short silence and the prince surprisingly made a very sympathetic comment. 'I must say that the differences – vast differences, I have to emphasise – in this England of ours are things that worry me. I have seen the workhouses and I can understand what a difficult start in life it would be for so many of our young people. In Whitechapel and the Elephant & Castle I was taken to see the conditions of the working classes and I was truly shocked when I saw how many of them were living and working in absolute poverty and in homes unfit for inhabitation. I hope that in my lifetime I shall see far reaching changes. When I ascend to the throne as monarch I shall be keeping in close contact with the Prime Minister and the government as to their progress on reducing poverty.'

Rudyard Kipling was not backward in coming forward. 'It is a question I believe of providing opportunities for everyone in work so that they are able to improve their lot in life. With a proper dedication to their duties and a respect for their seniors there could be no limit to what they may achieve in their lives.'

'Regrettably,' said Councillor Rattray who felt he also had something worthy to discuss in this conversation, 'there are more issues raised by those good intentions. It is not just ensuring work for all. It is about providing a decent living wage. Solve that problem and it will go a long way towards ending poverty.'

The conversation had taken a more serious tone. The prince, who was acutely aware of it, smiled and skilfully changed the context of it. 'It is obvious to me that not only shall I have to spend time with the Prime Minister but also the Cabinet.' He lit up a cigar and looked across to Chesney. 'Tell me Mr Chesney, like our good friend Rudyard, you spent many years abroad?'

'The best part of twenty years. Time spent in India, Ceylon and Australia.'

'Forgetting social differences for the moment – differences that we are all too painfully aware of – what sort of things did you cherish most about homecoming?'

'Not seeing England for twenty years, there were many things I had forgotten. I don't want to sound sentimental or overindulgently patriotic. That's not my way and I'd think it a sin if I were insincere. It all came back to me when I saw the white cliffs of Dover which I suppose must be every home-coming Englishman's landmark. Then I thought of what England really meant. Dewdrops on the grass. The hills shrouded by misty rain. Westminster Abbey and the Tower of London. The Strand. Piccadilly. The smiles of the elderly who've known lives only of drudgery and poverty but they're courteous and never grumble about their lot however hard it is. The young children, full of joy and enthusiasm whose future is so important for this country. The freedom that we know to walk down the street without hindrance from a hostile authority. Taking a quiet ale in a warm hostelry. The flowers in spring. The freshness of the fields in the early morning. Those are the things I thought of most when I came home.'

'Very eloquently put,' stated Rudyard Kipling, a man not easily impressed at the best of times.

'Indeed,' agreed the Prince of Wales.

From one side of the room Jimmy smiled in deep admiration at the way Chesney expressed himself.

'What hopes do you have for this country Sir?' Lady Bernadette asked with interest.

'Well my dear, to put it in layman's terms I have many,' he replied. In this he was genuine. It was well known that the Prince of Wales had privately and publicly expressed concern for the working classes of Britain. 'We've already spoken of the need to end poverty. In this century there have been enormous changes. The empire is at its finest stage in history. Don't you agree Rudyard?'

Jimmy returned to the kitchen to bring some plates back. 'What a night this is turning out to be!' he said to Mrs Price and Jessica who were hard at work. 'I was just listening to Kipling, the prince and Harry Chesney discussing the differences in class in England. Would you credit it? The prince is actually interested in improving the lives of the working classes. That's a turn up for the books isn't it?'

'Good for 'im!' Mrs Price said decisively. 'It'll do the future king a lot of good to get amongst his subjects and listen to what they have to say. Heaven knows that day can't be too far away when he takes over.'

'If I didn't know my place I would have joined in on the conversation and put my half-penny's-worth in. I'll say one thing for Harry Chesney. He's as honest and as straight speaking as the day is long. Even though he was in the company of royalty, a right fine lady in the mistress of our house and an old Conservative like Kipling, Harry took no airs or graces. He fair spoke his mind. Yes he might have won the VC and been successful, but at heart he's still one of us.'

'That's nice to know,' smiled Mrs Price. 'I liked him straight off y'know.'

It was a long night. The guests were all in a very happy mood. Jimmy poured coffee for the guests at one end of the table while Ravi did the same at the opposite. Chesney, by now totally relaxed and fully at ease, found himself caught between conversing with Georgia, who he was quite attracted to, and Kipling, always a good raconteur.

'I've read much of your work over the years,' Chesney said proudly to Kipling, but with straightforward honesty he felt compelled to add his opinion. 'I'm an honest man and I would have to say with due respect

I don't agree with all your views. But! – But there was a poem that you wrote which I really feel hits the mark on the bulls-eye. You sum up many an ex-soldier's feelings.'

'And which one was that Mr Chesney?' Kipling asked, already knowing full well which one it would be.

'*Tommy*,' replied Chesney unequivocally.

'*Tommy*. I thought it might be,' Kipling said with a quick smile. The Prince of Wales appeared to be listening.

'Yes Sir,' Chesney continued, 'when I first read that I thought to myself, now someone understands. I get a thrill when I hear *Mandalay*. I can see the place almost. *Gunga din* moves me. By golly it does. But if there's one verse that moves me and a thousand other ex-soldiers who find the civilian world frustrating then it has to be *Tommy*. I've read it so often I could recite it like a music hall artist on the same bill as Marie Lloyd.'

'Well let's hear you then my good fellow!' the Prince of Wales said enthusiastically.

'My word! I'll second that,' said Kipling eagerly.

Lady Bernadette responded as well. 'Bravo Harry!'

Chesney stood up and bowed slightly towards the prince. 'It seems I've won the popular vote! Sir, I take it that's a Royal command?'

The Prince of Wales happily joined in on the fun. 'Indeed it is Mr Chesney.'

'Then your Royal Highness, I am happy to oblige.' He moved out into the centre of the room behind the table. 'Ladies and gentlemen will you bid me welcome to the centre stage!'

Everyone at the table applauded. Bobby Grey, Jimmy and Ravi moved to the back of the table where they too would view Chesney's performance. From the table all eyes were directed at Chesney and in the kitchen Mrs Price and Jessica, aware that something was happening, watched through the window.

'Thank you your Royal Highness, Mr Kipling and distinguished guests. May I pay tribute to Mr Rudyard Kipling with a recitation of his extremely fine verse entitled – *Tommy*.' He put his thumbs in his lapels and struck up the poise of an old time music hall performer.

Chesney recited the words of Kipling's poem *Tommy* to a very receptive audience. In the kitchen Mrs Price and Jessica smiled as they listened to Harry Chesney's music hall antics. Bobby and Jimmy looked at each other and laughed. The other guests were all variously enthralled, astonished or amused. Rudyard Kipling's face registered approval.

Strangely enough, Chesney felt his confidence grow as he recited the verse. In another time he would have made a great showman on a stage. His voice, facial expressions and hand mannerisms became more diverse and expressive. When he had finished his recitation he stood back and bowed. The guests at the table were on their feet and applauded.

'Good show Mr Chesney!' Rudyard Kipling said happily. 'A fine recitation of my verse.'

Eighteen

The next morning Chesney stirred in his bed, which was situated in the guest bedroom. Outside the birds were singing in the early morning light. Chesney rose from the bed and walked to the window. He ruffled his hair and gazed outside at the roll of the Sussex Downs. In the distance there was a farm and some crofters' cottages. There was a knock on the door which disturbed his train of thought.

'Come in,' he said, fully expecting it to be Ravi.

In fact it was Jimmy who entered carrying a tray.

'Good morning Sir. Up already?' he said cheerfully. 'I thought you might appreciate an early morning cuppa.'

'Just the job Jimmy,' Chesney responded.

Jimmy placed the tray down and poured a cup. 'Last night was quite an occasion wasn't it? It seems very quiet this morning. The prince didn't leave 'til the early hours. I believe he was travelling overnight to the Isle of Wight. Mr Kipling and his wife went home very late too. Wonderful night though wasn't it?' He handed Chesney a cup of tea. 'You were a bit of a star last night. I'll tell you what though, if the tea business goes bad you can always make yourself a crust in the music halls!'

Chesney laughed. 'I'll remember that.' He took a sip of tea.

'Another thing Sir.' Jimmy seemed serious but he was quietly sincere. 'I like the way you express yourself. You and me, we both come from a similar background, although our lives could not be further afield if they were prised apart by two Indian elephants. Yesterday when you were talking to the prince and Kipling, even though you were in the company of distinguished men, you weren't afraid to speak your mind and to say your piece in a firm but polite manner. I admired that Sir. You don't bow to anyone. You only bow to courtesy.'

Chesney sipped his tea and thought over Jimmy's kind words He appeared to be touched. 'Jimmy it's my turn to say a few kind words to you. Thank you for keeping a fatherly eye on Ravi. The word is you took three thugs on, two who set about Ravi. I don't know where you learned your fighting trade but neither is it any of my business. I'm grateful to you. You're a decent man Jim and if you ever get in strife and need a job or a place to stay, promise me you'll knock on my door.'

'I will Sir.' Jimmy said, delighted at the alternative he might one day take up. 'No insult meant, but I hope it never comes to that. I love the old manor. But I'll remember your kind offer. Lady Bernadette has asked me to tell you she would like you to join her for breakfast in the conservatory in about an hour's time.'

'Thank you Jimmy. I'll wash and be there.'

At the back of Shervington Manor there was a spacious conservatory full of plants and rustic furniture. A shaft of sunlight penetrated the windows and illuminated the area where Chesney joined Lady Bernadette for breakfast.

'I'm so glad you came Harry,' the lady said, as gracious as ever. Chesney felt it was his pleasure to be there. 'The others enjoyed having you as company. The prince and Mr Kipling are men with strong opinions. They seemed to admire the way you spoke your mind.'

Ravi entered the room carrying a tray. 'Would you like coffee or tea this morning m'Lady?'

'Tea thank you Ravi.'

'Mr Harry?' asked Ravi.

'Coffee please,' replied Chesney and he added thoughtfully, 'I'll drop by and see you before I leave.'

Ravi nodded and smiled. He poured their drinks and then left quietly. The door closed. Lady Bernadette looked at Chesney; her expression indicated that she wanted to say something of a more serious nature.

Softly, with some emotion in her voice she spoke; the words seemed to strike Chesney with a stony effect. 'Ravi is very much like his father.'

Chesney sipped his coffee. He lowered his cup slowly; his face revealed a mixture of shock and horror. Lady Bernadette leaned across and gripped his wrist warmly.

'It's alright. I know.'

'How?' gasped Chesney.

There was a silence of almost deathly proportions. Lady Bernadette managed a slight smile, which broke the ice. She looked at Chesney knowingly. 'Rex told me.'

A shadow crossed Chesney's face. His voice betrayed a sense of deep shock. 'You knew?'

'Oh yes,' Lady Bernadette replied quietly. 'I've known for many years. I'll recapitulate! I met Rex when he came home on leave from India. He was the gallant, sparkling hero of the regiment who swept me off my feet and married me within a few weeks of meeting him. When we arrived in India it was then I learned of his very colourful past.' Her voice took on a different tone. It was one of sadness. 'His women. His conquests. Even during our marriage I knew there were others in his life. Then one day, when he was considerably the worse for drink, he told me of Sarah Armatradj; an Indian woman who had died not long after giving birth to Ravi. I was shocked and distressed of course. I loved him madly though. Like many a woman before with unpredictable, wild, exciting men as husbands I could forgive him anything. I learned that his son was being looked after somewhere. Just where he wouldn't say.' She seemed anxious as an old betrayal returned to haunt her. 'He could be so maddeningly infuriating! I told him to take me to see the boy. Finally he agreed. The day before we were due to visit the boy, Colonel Anderson sent Rex on a patrol. I never got to visit the boy – Ravi. Rex and his men died on that patrol. I assumed that Rex's son was known only to him. I never knew what to do about him.'

Such was the selflessness of Chesney's character he automatically thought of the pain this would have caused Lady Bernadette. 'So you carried the burden of this all these years?'

Lady Bernadette appeared surprised at this question. 'If any burdens were carried Harry, they were carried by one man. You. Why? What generosity of spirit and deep sense of compassion drove you to take financial care of another man's son? An officer's son at that!'

'Loyalty. Respect. A sense of ongoing duty if you like, for a man who gave me the greatest honour a workhouse boy could have ever wished for.'

'The Victoria Cross,' Lady Bernadette assumed.

'That was the least of it. No. It was self-respect. A sense of being someone. A feeling of usefulness. I owed him that much. I wanted to give that lad a good start.'

'And you have done.'

'There is something I would like to say. When I came to you for advice about Ravi, I didn't come here intentionally hoping that you would employ him.'

'I know that,' Lady Bernadette told him softly. 'It was strange though. His profile. His hair. He's so much like Rex. But he's slight where Rex was very well built. The similarity between the two is so strong I should have recognised it earlier.' After taking a sip of tea there was a hesitant pause and then Lady Bernadette changed the context of her conversation and with it the gravity of the tone in her voice. 'Harry, does the boy know who I am? Does that boy know this is his father's house?' Chesney nodded 'yes'. He felt embarrassed and almost ashamed for having concealed so much. 'More to the point, is he aware that I know?'

'No he isn't,' Chesney replied firmly. 'I told him this was his father's house and he was to respect his memory, and to be kind to you.'

'He has. I want to ask you Harry to keep this conversation between you and me. He must not know that I am aware he is Rex's son. I am effectively that boy's stepmother. I love him like the son I never had. Another thing, because you have been providing some financial assistance towards Ravi for many years I think that I should make some sort of bequest to you.'

Chesney was horrified. 'Oh no Lady Bernadette I won't hear of it!'

'I believe Harry that you have an outstanding loan of two hundred pounds on your teashop and the warehouse.' Chesney's eyes showed a look of disbelief. He was stunned that this lady had actually checked out his financial affairs. 'I had a lawyer friend of mine look into it. I could pay it out for you.'

He was not sure whether to be angry that she had inquired into the matters that were his personal concern or to be pleased at the offer to pay for his loan. Instead, after quiet deliberation he answered firmly, without aggression or causing offence to anyone.

'I am a proud man Lady Bernadette. I did what I did because I've no family, and although it may sound trite, it felt good being responsible for someone. It may sound ridiculous even, but in all of my life my greatest feeling of achievement was in helping someone, almost a stranger, who I now regard as an adopted son.'

Lady Bernadette was almost in tears; for she was moved by his compassion and knew that this was not a false display of revelation. Men like Chesney were above that sort of thing.

'They don't make too many men like you Harry,' she said quietly.

Before leaving the house Chesney called into the kitchen to say farewell to the staff. Only Ravi and Jessica were there. Jessica looked up and smiled warmly at him.

'Will you have a cup of tea with us Sir?' she asked pleasantly. 'There's only Ravi and I here. The others are distributing the remainder of the food from last night's meal to the poor in the village.'

'They're a nice lot aren't they?' Chesney said, sitting down at the table. Jessica offered him a scone with a cup of tea. 'Lady Bernadette speaks well of you Ravi. She's very fond of you.'

'I'm very happy here, Mr Harry,' Ravi replied.

'I'm very fond of Ravi too,' Jessica added.

'Oh – are you?' Chesney was pleased that Ravi obviously had some emotional warmth too.

'We have spent our days off walking through the country a lot,' Ravi explained.

'Have you?' Chesney looked across to Jessica. 'Well, she's a nice young lady Ravi.' For some reason unbeknown to him he put his hand inside his pocket and clutched the locket that Karen had once given him. 'Will you both come up and see me soon?'

'We will both be up very soon, Mr Harry,' Ravi promised him.

Nineteen

In that same year of 1899 the war that had been pending in far-off South Africa commenced in a blaze of publicity. Chesney was casually walking through Horsham when the sound of a newspaper seller's voice reached his ears.

'War in South Africa! Official! War in South Africa! British troops to fight the Boer! Read all about it!'

Chesney stopped and bought a copy of the Evening Argus. Eagerly he scanned through the pages and read with fascination of the events that were unfolding in the Transvaal.

Ravi and Jessica, meanwhile, were taking a leisurely walk across the fields on one of their days off. From there they strolled hand-in-hand to the very quiet high street of Storrington village. In actuality it was not so much the main high street as a thoroughfare with a few houses and a main store. This was a favourite venue of theirs.

Inside the store, which also passed as a post office and a shop serving cream teas, there were big jars of sweets mounted on shelves. Every sweet conceivable it seemed was available: bonbons, toffees, boiled sweets, liquorice, caramels, fudges. A kindly-looking lady in her sixties who knew them well came from behind the counter.

'Hullo you two. Been out on your usual long walk?' she asked pleasantly.

'Yes. Lovely day for it too.' Jessica studied the inviting sweets. 'Could we have one of your lovely bags of mixed toffees?'

'Certainly my dear,' the lady replied. She turned her back on them for one moment while she scooped up toffees from several jars and put them in a bag. The lady then weighed the sweets on a scale before handing the bag to Jessica. 'There you are then.'

Jessica already had the right amount of money. She had bought these goodies so often. Ravi was looking at the newspaper on a stand. The headline read: British Troops to fight Boers in South Africa.

'How sad,' Ravi uttered.

Jessica took his arm. 'Yes it is. Come on Ravi.' The two of them smiled at the lady and continued on their way.

For a while they walked arm in arm. It was obvious that Ravi was thinking deeply. He turned to Jessica quickly.

'In that newspaper the article says that troops from all over the empire will go to South Africa to fight. Does that mean they will come from my country?'

Jessica looked apprehensive. 'I don't know about these things. Probably. The empire covers a lot of countries. New Zealand. Australia. Canada.'

'And India,' added Ravi. 'There will be many people joining up here.'

'I expect so.' Jessica looked serious as she realised Ravi was leading up to something. 'Why?'

'Do you think I should join up?' he asked her sincerely.

'It's not your battle Ravi. You don't have to go.' Her voice betrayed her deep feelings. 'Besides, I don't want you to go.' Jessica stopped walking and tugged his arm affectionately. She looked at him lovingly. 'I love you, Ravi.'

He held her in his arms tenderly. 'I love you too.' Ravi spoke shyly. 'We have been close for a while now. I love you enough that I would marry you if you wanted to.'

'Of course I would,' Jessica stated without hesitation.

'If I go... ' Ravi tried to find the words. '... If I join the Army will you wait 'til I return?'

'I'll wait if you really must go,' said Jessica in a voice that seemed to register protest. 'But you make sure you come back here.'

They carried on walking for a while and began to start up the Downs back to Shervington Manor. There was a lovely spot where they loved to sit. Below, the green and golden rolling Sussex countryside spread out in all of its ethereal beauty.

Jessica lay back and chewed on a cud of corn. 'Harry will be pleased if you join up.'

'I'm not sure,' Ravi said in an offhand manner that surprised Jessica.

'Why do you say that? I thought he loved the Army.'

'He did!' Ravi confirmed in the past tense. 'It meant everything to him. But shortly before he was due to re-enlist, he was court martialled.' Jessica looked astonished. 'Yes, it is true. He was in a battle where he was the only one to survive. It's a long story. Very involved. He was innocent of course. Poor Mr Harry. He did not want to go on in the Army. So he took his discharge and went on his own travels to different parts of India, Ceylon and Australia.'

'The others like him a lot. Mrs Price says Harry is the salt of the earth. Jimmy likes him; really admires him in fact. He thinks Harry represents the best things about a working class Englishman: courage, decency, fair play, good manners to everyone but always speaks his mind in a firm and honest way. I like him. Funny thing is, I think Lady Bernadette is more than just a little fond of him. I think dear old Mrs Price wishes she was a few years younger too. She fancies him I'm sure!'

'Mr Harry has his own personal code which he lives up to. He always says to people, 'never brood on anything that has happened to you, never bear a grudge against anyone who was the real or possible cause of your humiliation or misery; be strong, have faith and always show courage under the greatest of stress'.'

'Now I know where you get your best qualities from,' Jessica said in a simple and gentle manner.

They looked at one another in loving affection. He took her hand and they made their way back to the manor.

It was late in the night when Ravi told the rest of the staff his decision to join the Army. They sat around the table talking and sipping tea. Ravi's decision had astounded them.

'Join up!' Bobby Grey exclaimed. 'Join up? You want to fight the Boer? I don't even know what it's all about! The papers talk about fighting for the empire. What's the empire for goodness sake? This is my empire.' He banged the table gently with his fist. 'Sussex. That's the only thing worth fighting for.'

'A lot of people don't see it like that, do they Bobby old mate?' Jimmy intervened. 'They believe anywhere there are English people is part of the British Isles. If their way of life is threatened then it's got to be protected. Simple as that.'

Bobby was no slouch in speaking his mind. 'That might be so. But aren't there plenty of things here worth fighting for? People living in poverty and them that work in sweatshops for a pittance. The miners in Wales and Scotland and the North Country who die of the coal dust in their lungs. The little children running barefoot in the streets. Some of the houses in this lovely land of ours are fit only for destruction, let alone living in. Why fight other people's battles?'

'I agree with you Bobby,' Mrs Price gave him her approval, although only slightly. 'For myself, I have to say I am well satisfied with my lot. We live in a lovely house in a lovely part of the world. Even if our hours are long and after a long day's cooking I feel dead tired on my feet, I wouldn't swap this life. But when the going gets rough it's the younger ones the country looks to. Old Mr Price's grandad went to Waterloo. He actually saw old 'Bonie' through his telescope. Now they've got problems in South Africa. That means a little bit of the empire is at risk. So they ask for volunteers to go to their aid. The problems we've got at home don't count for a bag of beans when an Englishman's castle overseas is under threat.'

Ravi appeared to be thinking deeply about the words he had just heard. A clock in the background chimed on the hour.

'I think Mrs Price has summed it up,' Jimmy murmured.

'I shall go,' Ravi said with certainty. 'Other young men will go.'

Jessica could not conceal her sadness. 'I'm proud of you.'

'We all are,' Mrs Price reaffirmed. 'We'll miss you terribly. So you make sure you come home. Do you hear me?'

'I will do my best,' said Ravi. He looked up at the clock. He had no wish to prolong the evening. 'It's late now. It will be a big day tomorrow. I shall have to talk to Lady Bernadette.'

'Yes, I think it's time for some slumbers,' said Bobby rising from the table. Everyone rose on this glum news of Ravi's pending departure and returned to their rooms.

All except Ravi. He stole a tranquil moment to ascend the stairway and study some portrait paintings that hung in the upstairs hallway. There were several of Captain Rex Shervington. Ravi studied them with interest. The paintings of Ravi's father seemed to capture the glamour and the dynamic personality of this man who was now a distant memory.

Unbeknown to Ravi, Lady Bernadette was at work in her study.

The door of her room was slightly ajar. She lowered her quill pen after completing a letter. Gazing from her study she caught sight of Ravi looking at the painting of her late husband. Lady Bernadette watched with interest. She wondered just what Ravi was thinking.

Twenty

That night Ravi dreamt of his childhood in India. It was fourteen years before. Ravi was nine years old and an orphan playing in this river with other boys who had no parents. It was the world of his childhood. He remembered it all so well. The shanties on the river banks; the villagers bathing in the water. That aroma of eastern spices, mingled in with the sultry heat and the scent of Indian plants, seemed to drift down over the years.

His memory switched to the house where he spent his early years. Mrs Patell entered the room. Close behind came an Army officer who bore the rank of captain. The man followed Mrs Patell through several rooms of the waterside shanty to an opening by the water. Mrs Patel waved to Ravi who was playing in the water.

'Ravi! Will you come here!'

Ravi came racing up from the river bank. He climbed up to the opening and shyly stood by Mrs Patell who put her arm around him. Ravi smiled at the man. To a nine-year-old this six-foot-five-inch tall man of huge build looked an imposing figure.

Mrs Patell tried to reassure him. 'Ravi, your father Captain Shervington has come to see you. I shall leave you two alone for a while.'

She left the two alone. Ravi looked up into the smiling, handsome face of his real father, Captain Rex Shervington. 'Hullo lad! How are you?' he boomed in a warm friendly voice.

Ravi was reticent. His father was not a frequent visitor. 'I am very well thank you, father.'

Captain Shervington sat down next to his son. 'That's good. I'm sorry I don't get to see you very often.' He tried his best to be warm and fatherly. 'You know I'm a very busy fellow. Often I get called away to lead patrols in the mountains far away. I'd like to see more of you. Would you like me to come far more often?'

'Yes,' Ravi said, still shyly.

'I will when I come back,' he promised. 'I've got to travel up to Prakaresh with a patrol. I'll be away for a few weeks.' He looked down into the sensitive brown eyes of his son. These infrequent visits made it hard for Captain Shervington to engender enthusiasm in Ravi. He changed tack. 'Listen, would you like to go on a journey with me one of these days?' Ravi nodded his head and smiled revealing a set of sparkling white teeth. 'Would you like to go to the green land I come from and swim in sparkling streams and walk through lovely fields with beautiful, crisp, golden corn; and see houses with thatched rooves, old antiquated villages that haven't changed in centuries? Would you? Would you?' He was boosting the boy's enthusiasm. 'Would you like to come to London with me one day? I'll show you Big Ben and the Tower of London; the River Thames and Richmond. We'll go for walks in Hyde Park and down Piccadilly. We'll dress up like a couple of toffs and I'll show you where the Queen lives at Buckingham Palace.'

'When will we go, Father?' the boy asked. It was a question asked in sadness, for Ravi had waited and waited; his father had promised things before that did not happen.

'Oh I'm – I'm not sure when that will be.' The tone of Captain Shervington's voice took a marked change 'But it'll be soon. You mark my words young fellow.' He didn't sound very convincing. He was struggling with his words and didn't really know how to talk to the boy. 'Tell me. Do you swim in the river there?'

'Every day,' Ravi said proudly. 'Sometimes I swim to the other side.' He pointed across to the opposite bank where there was a bazaar and a few houses. 'We play in the markets. My friend's father has a donkey. Sometimes I go for a ride on the donkey.'

Captain Shervington suddenly became sensitive and serious, showing a brief glimpse of the caring father he might have been. 'You're happy then?' Ravi nodded and smiled. 'You have friends? Mrs Patell looks after you and feeds you well.'

'Yes.' Ravi appeared sad. 'Father, why don't you live with us?' the Captain felt a surge of emotional pain within him. It was not helped by Ravi's following question. 'What was my mother like?'

For a handsome daredevil brute of a man who cared little for anyone but himself the pain of it all was too much for him. He leaned forward and hugged the boy.

'Oh it's so unfair isn't it?' He said agonisingly. 'You're much too young to understand. I have to live where the Army sends me. And your mother…' His voice faltered and his eyes showed pain at the memory. 'She was a…' A long silence followed and then he completed the sentence with emphasis, '… a beautiful woman.'

'I wish I could see her again,' Ravi said almost tearfully. The pain was almost too hard for Captain Shervington and he rose to his feet, putting his arm around the boy. He looked hard at the boy, then tried to smile warmly. He felt much affection for his Indian-born son. 'You don't deserve an old rapscallion like me for a father.'

'Will you come and see me again?' Ravi asked almost pleadingly.

'Tomorrow,' Captain Shervington confirmed. 'I have to lead my patrol tomorrow. But I'll see you before I go. Look,' he turned and pointed through the doorway, 'if you and Mrs Patell wait in the street over there I'll ride up on my horse. Will you wave goodbye to me?'

'Yes Father,' Ravi replied meekly.

'You promise now?' his father said sternly but with a friendly smile.

'Will you definitely come, Father?' Ravi asked almost pleadingly.

'I'll ride up at ten o'clock sharp tomorrow. I promise.' And this time Ravi was smiling.

Captain Shervington hugged him again; his eyes appeared moist. 'God bless you lad.'

At ten o'clock the following morning Ravi and Mrs Patell waited outside the front of the house. Sure enough the sound of horses' hooves could be heard. It became louder and louder. In the distance at the far end of the town fifty horsemen of the Queen's Light Northern Regiment could be seen. They approached in an orchestrated and orderly fashion. At the head of the riders could be seen one man who occupied centre stage. Ravi looked incredulously down the street.

Almost as if she sensed what Ravi was thinking Mrs Patell whispered in his ear. 'Here comes your father leading the men.'

Ravi looked at her quickly and smiled. The men of the regiment drew closer and closer. Captain Rex Shervington rode astride his horse in a manner that exuded authority and leadership. Finally he was almost parallel with Ravi and Mrs Patell. Captain Shervington virtually drew his horse to a halt. He looked across to Ravi and smiled the most beautiful of smiles at Ravi. The boy waved and his father gently tipped his helmet. Ravi did not realise it then but he had seen his father for the last time.

All of the horsemen seemed to increase the gentle pace of their horses to a trot and then almost as quickly they began to canter. Ravi and Mrs Patell watched as the riders streamed past. Dust from the street swirled up into the air. The two stayed on watching until the riders had disappeared from view.

Ravi was still dreaming of his childhood. Memories of India were still strong in his mind. They were clear warm visual images that were so strong, even the emotions of then could be felt now.

For some reason Ravi's dream changed location. The young boy Ravi, together with another little boy, swam across the river to the bank on the other side. Ravi and his friend scrambled up the river bank. At the top were some shanty dwellings and markets selling colourful fruits. The two boys disappeared under a market stall. In the next instance Ravi emerged in the middle of the market, riding a donkey that he obviously had great affection for. He stroked it and petted it. Ravi's friend walked by the donkey.

Three happy smiling British soldiers passed by. They were oblivious to the boy but one of them would play a prominent part in shaping Ravi's future. The three soldiers were RSM Sandy Blackshawe, Colour Sergeant Chesney and Corporal Bill Dunham.

That time of distant memories faded quickly as Ravi woke up in the early morning hours. He rose slowly. His dream had reactivated old thoughts and emotions. He stood at the window looking out at the Sussex Downs. In the distance a magnificent wild specimen of a deer ran across the contours of green and gold countryside.

Ravi stared in wonderment at the creature, likening its freedom to that which he himself once knew. He turned round from the window and remembered something else from a time gone by.

It was at the Officers' Club in Calcutta where Ravi had found work in 1895. He had moved on from the warmth of his carefree childhood home to work as a waiter in this most British of stiff British institutions. It was typical of so many clubs where British expatriates tried to carry on the traditions of their homeland, even though they were far away from home.

On one occasion Ravi was serving behind the counter when two men entered the room simultaneously and walked to the bar. They looked at each other in recognition.

'Good God man!' one exclaimed. 'Where do I know you from?'

Almost straight away he proffered his hand warmly. Henry Allason shook it. He recognised the man as Captain Bruce Harrison who had been on the presiding committee at Colour Sergeant Chesney's court martial.

'I know where we've met before,' Henry Allason said apprehensively. 'You won't thank me for reminding you.' Bruce Harrison seemed puzzled. Henry Allason gave him a clue. 'It was a decade ago. That should strike a chord in your memory Sir.' Bruce Harrison was still mystified. With a smile Henry Allason reminded him. 'It was at Colour Sergeant Chesney's court martial.'

At the mention of the name Chesney, Ravi immediately recognised the name of his guardian. He listened intently.

'Chesney's court martial!' Bruce Harrison was shocked at first but his look soon gave way to a faint smile. 'It's Henry Allason isn't it?' There was a pause as he remembered the incident. It seemed that he had developed a sense of humour in the intervening years. 'My word, we had the most spectacular dust-up didn't we?'

Henry Allason could make a concession too. 'It was a particularly difficult trial for all concerned. Look, it was a long time ago. Would you join me for a drink?'

'I'd be delighted. Barman!' Ravi, who was not far away, listening to the conversation, came across to the bar. 'Make mine a Singapore Sling would you old fellow. Henry what's yours?'

'A pink gin for me, thank you.'

Ravi heard and organised the drinks. Bruce Harrison paid. Then the two men sat down at a nearby table within earshot of Ravi who pretended to be busy but was in fact keenly listening to the conversation.

Bruce Harrison looked across the table at Henry Allason 'I'm very close to retiring as a legal advisor now. Do I take it you're not in the Army these days?'

'You take it right,' replied Henry. 'I'm now a magistrate. The Chesney court martial was the turning point for me. I firmly believed in that man's innocence and had he been found guilty I would have fought hard and long to overturn the verdict. I made up my mind that when my Army career came to an end I'd make the law my domain. It's been much more interesting pursuing a legal career here in India. In England, a magistrate at the Old Bailey needs to have the patience of God, the wisdom of Solomon and a fine line of judgement. In India I think one needs compassion, understanding and strictness.' Bruce Harrison listened courteously and lit a cigar. There was something Henry wanted to know. 'Do you mind if I ask you something?'

'Go ahead.' He looked back at Henry, aware that some old ground was about to be covered.

'The Chesney court martial is something I have often wondered about.' A beat of silence followed and then Henry Allason spaced his words carefully. 'Were there directions from Army headquarters to find Chesney guilty?'

Bruce Harrison stared straight into his eyes. He took a puff on his cigar and then lowered it. His eyes flickered from left to right, as he checked to make sure no-one in the immediate vicinity was listening. Ravi was unable to hear Bruce Harrison's reply which was spoken in hushed tones.

A nod downwards signified the reply that Henry Allason had fully expected. Yes. The answer was yes. So it was true after all. 'But,' added Bruce. 'Your very convincing argument that day swayed me. The even more astonishing evidence left no doubt in my mind. When I returned to Army headquarters with a 'not guilty' verdict I had a great deal of explaining to do; as far as they were concerned it was a cut and dried affair. All the same, you have to agree that it was a most astounding story.'

'Yes.' Henry Allason remembered the details of it so well. The Chesney court martial had been influential in changing the course of his own career. 'The truth was more fascinating than fiction. Strange to think how that encounter with Nadur Sohari generated so many incidents. Chesney must have had someone watching over him that day. One earlier patrol led by Captain Shervington...' he grimaced at the memory. '... one earlier patrol was absolutely devastated. The Captain was unrecognisable when they found his body.'

Ravi's eyes froze at the mention of his father's name. He almost lost consciousness and clutched the edge of the bar.

All that had happened years before. Ravi stood looking out of the window of his room in Shervington Manor. His face bore the same frozen expression as it had done on that night in the Calcutta Officers' Club when he had learned of the brutal way in which his father had died. Now he was an employee in his father's house. It all seemed so strange; so full of irony. It had never occurred to him that he was technically the heir to this house and all of its possessions. Not once had that thought even entered his head.

During his time at Shervington Manor, Ravi had often studied the house and the countryside; he had tried to imagine his father Rex in that environment. It seemed so hard to envisage the handsome stranger with the moustache and the sparkling eyes growing up at Storrington.

The clock chimed on the hour, jolting his senses into action. It was time to prepare Lady Bernadette's breakfast and to talk to her of his decision to join the Army.

Lady Bernadette entered the conservatory and took time to smell the flowers that hung in baskets. She walked to the door leading to the garden and opened it. A breath of fresh morning air filled her lungs. It was splendid to absorb this view of the Downs and the scent of the flowers every day. She turned round in a very appreciative mood and saw Ravi placing her breakfast on the table.

'Good morning m'Lady,' he said amiably enough, although inside he was a tremor of nerves.

'Lady Bernadette took her seat for breakfast. She noticed that Ravi was waiting. 'Thank you Ravi.'

'M'Lady...' he said suddenly.

Lady Bernadette became acutely aware he was about to ask something. 'Yes Ravi. Is there something else?'

Ravi found the courage to say the necessary words, 'M'Lady, I wonder if I could talk to you about something. In fact there are two things.'

'Sounds serious,' Lady Bernadette mused, although she spoke with a smile. 'Certainly. Take a seat.' Ravi drew a chair and sat down. He seemed nervous and unsure but Lady Bernadette, for all her aristocratic bearing, was a warm-hearted person. She immediately sought to put him at ease. 'Now then Ravi, tell me what is on your mind.'

Ravi began to explain. 'The first thing is that the Government is sending troops from all over the British Empire to the war in South Africa.

I feel that – perhaps I should join up.' He looked at the astonished Lady Bernadette in a manner that reflected the tone of his voice: apologetic, almost ashamed. Then after delivering this body blow, Ravi came to the hardest words he had ever had to say. 'M'Lady, there is something else I need to speak to you about. It's very difficult for me and it has worried me greatly.'

'Go ahead Ravi. Don't be afraid.' Lady Bernadette did not continue with her breakfast. She could see the young man before her agonising.

'It is about my …,' and then after an enormous effort, '… my father.'

'Your father?' Lady Bernadette's voice was shaking.

Meanwhile, Mrs Price and Jessica were out picking flowers in the early morning. Jessica was a little way ahead of Mrs Price. It was a golden morning. Jessica should have been smiling but she was downcast over Ravi's pending departure. Mrs Price caught up with Jessica and noticed the sad look on her face.

'Are you alright, young Jess?'

'Ravi will be telling Lady Bernadette that he's joining the Army. He's probably telling her right this very moment.'

'I know dear.'

'I don't want him to go,' said Jessica sadly. 'I don't want him to go out there – to South blooming Africa of all places! In a war. In a land we know nothing about. I'm sure it's a beautiful country. But why should he go and fight a war with people none of us have got a quarrel with? I don't understand this fighting for the empire stuff. Ravi is so mild and gentle. He'll never make a soldier.'

Mrs Price was quick to correct her with all the wisdom of someone who had lived many years and who understood people and situations. 'Those who talk the toughest and act the hard men are nearly always the weakest. It's the mildest and gentlest who are more often or not the strongest and most fearless amongst us. You remember that, my girl.'

Twenty-One

All the house staff, together with Lady Bernadette, came to the railway station to bid farewell to Ravi. A hissing steam locomotive train approached in the distance. In a moment Ravi would pick up his travelling bag to catch the train and make his way as a new recruit to Aldershot.

Bobby and Jimmy shook his hand. Mrs Price hugged him. Jessica did her best to control her emotions and she embraced him, trying desperately not to shed any tears. Finally Ravi came to take leave of Lady Bernadette. The truth about Ravi's identify had not been revealed to the other staff. It was a closely guarded secret between them. Lady Bernadette shook his hand lightly and smiled; her eyes told the story.

'Goodbye to you all. Take care. I will see you all soon when I come home for leave before I sail for South Africa.' With this Ravi entered the carriage and sat down by the window. The train moved off and Ravi made one final wave. Behind him on the station platform the others' faces showed mixed emotions. Jessica, predictably, had a tear in her eye. Jimmy, true to form, winked at Ravi in his usual fatherly fashion. Bobby gave him a mock salute. Mrs Price managed a tiny smile. Lady Bernadette, who was dressed beautifully, with a large hat, appeared to be beaming with pride.

In the carriage Ravi sat down and opened a book. He began to concentrate on a verse by Rudyard Kipling. It was called *The Young British Soldier*. He could not help but compare himself to the role he would now play.

At Aldershot, Ravi fell in with the other young recruits on the parade ground. They were a mixed bunch of fellows; ordinary working lads seeking adventure and not really knowing what they were doing there; bank workers, civil servants, account clerks; people who wanted to escape the humdrum lives they led in provincial towns to fight a war in South Africa, which in all probability they did not know the reason for.

Discipline and parade ground square-bashing were something new to Ravi. He had not reckoned on the tough continuous training he was made to go through. The sergeant-major was so loud and aggressive, and delivered his orders at a sharp volume Ravi did not think possible of a human voice.

In the barrack room Ravi learned to clean the brass work on his uniform and to polish his boots so shiny that they were like mirrors. It was the art of spit and polish that soldiers became so conversant with during their training.

The local public houses in Aldershot did a good trade with the young recruits. Ravi spent several evenings with his new comrades at these establishments. He found friendships with the most unlikely people, with whom in civilian life he would have had little rapport.

For the first time in his life Ravi picked up a rifle. On the first occasion it had been as part of rifle drill. This time he had been trained to use a 303 rifle on a range. To use a weapon such as this was totally alien to his peace-loving and gentle nature; but he accepted that he had joined the service and this was part of his training.

Harry Chesney was about to open up his teashop one morning when the postman pushed a letter through the door. He walked over from behind the counter and picked the letter up. Chesney was startled. The postmark indicated that it had come from Aldershot.

'Aldershot!' he murmured in amazement to himself. For a moment he joked with himself that perhaps his discharge papers had gone missing and he was being asked to report for duty. He began to read the letter out loud. 'Dear Mr Harry – ,' Chesney at once recognised it was from Ravi. He read on. 'I am a young British soldier like one of those in Rudyard Kipling's verse.' He stopped and put the letter down on the counter. 'He's joined up.' Chesney's face was a picture of shock. 'Ravi's joined up!'

Somewhere in Hampshire, as Chesney read the letter, Ravi was on a route march with other recruits. They marched with packs on their backs. Ravi found himself being stretched to limits that he didn't know he had.

On one parade Ravi watched from the ranks as huge canons were wheeled into line. It was at that moment he realised just how imposing the weaponry was that would be used in battle.

Lady Bernadette was hard at work in her study examining the financial turnover of some of the Shervington family companies. There was a knock at the door and Jimmy entered.

'Sorry to disturb you, m'Lady. Your solicitor, Mr Fielding, is here to see you.'

'Thank you Jimmy. Would you show him in and bring some tea for Mr Fielding and I?'

'Very good, m'Lady.' Jimmy left the room and within a minute re-opened the door. Mr Fielding entered. He was a distinguished-looking man with grey hair and spectacles.

Lady Bernadette rose to greet him. 'Mr Fielding! Thank you for coming. Please take a seat.'

'Good evening to you Lady Bernadette.' He took a seat and removed a number of documents from his briefcase. He placed them before Lady Bernadette. 'I've had the appropriate legal correspondence drawn up for you. I think you'll find that as your family solicitor I've not missed any fine details.'

Lady Bernadette looked through the various documents and appeared to re-read one piece of information. 'That's very good. I can always rely on your firm for efficiency.' Jimmy entered the room and placed a tray on a side table. 'Thank you Jimmy.' She continued to browse through the documents. Then she fixed her gaze on Mr Fielding, indicating that there was more formal business to attend to. 'As you probably realised, I've not brought you here tonight purely to examine the family deeds of ownership to our enterprises, although I do appreciate the work you've done. I can retain these copies for my records can I?'

'Of course,' replied Mr Fielding. 'You have there the copies for the Shervington Sawmill at Pagham, Coltry Farm Estates, the share of the boat building business at Hove, together with a revised financial statement for all these. I have drawn up separate balance sheets and legal deeds for the Shervington companies in Belfast and the North of England. If I may say so, the combined output of all these companies looks very healthy indeed. I think the income generated from them all is assured for many a year.'

'I am very pleased to hear that – because – that brings me to my next request.' Lady Bernadette allowed the words to sink in. 'I want to draw up a Will and arrange for the ownership of these companies to be passed on to those I nominate. Naturally, I hope to be around for many a year but then one never knows, do they?'

Mr Fielding agreed. 'I would say that was an extremely wise decision. Do you wish me to draw up the relevant papers?'

'If you would please, and bring them to me at our next meeting.'

'That will be done, Lady Bernadette.' He began to make a few notes. 'If I could ask you, just so as I can prepare the framework for the Will, is there anything special you require?'

Lady Bernadette had thought long and hard about this. 'My main concern, apart from the companies, is for the welfare of my staff. I would like to ensure my staff have a job for life if they want it, and if they need it a home too. I know Mrs Price, Mr Grey and Jimmy the butler have nowhere else to go. I would like to see they are well looked after. Jessica the parlour maid – I suspect she may marry eventually. However, she works well and although she's only twenty-one I'd like to guarantee her employment for as long as she needs it.

'That is very generous of you, Lady Bernadette. You obviously think a great deal of your staff.'

Lady Bernadette smiled. 'They are as near to family as any that I have.'

'I will prepare the Will with those contingencies in mind. The wording will be slightly flexible but of course you can amend it as you see fit.'

Mr Fielding began to put the documents away, incorrectly assuming the conversation was now at an end. Lady Bernadette leaned forward across the table suddenly. 'I also want to make a separate provision for one other very important beneficiary.'

'Oh! Who is that Lady Bernadette?' Mr Fielding seemed to be surprised.

Lady Bernadette took a deep breath. 'Rex's son.'

Mr Fielding removed his spectacles and stared directly at her. He was not sure he had heard her correctly. 'Rex's son! This is some sort of joke surely?' Lady Bernadette nodded solemnly that it wasn't. 'Rex had a son? I didn't know that Rex had been married before. No-one in the Shervington family ever mentioned that to me.'

Lady Bernadette let slip a faint smile at Mr Fielding's assumption that her late husband had been married previously. 'I do not want to shock you too much, Mr Fielding. I have to tell you the son was a result of an association Rex had with an Indian woman during his service there.'

'I see.' Mr Fielding was visibly astounded.

'Rex didn't find out until after we were married. A colour sergeant in the Queen's Light Northern Regiment – a Mr Harry Chesney – became the boy's guardian and eventually brought him to England. Until recently he worked in this house as an assistant butler.'

'In this house? As a... You really must excuse me, Lady Bernadette. This is all extremely hard to comprehend. Where is this young man at the moment?'

'He's now in the army and will shortly be leaving for South Africa to take part in the Boer War. When he returns – as I pray to God above he will – I want him, as my stepson, to live in this house and eventually inherit a share of it.' Mr Fielding continued to look stunned. Lady Bernadette reached for the tea. 'Would you care for a cup, Mr Fielding?'

It was a few weeks later when Harry Chesney was about to close up for the day that he paused to sit down in the teashop and read the latest of the happenings in Transvaal. The door of the teashop opened very quietly and someone entered without Chesney becoming aware. Chesney put down the newspaper and went behind the counter to sort out the day's takings.

'Hullo Mr Harry,' a quiet voice spoke to him.

Chesney looked up, absolutely surprised. He was doubly surprised when he saw Ravi in uniform.

'Ravi!' he gasped, and then he stepped forward and embraced him. Chesney was delighted to see him.

'I hope I didn't shock you too much. I have a few days embarkation leave before departure.'

Chesney drew up two chairs for them. 'Sit down. It's good to see you. I can't say I wasn't shocked when I received your letter telling me you'd joined up. But I wish you well old mate.'

Ravi looked at him with some apprehension. 'It seems Lady Bernadette has long suspected who I am. When I told her I was joining up I also spoke to her about my past in India.' He noticed that Chesney was looking at him with dismay. 'I felt I had to, Mr Harry.'

'No, you did the right thing. You were justified. In fact, if truth be known, she asked me about you. She told me how similar in looks you were to Rex. Still, it's all water under the bridge.'

'I'm leaving for the Cape in a few days' time. I wanted to see you – and thank you for everything you have done for me. There is no way I can ever repay you for your kindness and for allowing me to enjoy two of the happiest years I have ever known. I feel privileged and humbled to have had the good fortune to have known you. I have learned much from you and I thank you Mr Harry.'

Chesney's eyes were glowing. 'You were a born gentleman, Ravi my son. You needed no prompting from me. From the time you spent with Mrs Patell back there in India I think you learned far more. In you I see kindness and respect for others, polished manners, and a responsible young fellow who was gutsy enough to join Her Majesty's forces without any pushing from anybody. Good for you son! Bloody good for you! And if you'll take my advice when you're out there in the old Transvaal you'll keep your head down, learn to duck very quickly, run fast and when the show is all over you'll get back here and marry that sweet little thing Jessica who loves you so much.' Ravi smiled at the thought of her. 'I let go of a girl who loved me once. My God, she was a dark-haired beauty; a sparkling Irish colleen called Karen Kelleher. I met her out in Ceylon. I didn't take the lifetime opportunity of happiness she offered me. So if you think about it you've got every reason to make sure you come home.'

'Will you come and see me off at the dock?' Ravi asked him.

'Wouldn't miss it for the world,' Chesney replied enthusiastically.

'I am going down to Shervington Manor tomorrow to say goodbye to everybody. When you see me at the dock, Mr Harry, there will be a number of other regiments there: the Royal Hampshires, the Scots Guards, the Sussex and Surrey regiments.' He smiled. 'I'm not with any of those.'

'Which one are you with then?' Harry was curious.

Ravi could hardly restrain himself from bubbling over with enthusiasm. 'I'll be with the best regiment in the British Isles Mr Harry. I will be sounding the bugle for the troopship at sea. Listen out and pretend to hear. I'll be playing for you. For my father Captain Rex Shervington. For you, Harry Chesney, and your comrades. I will be with the 25th Queen's Light Northern Regiment. I will be so proud to serve.'

Chesney looked stunned. Then he broke out into a happy smile.

At Shervington Manor, Ravi presented himself in uniform to Lady Bernadette and the staff. The occasion was recorded by an old time photographer. Ravi in full uniform was seated beneath a portrait of his late father. Lady Bernadette then sat next to Ravi and the photographer managed to produce what was in effect a family picture.

For the next photograph the entire household was included. Ravi and Lady Bernadette sat in front. Jessica and Mrs Price stood behind. Immediately behind them were Jimmy and Bobby. In the flash of an instant a very happy picture was recorded for posterity. Ravi stood up and looked quickly at Jessica who smiled at him lovingly. Lady Bernadette moved forward and whispered quickly to him.

'Your father would have been very proud of you.'

Ravi smiled back; for only he knew what she really meant. Jessica tapped him on the shoulder. Ravi turned around.

'Come home soon. Won't you Ravi?' Jessica asked him quietly.

Twenty-Two

Harry Chesney watched the troops embarking for South Africa from the London Docks. It was an emotional and inspiring sight. He had watched the regiments march to the ship in a blaze of colour and with an accompaniment of military music. Just for a moment, Chesney felt the thrill of a bygone age when he himself had departed on similar journeys.

Ravi had looked so happy as he marched in his father's old regiment and the one in which his guardian had served with distinction until the incident at Prakaresh. Keep your head down boy! Run like mad! Chesney wondered if Ravi would follow his advice. This was a different type of war; the troops of the empire versus the Boer. What sort of contest was this?

Wives and sweethearts waved. Mothers and sisters cried and wept, and waved handkerchiefs. Fathers and brothers cheered. Older men, who had fought in Crimea or against the Zulus at Rourke's Drift, and in the Sudan, watched in awe and admiration as the young soldiers boarded the ship for the fight ahead.

The musicians on the wharf began to play *Soldiers of the Queen*. A great roar came up from the crowd as the gangplank was raised. The ship at the wharf was being guided away. Streamers broke and the band played louder and louder. Give the lads a good send off! That was the message. It was coming through in every note of rousing marching music played.

Chesney stood there completely mesmerised by the occasion and deeply immersed in his own thoughts and memories. He was totally oblivious to the fact that not less than two feet away stood a man in top hat and cane whom he knew so well. The man took a pace nearer to Chesney and spoke to him quietly; his familiar voice completely caught the colour sergeant off guard.

'Do you remember India, Harry? Do you remember the times of the 25th Queen's Light Northern Regiment's greatest days at Fort Valaka?'

The soft voice seemed to cause an immediate transformation to come over Chesney. His grin collapsed. A look of shock spread over his face. Slowly he turned his head and lowered his cigarette. He found himself facing Graham Whittaker, the military journalist who had accompanied the men of the regiment to the battle at Prakaresh.

'Mr Whittaker,' he gasped. 'By God! That's right isn't it? Mr Graham Whittaker.'

Whittaker beamed with delight. In fact he was thrilled to see this piece of colour once again after so many years. He looked at Chesney who wore a cockeyed felt hat, a dapper orange suit and a chequered bow tie.

'Hullo,' Whittaker said with a warm smile, and after a short pause he remembered the name and rank of this man, 'Colour Sergeant Chesney.'

In a smoky dockside public house, full of unruly looking characters, the two men talked for a long time. Whittaker had listened with absolute fascination as Chesney recounted his story of the past years. But it was the news of Captain Shervington's son which had intrigued Whittaker most of all.

He looked hard at Chesney, trying to absorb what he had just heard. 'So – as we sit here tonight Ravi is at sea on a troop ship.'

'Yes,' Chesney said meekly, knowing that Whittaker was stunned by this revelation.

Whittaker attempted to put this in perspective. 'Rex Shervington had a son. Ravi – who was brought up in a women's hostel; whose upkeep was paid for by you. You – who in turn brought him to England where he worked as a servant in the home of his real father.' Whittaker's face was full of disbelief. 'And now Ravi is in the old regiment – the Queen's Light Northern.' He allowed himself a smile. 'If it wasn't true it would be some sort of ale house yarn spun at the height of someone's drunken dishevelment.'

'I don't drink so much these days Sir,' Chesney retaliated quickly, but in good humour. 'With the passing of the years I've become a man of far more sober habits and my gaze of past, present and future is as clear as the pure light of crystal chandeliers. I've volumes of memories in my mind, stained like indelible ink.'

'Don't doubt you for a moment Harry.' There was something else on Whittaker's mind. It was not like him to pass up the opportunity that journalists were quick to spot. 'I could write this story for a newspaper if you like.'

Chesney was no fool. He came back smoothly and quickly, grinning at Whittaker's opportunism. 'Really Sir. I think a well-educated man like you should show more tact than that. It's not a good thing to revive too much of the past. Don't you agree? Life moves on, Sir – it does for me. I know that.'

'Perhaps you're right Harry.' Whittaker still had a huge measure of respect for Chesney.

Chesney rose from his chair. 'Sir I've enjoyed meeting you again but the clock's ticking late and I really must go. It's been a pleasure to have recounted a mixture of harsh and beautiful memories of India: mountain ranges and regimental parades; Major Jack Clancy and Regimental Sergeant Major Sandy Blackshawe – fine men of colour and character – the like of which I'll not know again in my lifetime; elephants with platforms and passengers; Indian castes and maharajahs and princes; skirmishes and battles. Yes – that any man should know all that and live to tell the tale.'

Outside the public house the two men stood in the shelter of a doorway. The night air was cold. It was beginning to rain now. Across the road there was a hansom cab. Whittaker looked at Chesney as if he was trying to find some warm words of farewell. Finally he found them.

'It's been a pleasure to have met you again Harry. I may call in and see Lady Bernadette sometime. Perhaps we may meet again.'

'Possibly we will,' Chesney said with a smile.

Whittaker felt inclined to take leave of his friend with warm words. 'Speaking to you tonight and hearing your own story, I believe you can walk tall in any company you choose. You have good values. Courage. Strength. Valour. Dignity. Honesty. Loyalty. Great values Harry. Real values. The things that we British have placed more emphasis on, than any military might, than any aspirations of extending the colonies, or even the accrual of wealth. In years to come when we have left the colonies – and we will – and the British Empire is history, we will leave those values. People like you. The ordinary Tommy. They contributed so much.'

Chesney felt a mixture of cheerfulness and embarrassment. 'I've only got to walk down the road to where I'm staying. You might like to take the hansom cab over there.' Whittaker glanced across and waved his cane to the driver, indicating that he would take the cab. He turned to Chesney and shook his hand. Chesney added his final words. 'Thank you for your kind words, Mr Whittaker.'

'Good-bye Colour Sergeant,' Whittaker said with finality. He crossed over to the hansom cab and entered. He sat down, gave instructions to the cabbie and looked out.

Chesney stood in the shadows lighting a cigarette and covering the flame with the collar of his jacket. Out of respect Whittaker tipped his top hat to Chesney with a gentlemanly courtesy. Chesney replied by raising his own felt hat and smiling almost laughingly. The hansom cab moved off down the damp dockyard road. When the cab had turned round a corner out of view Chesney began to walk along on his own.

Apart from a couple of sailors and a lamplighter he was virtually alone. It was dark, damp and chilly. He stopped by the Thames and looked out at the murky waters. Chesney glanced at his pocket watch. He realised that on board the troopship Ravi would be sounding the Last Post on the bugle. In his mind Chesney was a lifetime away. He could envisage the sound of the bugler playing. There were a few lights in the distance. They sparkled on a smoky rainy evening.

Out at sea Ravi stood beneath the colours of the Union Jack. He played the bugle with consummate skill. In the background the waves constantly rolled on a restless sea. The stars in the sky sparkled generously.

Chesney continued to look out at the Thames. It was almost as if he could hear the playing of the bugle from afar. Some hidden command from his past perhaps rang in his ears. He suddenly stood tall and ramrod still, almost at attention and removed his hat; he clutched it to his chest.

Prakaresh was far away on the North-West frontier of India. Chesney relived that sad and splendid moment when he had stood alone on the ridge there, playing the bugle in tribute to his fallen comrades. He remembered it all so vividly; the brilliant red sun rising up above the mountains, the regimental colours fluttering in the early morning breeze. That moment had been so emotional it had brought tears to his eyes and he had lowered his bugle with a tremble.

At sea Ravi lowered his bugle. He stood to attention for a moment.

Harry Chesney did exactly the same by the banks of the Thames. Then after a short while he put his hat on and started to walk. He began to whistle *D'ye Ken John Peel*. His imagination ran riot. It was as if there was a military band accompanying him and an Indian sitar thrown in for good measure.

Instead of walking he began to stride. His pace quickened. He marched in a proud and confident fashion, whistling loudly with the rain now pouring heavily on him as he splashed through puddles happily.

From the shelter of a corner shop doorstep a peeler in a mackintosh gazed on in bemusement at the whistler's moment of eccentricity.

'Who does he think he is?' the peeler said to himself under his breath, 'A Victoria Cross winner?'